KEITH AUSTIN

RED FOX

SNOW, WHITE
A RED FOX BOOK 978 1 849 41558 3

First published in Great Britain by Red Fox,
an imprint of Random House Children's Publishers UK
A Random House Group Company

This edition published 2014

1 3 5 7 9 10 8 6 4 2

The Random House Group Limited supports the Forest Stewardship Council®
(FSC®), the leading international forest-certification organisation. Our books
carrying the FSC label are printed on FSC®-certified paper. FSC is the only
forest-certification scheme supported by the leading environmental organisations,
including Greenpeace. Our paper procurement policy can be found at
www.randomhouse.co.uk/environment

Set in 12/16 pt Bembo by Falcon Oast Graphic Art Ltd.
Red Fox Books are published by Random House Children's Books,
61–63 Uxbridge Road, London W5 5SA

www.**randomhousechildrens**.co.uk
www.**totallyrandombooks**.co.uk
www.**randomhouse**.co.uk

Addresses for companies within The Random House Group Limited
can be found at: www.randomhouse.co.uk/offices.htm

THE RANDOM HOUSE GROUP Limited Reg. No. 954009

A CIP catalogue record for this book is available from the British Library.

Printed in Great Britain by Clays Ltd, St Ives plc

Also by Keith Austin

GRYMM

Once upon a time there was an agent who fought the good fight when everyone else had given up; so, thank you, Alan Davidson. Thank you also to Judy and Tony O'Neill for letting me disrupt their lives at their idyllic home while finishing this manuscript. And, of course, none of this would have been possible without my partner, Helen O'Neill, who believes in me even when I don't; *especially* when I don't.

What a tender young creature! What a nice plump mouthful . . .

Little King by the Brothers Grimm

PROLOGUE

Deryk McDougall didn't mind the cold – living this far north, you had no choice. Or rather, it *was* a choice. Most of the kids he'd been to school with had *chosen* to leave; to head south for work or uni or love. It certainly wasn't for everyone: icy for nine months of the year, teeth-achingly freezing for four of those, dark at four o'clock most afternoons and not really light until nine a.m.

And yet he stayed. Anyone asked, he said it was because of his poor old mum. She had trouble getting about, she could fall down the stairs in their cottage on the edge of the forest and . . . Well, she wasn't quite right in the head – dribbling on as she did about the people in the mirror. Old Mrs Dalgleish in the village shop didn't know what to say the first time it happened. Now she just gave him her *your-poor-old-nutty-mother* look.

That said, apart from her obsession with the 'poor wee bairn with the face', she wasn't too bad: she was perfectly able to look after herself – always telling him to get out and see the world. 'Go, Deryk, go. Find yourself a lovely wee girrrl!'

The thing was, his mother was just an excuse. He loved living on the border of the National Park, on the cusp of the wilderness. He loved his job as a ranger and wouldn't want to do anything else. No, he was better off here: 3,000 square miles of nothingness and only 17,000 widely scattered people. He had mountains and lochs and valleys in which to hide from the world.

Deryk eased off the throttle of his snowmobile, slipped it into neutral and coasted to a stop on a flat bit of land; snow had been falling for days and the pine trees were sagging under the stuff, laden like tired shoppers at Christmas.

Through the trees behind him he could see his small two-storey cottage, cosy and dark against the white. Snow clung to the gutters and windowsills, and puffs of off-white smoke chuffed from the chimney like some Native American call sign. They had central heating, but Mum did like what she called a 'real' fire.

He was about to restart the snowmobile when, out of the corner of his eye, he saw something move. Something dark, something slinky. Fox? Badger? No, both too small. He slipped off the seat and crab-walked sideways up the slope. He came to the crest and his heart rate shot up.

It was a wolf. A *big* one. That was impossible, surely? Wolves had died out here a hundred years ago. No – no mistake: it *was* a wolf. Black as pitch and stealing through the snow.

Deryk crept back to his vehicle, swung a leg over the seat and was about to fire it up when he saw another wolf lurking round the back of the cottage. He squinted. He was a long way off, so maybe . . . maybe it was a stray dog? It moved slowly through the snow, head turning this way and that, big, black and vicious looking. He slammed the snowmobile into gear and shot off down the slope at breakneck speed. If they were wolves, the chances were that they would be as scared of him as he was of them – especially when he burst out of the tree-line astride his own growling mechanical beast.

He rounded a bend and lost sight of the cottage for a moment. By the time it came back into view the wolf was gone – or just prowling around the side he couldn't see. Deryk didn't take any chances, deliberately pushing the snowmobile hard through a gap in the trees and slewing sideways up to the house. It hadn't even come to a full stop before Deryk was off and running full pelt for the front door.

'Mum?' he shouted, shutting the door behind him and shaking his gloves off. Silence. He stepped through into the lounge, where the fire was crackling away. Maybe she'd gone to get more wood? He dashed back to the hallway, skidding on the polished wooden floor, and turned through to the kitchen, a shiver of cold air telling him that the back door was open.

Wide open.

And standing right outside it was the huge black wolf. It faced away from him, sniffing the air, its coat shiny, its shoulders rippling with muscle. Deryk froze. Was his mother out there? Had she been trapped in the garden?

He remembered the gun. There was a rifle upstairs that had belonged to his father. It hadn't been out of the closet for years, but this was a good time to get it. As he turned to go, the sleeve of his padded jacket brushed against a cup on the kitchen counter. It was just a clink, but it was enough: the wolf's ears twitched and its head angled to one side, listening.

With one eye fixed on the back of the animal's head, Deryk began to edge out of the room. It was too late. In a sudden explosion of movement the wolf whirled round, saw him and bared its fangs in a slobbering snarl. For a split second Deryk was rooted to the spot, but as the wolf leaped towards him, its legs failed to gain any traction in the snow and it fell awkwardly, scrabbling to get up again. In those few precious seconds Deryk raced for the stairs.

'Mum? You there? Mum?'

Even over the sound of his own voice he could hear the distant huffing of the wolf, the scratchy pitter-patter of its nails on the kitchen floor and then the floorboards at the bottom of the stairs. He raced along the landing and burst into his mother's bedroom. She wasn't there. He slammed and locked the door just as the wolf threw its weight against it. Deryk pushed back and, after a while, the snarling and scratching ceased – though he could still hear heavy breathing as it paced up and down outside.

He moved quietly away from the door. The room looked the same as usual. There were a few clothes over the back of the chair by the dressing table, two Agatha Christies beside the bed, and in the corner the large mirror they'd dragged home from an auction last year; it reflected the image of a tubby man/boy – a large, overfed baby, as he'd once heard Aileen Campbell describe him to her giggling friends – with an impressive ginger beard and scared eyes. He noticed then that his mother's spectacles lay on top of her books; she never went *anywhere* without her spectacles. Deryk felt a sob building up inside, a big bubble of fear that he was afraid might pop and leave him a blubbering wreck. No, he had to be strong, for her sake, wherever she was.

Gun – he needed that gun, and he needed it now. He went into his mother's small walk-in wardrobe, unlocked the gun case, hefted the rifle out and loaded it, nerves and fear making an unaccustomed act even more foreign. Finally he stepped quietly back into bedroom. As he did so, a sleek blue-black raven dropped out of the sky onto the snow-covered windowsill, scaring him half to death.

Caw, it screeched. *Caw! Caw!*

Deryk stared at the intruder. There was something odd about it . . . He waved at the bird to shoo it away, but it stood its ground and stared at him before tapping three times on the glass with its beak.

Tap tap tap!

No! He had to be seeing things. He tiptoed hesitantly towards the window, squinting at the bird. He was right: it was a raven, but . . . but it only had *one eye*, a glistening ebony pearl, alive with fierce malevolence, right in the middle of its forehead.

The bird tapped again and the wolf threw itself against the bedroom door and howled. Deryk backed away from the raven and crossed the room, gun raised, coming slowly to a halt with his back to the mirror. What was *happening*?

'Mum?' he hollered. The only reply was another attack by the wolf. The door wouldn't last long at this rate. He aimed where he expected the animal to come bursting through, but then became aware of a cloying, rotten stink. It was the smell of the dead, swollen animals he sometimes found in the woods.

He spun round, slowly, deliberately, not wanting to turn his back on the wolf behind the door but knowing he had no choice.

From a head that was as large as Deryk's body, two baleful golden eyes the size of boiled eggs gazed at him.

What big eyes you have . . .

And what big . . . teeth.

He just had time to register that the warm feeling was the breath of a massive white wolf standing right behind him.

Deryk suddenly found he had no strength to hold onto the gun, and it dropped to the floor with a crash that he barely registered. A warm wet patch spread around his groin as the wolf huffed and puffed.

In the final few seconds of his life, before the wolf tore his head from his body, Deryk McDougall had only one thought. 'Mum?'

A little later, the white wolf was standing outside in the snow. She could hear the sounds of snarling and ripping behind her in the house, but her attention was elsewhere. She sniffed the air. The one she had long been searching for had been here; she could smell him – faint but unmistakable.

But where was he *now*?

She looked up, unperturbed, as an explosion of one-eyed ravens came spewing out of the bedroom window where Deryk McDougall had met his fate. The papery rustling of thousands of wings grew louder and louder as the flock rose up into the air and began to swell like some gigantic black fist.

Fly! ordered the wolf with her mind. *FLY!*

The great mass blew apart as if a bomb had gone off in the heart of it, heading north, south, east, west. Within minutes they were gone, disappeared on the wind.

Fly, thought the wolf again, and turned back towards the cottage.

Find him.

PART ONE

1
BIRTHDAY BOY

He was used to it by now. The dream. It was, without a glimmer of doubt, his first conscious thought: the wolf, in a pure white, snowbound forest. And there was never any sense of having arrived, just of being there. Of always being there. Like being born.

The forest isn't dense; the trees only begin to gather together in the distance, further up the slope. Here the trunks are widely spaced, like black licks from a painter's brush — solid, and yet, because of the constant snow, insubstantial at the same time.

In one of the trees, just on the periphery of his vision, a large blue-black crow — raven? (He can't tell the difference) — is flapping its wings and jabbing its beak at a trio of what look like large, indistinct brown moths as they flutter around its head.

Sparrows! They are sparrows! Harassing and tumbling and rising and falling — protecting a nest perhaps?

And then, as he moves forward, leaving the birds to their

bickering, the snow, which has been falling softly and almost in slow motion, stops. It is as if, as the final flake flutters past his face, a curtain is raised . . . and behind it is the wolf.

It is huge — much larger than him even at this distance — and white; so white that it would disappear into the snow if it wasn't for the bright red smear beneath its front paws.

And he knows, knows in his bones, that whatever it was there in the snow — whatever the wolf had been worrying and biting and tearing into with such controlled rage, such concentrated energy — had been alive only moments before.

And that's when it happens; that's when the wolf stops eating and looks up and sniffs the air; that's when it turns its almond eyes — eyes of bright, luminescent gold — towards him.

That's when, snout matted scarlet with blood, it looks right at him.

And smiles—

'Mr Creed?'

John woke with a confused shudder, jerking like someone who's just realized he's drowning. He stuttered, 'W-w-w . . .' and cruel laughter tittered around the room.

Oh, no. He groaned; he had fallen asleep in Mr Christmas's Geography class. Again. Patches of embarrassment started to spread across his cheeks. Soon they would work their way up into his scalp and he would look like—

'I'm very sorry to interrupt your beauty sleep, Mr Creed,' said the teacher, his irony compounded by a pained grimace. He was standing next to John's desk, rolling backwards and forwards on the balls of his feet. 'Do you feel up to continuing the lesson?'

'Sir, s–s–sorry, sir,' he muttered. 'W–w–won't happen again, sir.'

He knew better than to talk back or argue. What would he have said, anyway? *Sorry, sir, but I was up at five a.m. delivering your newspaper!* No. He might *think* it, but he could never *say* it. No way. Creed's credo was: *Shut up and keep your head down.*

'Make sure it doesn't.'

'Yes, sir.'

'This wouldn't have happened in my day, of course. No, back then . . .'

Mr Christmas (English and Geography) was one of the school's more eccentric characters. A former military man (behind his back he was known as the Colonel), he was always ready for a trip down Memory Lane, and his pupils were always more than happy to open the gate and lead him up the garden path with a well-timed comment about the war – any war. Today, it seemed, he had opened the gate himself. The room went quiet; for while he was reminiscing, he wasn't teaching. Which was, in anyone's schoolbook, a result.

John was glad of the distraction and slumped back in his seat. It was a dangerous tactic because the room was sweltering – the old-fashioned iron radiators were going full blast – and he knew he could easily drop off again. How the Colonel stood it, he didn't know. The man was dressed, as usual, in a heavy brown tweed suit, complete with waistcoat, white shirt and green regimental tie. His grey hair was cut, short back and sides, with a razored parting and enough oil to choke a pelican. Neat cuffs decorated with gold cufflinks dwarfed liver-spotted hands, and his brilliantly shiny brown leather shoes creaked every time he moved.

He was also the owner of a nose that hung down like a bulbous teardrop; he constantly touched and dabbed at it with a white handkerchief pulled from an inside pocket. His appearance wasn't helped by the big black wraparound sunglasses that he wore all the time, even inside. One of the other teachers had explained it when the ribbing had got out of hand: something to do with a bad side-effect – extreme photosensitivity? – from anti-inflammatory drugs.

There were wild rumours of a mad brother hidden in Mr Christmas's old house. The impressive three-storey building wasn't far from school, and was on John's paper round. *Mr B. Christmas* it said on the delivery note. Nobody knew what the 'B' stood for. He was 'Mr Christmas' or 'sir' to anyone and everyone, even the other teachers. Even John, who knew him better than most, was too scared to ask.

'Ah, but listen to me prattling on,' said the Colonel. An irritated sigh went up; he had somehow found his own way out of the garden of memories. 'Now, where were we? Yes! So, as we can see from this diagram, Grimsby is a gap town. This means . . .'

As soon as he turned away to write on the whiteboard, a ball of scrunched-up paper flew across the room and hit John on the side of the head. *Here we go again*, he thought.

'Bull's-eye,' whispered a voice off to his right. 'You know, Creed, when you blush, your face looks like a baboon's bum.'

'According to legend,' droned the teacher, 'Grimsby was founded by Grim, a Danish fisherman, who . . .'

'Oi, scarface!'

John turned his head just in time to be caught in the eye by a second missile thrown from another direction. He flinched.

'You are *so* gay,' whispered the first voice. And then, when John refused to acknowledge the speaker's existence, added, quietly vicious: 'G-g-g-gay and p-p-pug ug-ug-ug-ugly.'

Still John didn't look up; just glared with impotent anger at his books without actually seeing them. He knew what he would see if he did: Caspar Locke tipping his chair back and smiling that wide smile of his, the one full of perfect white teeth.

At the front of the classroom the Colonel droned on about Grimsby and why it had no town walls, as if any of the thirty or so kids there gave a f-f-f . . . fig. John smiled at this mental self-censorship; maybe Grandpa Mordecai was having more of an effect on him than he thought. *There are so many better words than swear words, my boy.*

Yeah, well, that was all very well, but Grandpa Mordecai didn't go to school in inner-city London. Or even in the twenty-first century, for crying out loud. He'd gone to school on a donkey in the mountains of northern Romania! Probably a few years before they invented the wheel.

'Of course, in the early nineteenth century the town grew rapidly, helped by an Act of Parliament in 1796 which formed the Great Grimsby Haven Company for the purpose of . . .'

Outside, a light wind played with the branches of the oak tree that squatted in the middle of the playground.

There was a ramshackle circular bench around the trunk, and a wrought-iron fence to stop the kids climbing it. The lowest branches had also been removed for the same reason. Of course, this didn't prevent anyone from reaching through the bars and carving into the bark names, nicknames and startlingly unoriginal obscenities.

John liked it; with the lower branches gone, the tree's energies had been channelled into looking after the great rounded dome. Even now, in the depths of winter, with no leaves to speak of, it looked magnificently battle-scarred and defiant.

As he watched, a small squabble of sparrows appeared and settled on the branches. He liked sparrows; they were the only bit of the dream that he liked. They always seemed so angry, he thought; so puffed up and brave and indignant.

It wasn't even three o'clock, but the sun was low in the sky and preparing to disappear. It had been one of those bright winter days with a cloudless blue sky which are nonetheless freezing. Of course, the only peek they got of the sun was through the occasional gap in the maze of surrounding tower blocks. As if by some celestial signal, small white feathers began to float past the window. Feathers? No, not feathers . . . snow; it was snowing! Hadn't Mr Patel said that this very morning when John collected the papers? That it was cold enough to snow?

How could it be so sunny and still be so teeth-chattering cold that it snowed? He pictured a great snow-swollen cloud sitting right above the school and nowhere else. There's a question for you, Mr Christmas; one that we might actually be interested in. How come there are no clouds and yet it's snowing? Why don't you explain that, rather than going on about Grimsby. Where *was* Grimsby anyway?

2
ICE QUEEN

Fyre King didn't notice the snow at first; she was far too busy watching John Creed out of the corner of her eye. She'd never really got to know him. Who had? Creed was the class weirdo (the other one) and kept himself to himself. The Colonel was marching up and down, his shoes squeaking, going on about Grimsby, but she wasn't listening. She didn't really have to; she'd done the homework, read the next chapter – it never hurt to be one step ahead – so she already knew what Grimsby was: it was *boring*.

John Creed, on the other hand . . .

They had been in the same classes for more than a year now, and the most she had got out of him was a thin smile and 'S-s-sorry' when she had accidentally-on-purpose bumped into him in the corridor one day. He wasn't the easiest of people to befriend. She certainly felt sorry for him – it couldn't be easy having a stutter like that – and in a way they were freaks together. But where she had come to terms with her 'problem' (as much as you could), he had retreated into his and all but disappeared.

It was all her mother's fault, of course. If she hadn't been such a goody-goody and encouraged her to befriend the 'poor boy' with, as she had so kindly and so coldly put it, 'the face', he wouldn't have turned into such an obsession. She hadn't realized her mother had even *seen* him.

She had watched as the teachers gradually stopped asking him questions in class. How many times had she wanted to crawl into a hole and drag him in with her as he struggled to get his words out, as the tendons in his neck stood out with the effort, as his jaw muscles worked back and forth . . . ? She had seen his fear, his dry, panicked swallow, the unendurable tension and the blush that he couldn't stop. What was that like? To know the answer, but also to know that the words just wouldn't come, however much you wanted them to. There was that time with Mrs Cooper, the Maths teacher, for instance.

'S-s-s-s . . .'

Mrs Cooper, outwardly patient but somehow impatient at the same time, wanting to move on: *Time's a-wasting, kids.* The class, sniggering . . .

Caspar Locke – surprise, surprise – laughing outright and mimicking Creed's distress: 'Is it suh-suh-suh-sex, miss?'

'Yes, well, that's quite enough from you, Caspar.'

'Sssssssssseventy-sssssssseven!' John's answer had eventually came out as a gasp, almost a shout really.

'Well done, John,' the teacher had said, patronizing and glad it was over. It hadn't helped that she had tried and failed not to smile at Locke's 'witticism'.

And all Fyre could do was sit and watch as John Creed crumpled in despair, withdrawing into his shell, red-faced, shoulders slumped so that his head almost touched the desk. Only she had noticed the few fat tears that dropped onto his notebook. His eyes were wide open, staring inwards. She knew what he was doing: if he blinked, the drops would turn into a flood. She knew how *that* felt. And so he had sat there, cringing with embarrassment and anger at the teacher, at the other kids, at the world and, most of all, at himself.

That was the day she realized, with sudden empathy, that every day was like this for him. She knew what it was to be made fun of, but with her it only lasted a while, and then the others just got used to the way she looked. But Creed . . . *Every time anyone* talked to him was a nightmare. No wonder he just sat at the back and didn't speak. She imagined what it would be like if her classmates never got used to her appearance; if they just kept on and on and on about it.

Of course, the scars didn't help. There were three of them, thick livid ridges running from the corner of his right eye, one below the other in parallel lines, to his neck, just below the jaw line. It looked like some pre-historic animal or giant bird had dragged its claws through his flesh. The very bottom of his right earlobe was missing too. The scars stood out stark and white, like bony fingers, when he blushed – which was bad news because Creed blushed a *lot*. And he was unable to hide them, no matter how much he brushed his long mousy-blond hair forward over his face.

Attacked by a dog when he was a baby, some said. Others reckoned he was just born that way – possibly attacked in the womb by his evil twin, who was later consumed by John himself. Honestly, some of the stories would make your hair curl. But nobody knew the truth because nobody had got close enough to him to find out. Fyre would, though; she knew that without a doubt. It was dangerous, given what was going on at home. But wasn't that half the attraction? Was it the danger? Or perhaps she thought that he, of all people, would understand what she'd done . . .

She tried to concentrate on the Colonel as he droned on; she didn't want to dwell on her mother, all alone at home. If Fyre thought about it for even a moment, it would lead, logically, to how long she could keep it a secret; how long it would be before someone came knocking on the door, asking questions.

Instead, she listened to Creed. And right now it wasn't grim old Grimsby that was fascinating him, it was . . . Oh, snow! It was *snowing*. She felt her heart swell. She loved snow – there was something about it that made her soul sing. She hoped that, this time, it would settle.

3
THE TERMINATOR

At the back of the class Caspar Locke's mind was racing. Not that this was unusual; it was always running off this way and that, getting ahead of itself, falling behind, racing to catch up – like a dog that had been let off the leash, zigzagging around sniffing any whiff of pee that crossed his path.

The shrink he'd seen a few years ago had an answer for it: drugs to combat his ADHD. Which he took because he was a good boy in those days and the grown-ups knew best. Yeah. The tablets stopped the great out-of-control merry-go-round in his head all right . . . and replaced it with cotton wool. And more cotton wool – a whole pillow of the stuff, until his skull was bursting, his mind, well, stifled. The grown-ups liked it because he was so much *calmer*, so much *nicer* to be around.

Well, he'd put a stop to that. Just stopped taking them. His father didn't know, or care – too busy catching crims – but it was a hard act to keep up. Exhausting really. He'd had to cultivate a calm exterior while, inside, his head was a crazy mad jumble of images and thoughts and ideas.

He managed it, though. The teachers put up with his antics because he was near the top of his class in most things, but they certainly didn't *like* him. Not the way the girls liked him – all giggly and melty under his charming smile, witty banter and dark, brooding gaze. He was handsome but not too handsome, tall but not too tall, with thick, jet-black hair swept back from a perfect Roman nose. But inside? Inside he felt like the robot in that old film, *The Terminator* – emotionless, cold; computing, seeing, analysing, taking it all in, sucking it all down.

One day, he thought, he would just simply fill up. And then all that . . . *stuff* would come spewing out, flooding out in a great wave to drown them all.

He'd hardly noticed the paper ball he'd thrown at John Creed, and his words could have been spoken by someone else; he was really keeping an eye on Fyre King. Fyre was his girl. Well, not *his* any more – she'd made that pretty clear last year. But she had liked him once and she would do so again. Nobody said no to

Caspar Locke and got away with it. If only she would stop mooning over that freak Creed.

Creed, who was about the only one who could compete with him for class honours.

Creed, who embarrassed himself every time he opened his mouth.

Creed, who even though he didn't seem to know it, was Caspar's main competition for the affections of Fyre.

Creed who, worst of all, had somehow seen Caspar's true self.

Yes, Creed . . . everything seemed to come back to Creed. He was like a bone that had become stuck in Caspar's throat, and nothing he did, no matter how hard he tried, would dislodge it. And the harder he coughed, the more it hurt.

There *he* was, Caspar of the missing mother who spent too much of his time standing outside the head's office, while Creed – Creed with his doey eyes and the floppy hair he tried to comb forward in a pathetic effort to hide those creepy scars – got an easy run. It was the stutter that did it. The teachers didn't want to put pressure on the poor kid. Poor kid? *Poor kid?* What about poor bloody Caspar?

And then there was Fyre. What *did* she see in him? He knew that she liked Creed; after all, he was *The*

Terminator and he noticed everything. It might not all compute, but it all went in. That was the thing: he knew the 'what' but not the 'why'. Why Creed? Fyre – pale-eyed Fyre with her stupid name, her snub nose, long white hair and snow-white skin – she was – was . . . beautiful. It was weird because she was weird. And yet he couldn't take his eyes off her. In the same way as *she* couldn't take her eyes off Creed. Why? *Why?* Creed was ugly, deformed, a s-s-stuttering idiot with no friends. Talk about beauty and the beast.

Caspar pulled out his phone and surreptitiously texted Cem and Aziz. Time for another Creed Hunt after school. They'd be well up for it. And Baz would come along for the ride, he knew.

He turned to look out of the window. It was snowing. He hoped it would settle; there was just too much fun to be had from a tightly packed snowball kept in the freezer overnight. Right in Creed's ear when he wasn't expecting it . . . Burst an eardrum maybe? Bit of blood? Yeah, he wanted blood.

Then he remembered their first few days at the school, when everything was bigger and newer and frightening; how they had scuttled from lesson to lesson, sticking to the walls like mice or cockroaches. And then came *that* lunch break – was it their first or second week? And bloody John Creed.

4
WRITE AND WRONGS

John sat up with a start when the bell rang to end the lesson. He wasn't asleep again, but he *was* miles away. In an instant the classroom became a clamour of slamming books, talking, scraping chairs, shrieking, laughing . . . and above it all the Colonel's clipped military voice ordering them to read chapters eight and nine that week because there was going to be a test on—

The rest was drowned out by a girl's high-pitched squeal outside in the corridor, the slap of running feet on polished floor and the violent shove that sent John tumbling forward onto his desk, his books crashing to the floor.

'Oops,' sneered Caspar as he pushed past. Cem Nawab and Aziz Miah sniggered at their leader's audacity and, in the confusion, kicked John's books away across the floor.

'What's going on over there?' demanded Mr Christmas sharply, standing on tiptoe and peering in their direction. 'Is that you again, Locke?'

'What, sir? Me, sir? No, sir!' said Caspar, his usual mocking half-smile replaced with an expressionless mask. 'It was Creed, sir. He f-f-fell over, sir. We're just helping him p-p-p-pick up his b-b-books, sir.'

'Yes, well, that's enough of that, whatever you're up to. Haven't you got another class to go to?'

'Yessir!' Locke executed a perfect salute and strode, stiff-backed and soldier-like, to the door, where he turned on his heel and marched out of the room, Cem and Aziz in his wake as always, like ducklings behind their mother. They were off to make Ms Holles's life a misery in Art. John knew Locke's schedule as well as he knew his own: Thursday, last lesson, Locke to Art, himself to Latin. It was one of the few classes when their paths didn't cross and he always looked forward to it. Latin was a subject at which he excelled, thanks in part to the otherwise useless lessons his grandfather insisted he take at home, learning some blasted Carpathian gypsy language spoken only by Mordecai and the wretched donkey he used to ride to school.

'Are you OK?' asked Mr Christmas after John had picked up his books and was leaving the room.

'I am, s-sir, thanks.'

'John?' The cut-glass parade-ground bark was gone, replaced by a softer, more compassionate tone. He came round from behind the desk, closed the door. 'Wait a minute.'

'I'll be l-l-late for L-Latin,' said John, looking at the floor. Monsieur Sibellas, who taught French and Latin, was a notorious stickler for punctuality.

The Colonel sighed. 'I'll give you a note. Bear with me.' He guided John back into the room and sat on the raised dais so they were almost face to face – though John was staring at the floor.

'First of all, I'm sorry about all that earlier.'

'S-sir?'

'In class. I snapped at you. I just don't want anyone to think I'm playing favourites.'

'It's OK, s-sir. I understand.'

'And you *were* snoring.'

'I w-w-*was*?' John laughed.

'Quite loudly, yes. But, look, I wanted to talk to you in private about your last English essay. I know how embarrassed you get. The thing is, it was good, John, *really* good. I can't remember the last time I had to mark anything that good from someone your age. Well done.'

For a nano-second John managed to drag his gaze away from a particularly interesting whorl in the wooden floor and glance shyly at his teacher. The

Colonel might teach Geography with all the passion of a salted slug, but English was where he came alive.

'Thanks,' he said, blushing.

'I take it the extra lessons are helping?'

John nodded. He *lived* for the extra-curriculum English classes; just two hours after school on Wednesday nights, but everybody who was there had chosen to be there (mostly older kids, the eighteen-year-olds, the almost-men with dreams of studying English at university, of great novels, crusading journalism). The best bit? Nobody expected him to say much. At first the older boys sniggered, but the Colonel had soon put them straight. Now he was one of them. And Mr Christmas wasn't interested in what John had to say out loud; he wanted to see what he said *on paper*.

Writing was *freedom*, a glorious escape from the tyranny of the spoken word. On paper John didn't get stuck. On paper he didn't stutter. On paper nobody laughed at him. On paper words weren't recalcitrant; they didn't squirm and kick in his mouth, didn't decline to be p-p-pinned down or simply refuse to come out and play.

He smiled back. 'Yes, s-s-sir.'

'Good. I'm proud of you, boy. Now, what are we going to do about your friend Caspar?'

'S-sir?'

'Come on; I've got eyes, you know. I've seen him, John. I've seen that *look*. I know you know what I'm talking about.'

It was, John thought, something that Locke specialized in: a knowing smirk, a curl of the lip and a dead-eyed hatred all wrapped up; the work of a millisecond – and never noticed by anybody but the recipient. It was like some genetic virus intended only for one person: John Creed.

'I d–d–dunno.' He shrugged; the Caspar problem wasn't going to be solved by telling a teacher, that was for sure.

'I *do* understand, John. But you know you can talk to me. Right? That Caspar is an angry one. I've seen his type before, believe you me. If he's not careful, he's going to hurt someone one of these days – and I don't want it to be you. Not my future best-selling pupil.'

John smiled, and blushed again.

'Good, good. Now be off with you. Here's that note for Mr Sibellas.' And then, with a wink, the Colonel added: 'Oh, and as usual, my brother sends his best wishes.'

'Thanks, s–sir,' said John and headed for the door. When he got there, he thought of something and turned back. 'About Caspar . . . It was that d–d–day in the playground with N–N–Nate Davis, sir. That s–started it. I d–don't know why.'

'He's had it hard, what with his mother leaving so unexpectedly,' mused Mr Christmas. 'He's angry. And yet, at other times he can be charm itself. A real-life Jekyll and Hyde. Which, by the way, is a book we'll be looking at in the coming weeks. See if you can get it out of the library, OK?'

John nodded his agreement and quietly left the room. Thanks to the Colonel, he didn't have to rush to Latin, so he sauntered over to the window overlooking the playground, watching the snow fall, his thoughts drifting back to the events of the previous September.

The school was a large Victorian building, a great Gothic pile of red brick with a collection of steep roofs, bay windows and even a cone-shaped turret in the middle. The main entrance, at the top of a flight of white stone steps, was a huge, ornately carved wooden door – the sort of thing vampire hunters have to force open to get into Dracula's castle.

Inside, the hallway was dominated by a magnificent oak staircase that wound its way up through the building's four floors. Standing at the bottom and looking up past the flights of stairs into the interior of the turret was certain to induce dizziness and fear in any new boy or girl.

As with any place full of so many adolescents, it

smelled faintly of sweat, musky perfumes and rancid gym bags. Generations of boys and, in recent decades, girls had trodden those staircases, run their hands along the polished wooden banisters, rushed to and fro along the corridors and sat, half asleep, in classrooms with ancient iron radiators that were either off and cold or on and scalding. Here, history was only a touch away. You could even smell it. Underneath everything was the musty aroma of age, like old rolls of parchment – a smell that, thanks to Grandpa Mordecai and his old books and papers, John knew only too well.

In one corner of the playground there was a loading bay, a short flight of steps that led down to a padlocked double door. A set of rails on one side stopped kids toppling in and breaking their necks. However, it didn't prevent a curious ritual in which a group of older boys regularly rounded up half a dozen or so newcomers one by one and 'trapped' them down there for the duration of lunch. The older boys, the sixth formers who occupied a set of the newer classrooms, had had it done to them when they arrived and saw no reason to drop the tradition.

And so, during the first few weeks of the new school year, each lunch time saw a fresh batch of eleven-year-olds – boys mostly – chased around the playground, separated from their packed lunches, and dragged kicking, screaming or laughing (depending on character) into what was quaintly and affectionately dubbed 'The Hole'.

Some spent their hour down there trying to 'escape', while others made sure they smuggled in a book or secreted sandwiches in their underpants, just in case. John witnessed one nasty incident with an egg sandwich and saggy underpants that made him smile. And everyone got their turn in The Hole. He himself had meekly accepted his internment – the teachers certainly weren't going to put a stop to it – and saw his sentence out with the help of a book.

A few days later the sixth form Flying Squad, as they called themselves, decided that it was Caspar Locke's turn in The Hole. Up to that point he was just another boy trying to make his way through the maze of Big School. Of course John knew who he was; he might have kept himself to himself but this didn't mean that he didn't notice things. As Grandpa Mordecai said, 'If you're talking all the time you're not listening.'

Locke was much the same size as all of them back then; wiry and nervy, with an unfortunate habit of running his tongue along his lips like a snake tasting the air. In those days his hair was always shaved back to the skull, emphasizing the prominent cheekbones, the dark, slanted eyes.

But that wasn't the main thing about him, not to John. Although he'd only known him for a few weeks, he was aware of the sense of loss that followed Caspar around like underarm sweat or a particularly clingy fart. John didn't know whether the other kids had noticed it – he himself wasn't much of a mixer, after all – but to him it shone out of Locke like a searchlight in the night. Locke *never* looked happy. He wasn't like some sad clown, all droopy face and sad-sack dopey cow eyes, but neither did he ever crack a real smile.

Of course, none of them knew *then* that Locke's mother had suddenly left home only six months earlier. Gone, without a note or anything. Caspar Locke existed in a dark and lonely place. And only the teachers knew why.

And so there he was, sitting on the oak tree bench, old-fashioned metal lunch box on his lap and four burly sixth formers standing over him like giants around a garden gnome.

'Caspar, right?' said the leader, a slightly podgy boy called Nate Davis who was in the school rugby team. He was wearing grey trousers, a too-small school jacket and a white shirt whose buttons strained to contain his burgeoning stomach.

'Caspar!' snorted one of the other boys. 'What sort of name is that?'

'Caspar Locke, yes.'

John had been watching the exchange only half-heartedly – he knew what was going to happen, after all. You could run from the Flying Squad, but you couldn't hide for long. But something in Caspar's voice – a hitch; a sense of a mind being made up – forced him to sit up and listen.

'Well, *Caspar* Locke, it's time for The Hole. Are you going to come quietly?' The four boys laughed, their deep voices in stark contrast to Locke's little-boy squeak.

'Leave me alone.' Locke hadn't once taken his eyes off the leader, who loomed above him like a wolf over a lamb.

'Sorry, no can do,' said Davis with a happy smile. He liked it when they showed some guts. 'It's down The Hole with you. *Now.*'

'I said, Leave. Me. Alone.'

The repetition pulled them up short. Obviously they had been mistaken: the first sentence hadn't been a plea – it had been, inexplicably, an *order*. The laughter stopped. This was new; this was unexpected. They looked at each other. Did the little idiot know he was committing suicide?

John was suddenly alert to something in the older boys' stances; something about Locke's rigid body and blank stare. It was as if electricity had escaped into the air and was fizzing away between them.

'What did you say?' Nate Davis glanced at his friends. *Can you believe this little slug?* In reply Locke, head down, apparently realizing what he'd done, just mumbled something into his chest. Davis, confident and cocky, leaned further in.

'Caspar! *No!*' The words burst from John without permission from his brain. With sudden clarity he knew what Caspar was going to do. Even though every molecule in his body was telling him to mind his own business, he dropped his lunch box and began sprinting across the playground.

Nate Davis looked puzzled. 'What is *wrong* with y—' he began.

He never got to finish. Locke brought his stainless steel lunch box up with both hands and all his strength in a savage swipe that smashed into the other boy's chin. All at once the air was full of blood and teeth and screams, and what looked like the remains of a cold bacon sandwich. Before anyone could react, Locke shifted his hold on the box and brought it down across Davis's cheek.

The boy fell to the ground, clutching his face and screaming, just as Locke threw his lunch box at the nearest of his tormentors and then took up a boxing stance, ready to fight. John was shocked, and a little scared, by the look on his face . . . And then the three other boys descended on him like lions on a foal. John finally identified his expression: he was enjoying himself. The boy who never smiled was grinning like a madman, like someone who had found a reason to live.

It took the teachers several minutes to penetrate the wall of bodies that surrounded the fight, but when they did, they found Nate Davis – his face a bloody mess of raw flesh – and his gang kicking seven bells of hell out of Caspar Locke, who lay, curled up in a ball, on the ground.

John was the first to reach Locke after the teachers pulled Davis and the others away.

'C-Caspar?' he whispered, gingerly touching his classmate's back. 'It's OK. They've s-s-stopped now. C-C-Caspar?'

Slowly, like a tortoise coming out of its shell, Locke unfolded his arms from his head. When he finally looked up, John saw that his face was covered in blood – not all of it his. His nose looked slightly out of shape, one eye was bloodshot and the other was beginning to close up. Bruises were starting to appear on his forehead, and his white school shirt was torn and stained. And yet, through it all, his teeth were bared in a wide, happy grin.

'Are you all right?' asked John, putting his arms under the boy's shoulders, trying to help him up.

But suddenly the grin was gone. Locke pulled away and staggered to his feet. He pushed John in the chest with both hands. 'Leave me alone,' he snapped. 'I don't need your help.'

John backed away quickly, as if the other boy had tried to bite him. 'I was j-j-just trying to help,' he muttered.

'I don't *need* your help,' Locke repeated quietly before he was led away by a teacher. Behind them trotted Nate Davis, his face buried in a large and very bloody white handkerchief.

John jumped up on the bench below the oak tree and watched them disappear into the school. And that's when he saw that smile again, that vulpine grin, now aimed at him. It was the first time he'd seen Caspar Locke look truly happy.

And it chilled him to the bone.

Because he recognized that smile.

It was the smile of the wolf in his dream.

5
THE HUNT IS ON

Ms Holles was wittering excitedly in the background –
something about perspective – but Caspar's attention
was elsewhere. On either side of him, Cem and Aziz
were mucking about, drawing obscene charcoal pictures
in the hope of shocking the teacher when she came
round to monitor their progress. As if she'd never seen
one of *them* before.

The once blue sky was now just dirty grey clouds,
the beautiful day obliterated – though the snow had
stopped, leaving behind a dreary-looking sludge. The
weather hadn't deterred muscle-bound Mr Rabin, who
held dictatorial and slightly sadistic sway in the gym: he
was making his PE class run around outside in the freezing cold. What was the point in building a gymnasium,
thought Caspar, if you didn't use it in sub-bloody-zero
temperatures? Tough love? Character building?

He watched from the overheated confines of Room 216 as thirty or so pupils in T-shirts and shorts jogged around the perimeter of the playground below – the fat ones turning red with the effort and the spindly ones turning blue with the cold.

Among them, standing out like a single snowdrop in a field of poppies and bluebells, was the whiter than white, paler than pale figure of Fyre King. She had tied her long white hair up in a bun so it wouldn't get in her eyes while she jogged. When she let it down afterwards, Caspar knew, it would fall in long, perfectly straight lines to her waist.

After two circuits Mr R had them doing star jumps and crouches, after which it would be back to the gym for rope climbing or some equally rubbish pursuit before the bliss of hot showers and home. *Well, for some of them*, thought Caspar. *For others it was Creed-huntin' time.*

At that very moment Fyre stopped her jumping and crouching and looked up at the window where Caspar was sitting. She tilted her head to one side as if listening for something. Had she seen him? Not possible – he'd Googled albinos, and according to Wikipedia, they had atrocious eyesight. He leaned back a little, though, peering through his own reflection as the early winter night drew in and Ms Holles turned on the lights. Was he imagining the faint pink glow in Fyre's eyes? He remembered an albino rabbit he'd seen in the local pet shop, with its snow-white fur and pink-rimmed eyes that seemed to shine like that red-eye effect you get in photographs sometimes. She didn't like him any more; and it was driving him mad. All the kids liked Caspar, right? The girls especially. And if they didn't, he'd find a way to *make* them like him.

Then Mr R shouted something and they were off, in a mad rush to get back into the gym, even if it did mean climbing a stupid rope. Then it was quiet: just the playground, the tree and the bench. *Ah, that bench*, he thought. Good times. Fond memories. Memories to suck on like a boiled sweet, memories to *savour*. He replayed the 'incident' with Davis, turning it over and over in his mind's eye, admiring its perfection like a jeweller examining a diamond. It was a turning point, that day. It was the day he learned how to fill the emptiness inside, how to plug the mother-shaped void that his father could never fill. They kept telling him that the pain would fade in time, that only the good memories would eventually remain. Well, that, quite frankly, was crap. He was stuck with it for ever; stuck with the memory of his father telling him that his mother had walked out on them.

For weeks afterwards Caspar had waited for her to

walk in the door and tell him that it was all a huge, horrible mistake. But she never did. She was gone. Gone. Just like that. Like some magician's trick. Now you see her; now you don't.

As for Nate Davis and the rest of it – he knew what was coming. He'd managed to stay out of their way, but he knew they'd eventually get round to him.

His dad was the one who had come up with the solution:

'Punch one of them in the mouth, son.'

He thought he'd misheard to begin with. After all, his dad was a policeman, an upholder of the law. Judge Dredd in a suit.

'But . . .'

'But nothing, mate,' said his father, leaning down, taking his skinny shoulders in huge hands like bunches of bananas and looking him right in the eye. They were in the tiny kitchen of their flat, his father filling the space like a grizzly bear in a small cage. 'They're much bigger than you, is that it?'

'Yeah.'

'And they'll hit you back, right? Probably twice as hard . . . ?'

Caspar could only nod this time, his head filled with images of Nate Davis and the rest tearing his head off.

'Well, you just take it, mate, and you come home and

we'll patch you up. And then, the next day, you go up to them and punch one of them in the mouth again. And you keep doing it and doing it and doing it. You know why?'

'No.'

'Because bullies are cowards, son. Once they understand that bullying you comes at a price – a bloody nose or a kick in the, er, shin – they'll stop it and move on to some other poor kid. Right?'

Silence.

'Right?'

'Right.'

'The thing is, son, you have to deal with it. Whingeing about it won't help.'

He had refined it a little – never mind all that hitting and getting hit back. His first attack would be so over the top that no follow-up would be needed. And so it came to pass: the satisfying crunch of that lunch box against Davis's jaw, the stunned look on his face, the blood, that tooth bouncing along the ground . . . and, yes, even the beating he took afterwards – it poured into him like a tsunami, sweeping away all the hurt and sadness and fear and loneliness. It filled him up and made him strong.

And, apart from that scar-faced moron Creed trying to stop him, and then his bloody *care* and *concern* and *compassion*, he saw the expressions on their faces – a pleasing mixture of shock and awe and fear and respect, even from the teachers who led them away.

And it was all thanks to his father – Detective Sergeant Siimon Locke.

'Punch him in the mouth, son.'

'Yes, Dad.'

'And again.'

'Yes.'

'And you do it again, and again, and again . . .'

Fyre enjoyed Thursdays; having gym last lesson was a bit like getting off early. She wasn't the most athletic person in her year, but she wasn't the worst either. With her long limbs, most of the exercises were easy enough; the class always ended early so they could shower. And on deep winter days like this, you were left with a lovely warm glow.

Not that she disliked the cold. Far from it; while the others moaned and complained about having to run around in the freezing playground, Fyre quite liked it. While her friends turned blue, Fyre just seemed to turn whiter, and felt more alive. Sitting in those hot classrooms, she felt dreary; outside, with the bitter winds biting at her flesh, she felt awake, buzzing with energy.

It was against regulations, but she changed – as did

most of her friends – into jeans, and put on her over-sized white sweatshirt over the top. With her damp hair pulled back and her hood up she looked like everyone else. Of course, it helped that it partially obscured her face too. She didn't mind her looks, not one bit, but sometimes all the surreptitious stares just got a bit much. As she was tying her shoelaces, Mary Williams and Tracie James poked their heads round the door of the changing room.

'Fyre, you are *so* slow . . .' Mary was chewing her usual bubblegum. 'You must be, like, the slowest person on the planet for getting changed, innit. I swear you like being cold enough to freeze your tits off.'

'I'm making myself beautiful for my public.'

'Too late for that, ha-ha-ha!' guffawed Tracie, whose black hair was tied back in a ponytail so tight, her eyes were pulled outwards. 'What about, like, making your-self beautiful for Dave Mitchell? We're all going down McDonald's and he's going to be there.'

'So?'

'So, he likes you.'

'You know' – Mary grinned salaciously – 'as in, *likes* you. Know what I mean?'

'He does not!'

'Does so. He told Kylie, who told Trace, who told me.'

'Right. So it's official, then?'

'Don't be a— Ooh, look.' Mary looked at her iPhone, swiped a few buttons, and turned it to face Fyre. 'Look! Kylie sent a picture. He's, like, gorgeous.'

'Thanks, but I've got to help my mum tonight. Sorry.'

'Come on, everyone's going! Even fat Fiona.'

'I can't. Really. I just *can't*.'

'Oh, well, suit yourself,' said Mary, attention already back on her phone. 'Look! Look! Trace! Look! Garry's sent me a picture of . . . Oh, that's disgusting.'

Fyre waved goodbye as they left, both of them squealing with laughter as they pulled the iPhone back and forth between them. She'd already turned down an offer to go to the coffee shop in the new shopping centre at Stratford – something she would never have passed up before . . . before she'd done what she'd done.

By the time she left, the sun was gone; even though it was only just past four o'clock, it was dark enough for the streetlights to have come on. If the snow had kept up, the road outside the school might have looked pretty, but the dirty slush was like some thin gruel. And in that cold, wet landscape, lit by the burning orange beacons of the streetlamps, she saw the dark figures of Cem, Aziz and Baz slipping out of a side gate and falling into step behind the hooded shape of Caspar Locke.

Normally this wouldn't be noteworthy — those four were more or less joined at the hip — but today there was something different about them. They looked like they were tracking prey, with Caspar as Alpha and the others as his pack, just out of puppyhood and dangerously anxious to please.

Up ahead of them, a small black smudge hunched against the cold, she saw John Creed.

Oh no, not again.

And just as the thought entered her head, Caspar whispered to Baz and Cem, sending them down a side alley that, if they ran fast enough, would bring them out in front of Creed before he got to his flat. There had been other occasions when Caspar and his gang had started trouble with John Creed, but this time, thought Fyre, there was a sharper edge to everything. There'd been the usual pushing and shoving and name calling, the usual stuttering jokes and the odd half-hearted punch thrown . . . But now there was a violent tension in the air that she could almost see. She hung back until Caspar and Aziz turned into the alleyway after John, and then, heart beating with dread, ran as fast as she could without falling flat on her face in the slush.

John didn't need Spidey sense to know that Caspar was behind him: the boy was nothing if not predictable in his unpredictability. Heart on his sleeve, that was Caspar; he was honest with his hatreds.

Should he run? John wondered. He'd been on the end of a shoving several times now and had solved the problem by running away, but there was always that feeling of regret afterwards. But what was cowardly about avoiding a beating? What was it Grandpa Mordecai said? *Violence is the last refuge of the incompetent.* Some sensible rubbish like that.

Perhaps he could appeal to their better natures? Ha! Baz for sure, Cem and Aziz maybe, but not Caspar. Well, what would happen would happen. The street to his flat was up ahead; when he turned the corner into the housing estate, he'd try to do a runner before they realized it.

'Hey, John! This snow keeps up, we'll be right as rain this weekend, mate.'

John was surprised to find Davey Leonard, who was in the year below him and lived in the same block of flats, at his side.

John looked around nervously. 'Keep your v-v-voice down! Where d-did you c-c-come from?'

'Whatdya mean? I was sitting on the bench back there. You walked past me, you nutjob. I said hello but you just kept going.'

'I did? Sorry, Davey. Got a l-lot on my mind.'

'Anything I can help with?' Davey was eleven going on thirty, a cocky, scruffy, malnourished, badly parented kid with so many brothers and sisters he could have gone missing for weeks and nobody would notice. He had a face that had seen too much too soon. He was also the closest thing John had to a friend.

'No, n-nothing. Look, I'm a b-b-bit busy here, Davey, and—'

'Sumfin' to do with that mad Caspar kid?'

John smiled; there wasn't much Davey didn't notice. 'Yeah, and I'd p-p-prefer it if—'

'I ain't going nowhere. We'll sort 'em out together, me and you. Don't you worry, Johnny, I've got your back.'

John smiled down at his neighbour – a skinny little ball of excitement with enormous ears like TV dishes and a shaved head hidden under a bright red woollen bobble hat. In his threadbare, patched-up school uniform two sizes too big for him, he looked like a strong wind would knock him over, but John knew from experience that he was all gristle and sinew and guts.

'I c-c-can't— Oh, shit.'

With Aziz, an impeccably dressed boy who pushed the school-uniform code to its sartorial limits, by his side, Caspar had followed Creed into the alleyway between the two concrete blocks of flats. There were streetlights at either end, but the fluorescent light halfway along, although high and covered in mesh, had long since been vandalized. Which meant that while both ends were bathed in semicircles of light, the middle where John and Davey now stood was dangerously dark.

At the far end stood Baz and Cem, a gruesomely cadaverous boy with a mop of jet-black hair. Slowly, menacingly, they advanced on their prey. John took a deep breath.

'Who are you l-l-l-looking at, s-s-scarface?' said Caspar.

John shrugged off his greasy canvas school bag, worrying vaguely about how wet his books would get if this didn't finish quickly. He was, quite simply, shitting himself. Davey, who had the brains of a rocking horse, the heart of a lion and the body of a stick insect, swaggered up to Caspar and cockily stuck his chin out and up.

'And who do you fink *you're* talking to?'

Behind John, Cem let out a high-pitched giggle.

'This is s-stupid, Caspar,' said John. He looked the other boy in the eye in the hope of finding some empathy there. 'Wh-wh-what have I ever d-done to you?'

'S-stupid, is it? *S-stupid?* What's in the bag?' Caspar ignored Davey as if he wasn't there.

'What's it to you?'

It wasn't the most sensible thing to say in the circumstances, but at least it would move things along rather than going through the usual pushy-pushy-shove-shove preamble. Was he doing the right thing? John felt sure they could hear, and even *see*, his heart pounding in his chest.

'So you can go f-f-fu—'

As he was trying to get the words out, Cem darted in behind him and snatched up his bag. Stupid, stupid, *stupid*! He whirled round, but it was too late. Baz, about as wide as he was tall, with short little arms, insinuated his bulk between them and laughed while Cem emptied the contents – books, notepads, pens, pencils – onto the ground. Damn! Grandpa Mordecai would go mad! They didn't have much money as it was, without having to replace all his stuff. With a superhuman effort, he got an arm under Baz's and pushed him off balance so that he could squeeze past and try to rescue his belongings.

As John scrabbled to put his things back into the bag, he looked up just in time to see Aziz punch Davey on the nose – which seemed to collapse with a splat, blood spurting down his white shirt. With a grunted '*Umph*', the boy fell onto his bum in the slush and looking about in stunned surprise.

John started to get to his feet, but was grabbed from behind by two sets of hands and forced to his knees in the dirt and slush, his bag discarded behind him. This was it; this was the moment Caspar had been waiting for. He took a step back and lined the freak's ugly, scarred head up with his boot. Oh, the anticipation. The crunch, as it caught Creed's head, was going to put the memory of what he'd done to Nate Davis well in the shade. Bare fun.

Fyre tumbled round the corner, hood falling back as she slipped on the wet paving stones and skidded to a stop. What was happening? Creed was on his knees. There was another kid from school there too. He was on the floor holding a hand to a bloody nose, with Aziz standing over him. What had they done? And Caspar, running towards John, fists clenched and head down, as if he were about to kick a football out of a stadium. John, in turn, held down like some sort of sacrificial lamb.

'Caspar?' Her voice shocked even her, so grown-up did it sound, echoing loudly off the walls on either side of them. 'Caspar? What are you *doing*?'

★   ★   ★

Caspar skidded to an ungainly, slushy stop just a metre away from John. Behind him, at the edge of the light, was a tall, thin, white-haired angel. What was *she* doing here? He looked at the others, who had also stopped what they were doing. Damn! She'd ruined everything. Cem and Baz were suddenly bashful. They'd let go of Creed and were retreating as if this was nothing to do with them. He knew what they were thinking: it was one thing to do what they were doing, but it was another to be seen doing it. It certainly wasn't going to help his plans to win Fyre back, that was for sure.

'Fyre, I—'

'Get away from me,' she snapped, pushing past him.

Fyre pulled Davey to his feet, and together they stumbled further down the alleyway to help John pick up the rest of his possessions and put them back in his damp bag. She studiously ignored Caspar, keeping her back to him as much as possible.

'Are you OK?' she heard herself say to Creed.

'I'm g-good, yes,' he whispered, though he was struggling to get his breath and his eyes were full of despair. He turned to Davey. 'D-Davey?'

'I'm OK . . .' Davey's voice sounded like it was coming from under water.

Fyre turned her attention to the others.

'So, Aziz,' she said lightly as she stood up. 'How's your sister? I saw her the other day in Tesco. She got a job yet?' Fyre knew she was gabbling, but it seemed the only thing to do – to bring everything back to earth, back to the mundane. Maybe if she made them realize that they were all connected, were all human . . .?

Aziz, who was Caspar's second-in-command, looked first at his leader and then back at Fyre. She smiled disarmingly at him. In return, he grinned and ran a gloved hand over his closely shaved head. It made a harsh rasping sound.

'Er, yeah, she's good, innit. Yeah. No job yet but, you know . . .'

'Well, tell her I said "hi" next time you see her, won't you?'

'Yeah, for sure.'

Next she turned her attention to Baz.

'We missed you in Music the other day, Baz. No one sings those low parts like you do. You not doing it any more?'

'Nah, gave it up. Doing Woodwork instead.' Baz's voice was a strange combination of highs and lows as his vocal cords struggled to adjust to being a teenager. By the end of the sentence his face was as red as his ginger hair, which was a rigid mass of tight, almost girly, curls on a head as round as a pumpkin.

'OK,' said Fyre. 'Got to go.' And with that she slipped one arm through John's, the other around Davey's shoulders, and gave a final glance at Cem, Baz and Aziz. There was no point appealing to Caspar. She couldn't believe she'd ever liked him. 'See you later.'

All three smiled sheepishly and grunted. *This is what lions look like after the zebra gets away*, she thought. Caspar, on the other hand, just gave them a baleful look. He was beyond angry, a million miles past embarrassment. Fyre had humiliated him.

When they got to the end of the passageway, where the light began again, Fyre let her hand drop until she could grip John's. He didn't pull away. Instead he smiled, peered at her sideways and squeezed her hand in return. Later, thinking back on it, John would date everything else from *that* moment, when Fyre King came to his rescue in a dark alleyway just a hundred metres from home. The threat from Caspar and the rest had vanished like smoke as soon as she'd arrived.

He stole a look back and saw Cem, Baz and Aziz turn away and melt into the dusk, hoods up and hands pushed deep into their sweatshirts. Caspar lingered, staring.

'You sure you're OK?' Fyre's voice was so close that it startled him. She had her hood back up, so all he could see was stray wisps of hair peeking out. She was talking to Davey Leonard, whose nose had stopped bleeding but now looked like a very large and very squished raspberry.

'Davey,' said John, looking closely at his friend, 'I t-told you not to c-c-come with me. Oh, j-jeez, look at your n-n-nose. I'm s-so s-sorry.'

'Geroff!' Davey grinned, pushing him away. His eyes were blurry with tears, but if he was going to cry he would do it privately. And then probably work out how to get his own back on Aziz. 'Not your fault.'

'But—' said Fyre.

'I'm good, really. I just gotta get home quick and get this blood out before me mum gets home from work. She'll go mad if she finds out I've been fighting again. And these are me only trousers too. That bloody Aziz. I'm fine,' he reassured them with a happy grin that lit up a face smeared with dirt and blood. 'Apart from a wet arse.'

'Davey—'

'I've had worse at home, you know that, Johnny . . .' Davey's voice was accepting and bitter and years older than its owner. 'I'll see you later, all right? It's fine, really.'

And with that he was gone, turning up the little walkway to his section of the flats. The long, three-storey, red-brick building dated back fifty or sixty years, and was dotted at depressingly regular intervals with entry halls. The only new things about the flats were the bright blue steel entry-phone doors that operated on a magnetic lock system. They'd gone in a few years ago and had the desired effect of keeping the thieves and the druggies out of the stairwells and stopping them stealing anything that wasn't nailed down. John and Fyre waited until the front security door closed behind Davey and then kept going.

'And what about you?' asked Fyre after a moment.

'I'm f-fine,' he replied. 'Better than D-Davey, anyway. Thanks for' – he nodded behind them – 'that.'

'That's OK.' She looked up at him and smiled. Her teeth were whiter than white too, he noticed. *She's like the opposite of Caspar*, he realized. *Black and white*.

'No, I think you really saved me. Caspar's always had a thing against m-me, but . . . this time I think he . . . well, I think he really wanted to hurt me.'

'He does seem to have it in for you. And the others, well . . .'

'Oh, they just d-do what he says, mostly.'

'It's no excuse. Worse even.'

'Yeah, at least Caspar does what Caspar does. He follows nobody and nobody tells him what to do. I suppose you have to admire that. In a way. S–sort of.'

'Well, I think— Oh, look!'

They had come to a stop outside the flats where he lived.

Fyre had turned her face up to the dreary grey clouds. They seemed unnaturally low, as if you could reach up and touch them. And then she did just that: with a wide grin she reached up to touch the sky; or at least to let the first of a new batch of large white snowflakes melt on her fingertips.

'It's really coming down now,' she giggled, and then closed her eyes and let the flakes fall on her upturned face, like tiny copies of her own pure-white eyelashes. With bright white hair framing her face inside the white hoodie, she was like John's very own snow angel. 'I *love* snow,' she said.

Something clicked in him then, like the snapping into place of a particularly difficult jigsaw piece. He would, he knew, be friends with this girl for ever.

'It's my b–birthday tomorrow,' he confessed suddenly.

'Is it?' She peered out at him through air that was now thick with snow.

'Thirteen,' he said.

'Welcome to the teenage years,' she said. 'And happy birthday for tomorrow.'

'Thanks. Look, I've got to go. My grandfather will be waiting. He worries. A lot.'

'Sure. I'll go this way and get the bus. See you in school?'

'Yeah. And look, er, thanks again for tonight. You saved my l-life back there.'

'Well, I don't think it was *that* dramatic, but you're welcome,' she said brightly, and squeezed his hand, which he realized she still hadn't released. Then, just before she left, she frowned and stopped, seemingly struck by a new, unexpected thought. 'You know, in the last couple of minutes, you've hardly stuttered at all.'

And then she pulled her hood tight around her face and walked off towards the main road. He watched her go until the increasingly heavy snowfall, unhampered by any wind, swallowed her up.

John just stood there. She was right. The stutter, the bane of his life, had almost disappeared for a few minutes there. He marvelled, both at her and at himself. *See? It can be done.*

'John!' It was his grandfather, leaning over the balcony above him. 'Come on in, come on in, boy! There's a storm coming! You'll catch your death.'

'C-c-coming, Grandpa!'

Mordecai Creed was a big bull of a man who still stood ramrod straight in his black trousers, white collarless shirt and old-fashioned black waistcoat. Shirt sleeves rolled back revealed forearms that wouldn't have looked out of place on someone hammering a sword on an anvil. But he had seen better days; he was in his seventies and his body had begun to let him down. He was tired, and it showed in the sag of his shoulders and the hang of his head. Where muscles once bulged, loose skin now held sway.

His eyes, though, were still bright in his big, bald, bullet-shaped head. They were framed by great hairy caterpillar eyebrows above and heavy bags below, but they looked at John with fierce intelligence when the door opened and he threw his wet school bag down in the hallway.

'Hi, Grandpa. You g-g-good?'

'Never better – though leave that bag there and I probably fall over it, break my neck. Then, maybe I *won't* be so good.'

'Yeah, yeah, yeah, s-s-sorry.' John grinned, leaving the bag where it was. They hugged, and as they pulled apart, he stood on tiptoe, kissed the old man on the cheek and gave his bushy grey beard a gentle tug. 'Love you, Grandpa.'

'Come,' said the old man with mock gruffness, guiding his grandson into the small room that doubled as bedroom and study. It was in the usual mess, thought John as he moved old books and bits of parchment around to find a spot to park himself.

'So, I see you have new friend. This is good, ya?'

'Nothing g–gets past you, does it?'

'I only ask. Is simple, no?'

'Yes. L–look, I think so. Yes. Maybe. It's j–just . . .'

'Is a girl, then?' The old man smiled at his own wisdom.

'Well, yes, b–but . . .'

'Is no my concern, my boy. But . . . is good, no? Yes. So, how was school?'

John shrugged. It was his stock answer these days.

'Good? Bad? Ugly?'

'It was OK. Grimsby's a gap town. Oh, and Mr Christmas said m–my last essay was r–r–really good. He thinks I could be a writer if I w–wanted.'

Mordecai pushed a few tattered, leathery books onto the cheap, rickety bookcase they had rescued from the rubbish tip. Apart from that, there was a single bed that creaked in protest when anyone went near it, two mismatched and badly painted chairs, and a battered, shiny-topped table held together by odd nails and duct tape. Every surface was always covered in his grandfather's paraphernalia when he got home for his language lessons.

'He is good man, this Christmas, no?'

'He's OK.' Another shrug.

63

'I never meet him but I like him,' said the old man, giving an exaggerated shrug as well. 'He *sees* you, John – real you. This too is good, yes?' And then he shrugged again. And again.

John laughed. 'Yeah, yeah, all right. I g-get it.'

'So, where were we?' Mordecai grinned as he pulled some threadbare books towards him.

'D-do you see it too?'

'Huh?'

'The *r-r-real* me?'

The old man reached out and took the boy's hands – so unlined and young and plump – in his own wizened, ravaged ones.

'Yes.'

'And?'

'I see shining boy who cannot yet see past his p-p-problem, yes? Will pass, OK? That is what I see. I see boy who will realize is just bump in road, not wall or ravine. I see boy who will become great man, like his father. I see heart filled – *filled* – with love. Also *fear*. But love is most important, John; love. Remember this.'

'A g-great man? Like my d-dad?'

'Of course!'

'You d-don't half talk some r-r-rubbish, Grandpa.' John pulled his hands gently out of the old man's and screwed up his face. 'OK, let's g-get on with this. I've g-got a whole b–bunch of Latin v–verbs to conjugate. Which, compared to this s–stuff, is a p–piece of pi—'

'John!'

'Sorry!' John smiled, not sorry at all, pulling a note-book towards him and picking up a pen. 'Right, so, er . . . *Khareeshi tenpah*, er, *droycu?*'

Not for the first time, Mordecai Creed wondered if they were doing the right thing by his grandson. Didn't he deserve better than this half-life they lived? Maybe the danger was over. It had been almost thirteen years; surely they were safe . . . ?

But then there was the snow.

And the forecast he'd heard on the radio.

Huge amounts of snow.

In Scotland, where they had come from so long ago.

Falling, falling, falling.

That night the dream changed. Not much, but enough. The sparrows were still there; the crow/raven too. And the snow . . .

It wasn't so much the wolf that frightened John – though standing there in that patch of bright crimson snow, it looked like a demon from hell . . .

No, that wasn't the worst of it.

The worst was that it recognized him.

Its nose twitched once or twice and it looked up

from its feeding frenzy, fixing those gold ingot eyes on him and . . . and, as always, smiled that wolfish smile.

But then, for the first time ever, he heard its voice in his head.

Hello, little sparrow, it said in a deep, deep voice that dripped with honey and hunger. *I've been waiting for you.*

6
THEY'RE COMING!

The soft beep of the alarm woke him at 5.30 a.m., as it did every weekday. He didn't like getting up so early, but the money his paper round brought in helped keep – as his grandfather put it – the wolf from the door. He turned it off and looked up at the ceiling in the half-dark and laughed. *Wolf from the door* – bloody hilarious, given his dream.

He threw the covers back and sat up. Even to 'rest' his eyes for a second could mean disaster. The bed, after all, was snug and warm, while his room was so cold he could see his breath. Still half asleep, he pulled his jeans and two heavy sweatshirts on over his pyjamas. He was already wearing thick woollen socks, so he just pushed his feet into his boots. Only then did he sit back down on the edge of the bed and relax.

His room had enough space for the bed and an old

desk, and was almost like a normal teenager's – at least that's how he thought of it: posters of pop stars and footballers on the walls (mostly scavenged from Mr Patel, the newsagent), and clothes scattered everywhere (mostly from the army surplus store). But there were no mobile phones, no laptops, iPads, iPods or iDon't-Know-What-Else Pods (as his grandfather also put it). This dearth of modern artefacts was a constant source of friction. When John's parents died in the car crash in Scotland, they had left him with nothing. And even if they had ever gathered together enough money to buy a laptop, there were plenty of other things ahead of it in the queue.

He sat there, enjoying the quiet – a rare thing in the middle of London. But there was something wrong with the silence. It was . . . muffled. John crawled across the bed and opened the curtains. There was the reason: it had snowed in the night and the streets were centimetres deep in the stuff. It was the first time he had seen so much of it and he realized why the 'blanket of snow' cliché was so over-used. He looked up and down the street, then over at the tower blocks opposite. All the edges had been taken off the world: the roads had disappeared, along with the pavements and the kerbs. Cars were just extensions of the snow on the ground, growing up out of it like massive car-shaped mushrooms. The walls were topped with what looked like thick slices of vanilla ice cream, and the back yards of the garden flats had more or less vanished. It really was as if some god had thrown a chunky white blanket over everything.

There was the usual brick-sized cheese-and-cucumber sandwich on the kitchen table, left there by his grandfather, who would already be at work in the café that their downstairs neighbours, Fletcher Hunter and his son Kendall, ran in Hackney market. Sometimes the sandwich was cheese and pickle or, depending on how the money was going, just pickle. He shoved it into the pocket of his baggy army camouflage jacket, opened the fridge and took a swig of milk from the carton. It was 5.45: time to go. He would brush his hair and clean his teeth later – it wasn't as if he was going to meet anyone except Mr Patel.

He was surprised to find a white envelope taped to the back of the front door, his name emblazoned on it in his grandfather's ornately old-fashioned writing. It was a birthday card, cheap but cheerful: a laughing elephant printed on paper that had been recycled too many times. The elephant was holding a sign that read: *Congratulations! You're a Teenager!* Inside, behind a solitary five-pound note, it stated simply: *Happy 13th Birthday*. And below that, again in the same copperplate, his grandfather had written: *Happy birthday. Pahtech dreyschi chaoimh. I love you, boy. Grandpa Mordecai.*

He had to smile at that. Trust Grandpa to squeeze that damn gypsy language of his into everything. He had no idea what it said, which meant it would probably form the basis of his next lesson. Tucking the card and the money in next to the sandwich, he crept out, making sure the door didn't bang shut behind him.

It was grey and dim out in the communal hallway, lit by a feeble bulb that struggled to illuminate the furthest corners of the landing. Opposite, flat 21 was still boarded up behind a wrought-iron gate. It had been empty for years now; heaven only knew what sort of state it was in.

He trotted down the concrete stairs, to find Sarah, Fletcher Hunter's daughter, sitting on the steps outside her door, smoking. She sucked on her cigarette, making the tip glow lava-red in the murk, and blew out a thin white plume of smoke.

'Morning, JC,' she whispered, turning her face up to look at him as he squeezed past. Sarah was eighteen, a tall, athletically built girl with spiky hair dyed a bright, eye-watering orange, a square jaw, and a smile which revealed a set of double dimples that made the word 'cute' seem old and ugly and inadequate.

'M-m-morning,' he whispered, and swallowed hard. The Hunters had lived here for as long as he had – and he'd had a crush on Sarah almost from day one. When she wasn't working in her father's café, she hung around the flats, and he was always glad to see her, even if it meant making an idiot of himself. A simple glance from her was enough to make his throat close and force his tongue to take a vacation. She was wearing her usual tracksuit, but with a large fur-lined green army jacket over the top of it, and big, unlaced Doc Martens. Her orange hair was mussed up, as if she'd just fallen out of bed.

'Are you OK?'

'Yeah, I'm f-fine.'

'Don't feel any different?'

'N-n-no. Sh-should I?'

'Look, I ain't got any money, JC, so I couldn't get you anything. Sorry, mate.' She pulled on her cigarette again, making the space between them glow.

'I, uh, th-th-that's, you kn-know . . .' *Idiot, idiot, idiot!*

'Here' – she took the cigarette out of her mouth and turned it expertly towards him – 'want a drag? Thirteen today? Easy old enough . . . No? Fair enough.'

'Aren't you c-c-cold?' He was past her now, a few steps down, and they were eye to eye. Or would have been if John could bring himself to look at her. Instead, he picked at a non-existent thread on his jacket.

She smiled fondly and laughed. 'Bloody freezing, but Dad won't let me smoke in the house. And I swear he can smell it from ten miles away. So what you going to do to celebrate becoming a teenager?' She waved her cigarette around in the air. 'Not smoking, by the way, is a *good* start.'

He shrugged, and made a mental note to stop shrugging. It was even driving *him* mad.

'You've got to do something. I'll talk to your grandpa later. See if we can't rustle something up.'

'N-n-n— It's f-f-fine. W-w-we . . .'

'Suit yourself.' She stood up, ground her cigarette butt under her boot, gave him a cuddle and a peck on the cheek. Her breath on his cheek was warm and inviting, her lips softer than . . . than . . . well, everything. 'No, tell you what . . . Stay there for a sec.'

'B-b-but I c-c-can't . . .'

She turned to him with a mock glare. 'Stay. There.'

She was back in less than thirty seconds, holding an oversized cupcake. There was a thick red, sugary glaze on it that made it look like an active volcano. In the middle of that was a single lit candle. '*Happy birthday to you,*' she whispered, '*happy birthday to you, happy birthday, dear JC, happy birthday to you!*'

John smiled and took it from her. 'Th-th-thanks,' he managed to say.

'It's not much, but it's better than nothing, right? And you gotta blow the candle out,' she insisted. 'It's tradition. Can't have you not celebrating such an important milestone. Thirteen! You're a man now. In some cultures, anyway. That's it! And make a wish, right?'

John did as he was told, closed his eyes and wished he could talk to this girl without sounding like a coughing car that refused to start. 'Thanks, S-S-Sarah.' He smiled at her.

'It's nothing . . . a nothing muffin!' She laughed, and leaned in to brush his cheek with her lips again. It was a featherlight touch, and afterwards she whispered, '*Kharesh pentah droybu.*'

He looked at her in shock.

She grinned madly. 'I know! Cool, right? Your grandpa taught it to me. No idea what it means, though. I could be telling you to eat shit, but I don't think that's Mordecai's style. Dad and Kendall send their best wishes too. Happy birthday!'

And then she was gone, sliding into her flat in her unlaced boots and softly closing the door behind her. As usual, he felt like the encounter had been both a joy and a disaster. He stood there, savouring the moment, and found himself wondering what it would be like to be kissed like that by Fyre King.

One of the ground-floor flats was occupied by old man Glass – a quiet, intense fellow who looked like a Hobbit, with a pair of thick bottle-bottomed glasses; he worked in a furniture factory nearby making wardrobes and stuff. Opposite Mr Glass lived the Duchess, Grandpa Mordecai's ancient and regal sister. Like Sarah Hunter, the Duchess would be awake now, John knew, and so would her Dobermans – all four of them. He also knew that no matter how quietly he took that last turn of the stairs, they would hear him and start to snuffle at the gap under the door; they seemed to know it was him and not some unknown invader.

'Morning, John.' The Duchess's voice was faint, and accompanied by the click–clacking of the dogs' nails on her linoleum floor. He stopped as she opened the door a crack and peered out at him.

'Morning,' he whispered back.

'Happy birthday, sweet boy.' She smiled. 'Are you feeling OK?' Her accent was a strange mixture: eastern European like his grandfather's, but tempered by years of living in the city. At least you could understand her; sometimes Grandpa Mordecai was almost unintelligible – no doubt due to his insistence on speaking that ridiculous gibberish and going on about the 'old vays'. John loved him to death, but really – sometimes . . .

'Yes, I'm f-f-fine. J-just one d-d-day older, that's all.'

'Well, you be careful out there – it's very slippery. I'll see you later.'

'OK.'

If he thought it was cold inside, his shocked lungs told him it was even colder out. The first few breaths actually hurt, and his breath froze as soon as it left him. He shrugged his sweatshirt hood up, pulled on the leather gloves he'd found at a second-hand stall in the market, and headed off into the Winter Wonderland, his boots crunching in the crisp fresh snow. The world – the little of it he could see from within his hood – had turned black and white. Mostly white, of course, but it was as if the storm had sucked the colour out of everything.

He stopped at a piece of waste ground that the local council had the cheek to call a park, and pulled out his sandwich. It was his morning ritual: eating most of it, but crumbling some of the bread to feed the group of sparrows that had, in the year since he'd talked his way on to the the paper round, grown to about twenty. He normally sat on the park bench and distributed the crumbs judiciously, but today it was topped with ten centimetres of snow. A few pigeons floated down from nearby trees and window ledges, but he shooed them away. It always amazed him how he could wave his arms around at the bigger birds while the sparrows hopped about ignoring him, somehow knowing he meant them no harm. He smiled, remembering the only bit of his recurring dream that he actually enjoyed – the startling bravery of the sparrows.

It was only then that he noticed there were *way more* sparrows than usual. His little group had been joined by dozens of others, perched in the trees nearby; brought out, he thought, by the snow. Lucky he had a volcano of a muffin with him. He broke it up and distributed it across the snow. As he went on across the park, he spotted a large crow – an ebony ink smudge against the whiteness – collapse out of the sky and squawk greedily.

The snow was falling faster, great feathery pieces of foam. It was difficult to see across the road. A big red double-decker bus loomed up and swept past in a buffeting roar. He pulled his coat closer and trudged onwards.

Mr Patel had already been busy. A neat path had been cleared from the kerb to the front of his shop. Through the large plate-glass window John could see that there was a light shining out the back where Mr Patel sorted the morning's papers. He opened the door and stepped through into what was relative warmth, stamping his feet to dislodge the snow.

'Mr Patel?'

'John!' said a voice from the rear. 'Have you ever known such a terrible day?'

'Oh, it's not so b–b–bad,' John shouted. 'It makes a ch–change. I like it.' He bent under the counter flap and headed for the brightly lit storeroom, where Rajesh Patel was sifting through a stack of newspapers. A three-bar electric fire glowed redly in one corner, throwing out an amazing amount of heat for something so small. John was suddenly too hot, his hands tingling as the feeling came back.

Mr Patel was a small brown peanut of a man, with short grey hair and a neatly trimmed grey-white goatee. As usual he wore brown trousers, a brown shirt and a brown sleeveless pullover. On his feet, thin, darned, grey socks poked out of brown sandals. He was a man who smiled a lot, showing sparkling teeth that were far too white to be real. The smile was echoed in his eyes, which crinkled merrily at the edges. He was a bright point of light in what John saw as his otherwise pretty dull life.

'Are you ever going to call me Rajesh?' he asked without looking up from his task.

'No, Mr Patel.'

'Oh, so, so polite, yes? When you attain eighteen, perhaps?'

'OK. P'raps.'

'Very good. And how is your grandfather? Well, I hope?'

'S–s–same old, s–same old,' said John. 'You know him.'

'Good, good, that is good. Now what are we to do with this morning? This snow is a real problem, is it not?'

John peered through to the shopfront, assessing the weather. 'I reckon it's OK for now. It m–m–might even be easing up a bit. I sh–should be f–f–fine. I don't know about tomorrow, though, if it k–keeps up.'

As he turned back, there was a sharp intake of breath behind him. He looked back to find Mr Patel staring at him with real concern.

'John, what has happened to your face?'

'My f–face?' John ran his fingers over his eyes, chin and mouth: everything seemed to be in the right place. Though he hadn't bothered to even brush his teeth, let alone check if his eyebrows had moved in the night.

'Look! Look!' said his employer, and moved him across to the small mirror tacked above a stained basin. John looked, and gasped: the three scars that ran down the right side of his face were now a vivid red, as if they had only just been made. And then, like the feeling earlier in his fingers, they started to throb.

'What the—?'

'They look quite painful, John. Are you feeling OK?' Mr Patel hovered next to him, obviously distressed. He placed a gentle, fatherly hand on John's back and leaned in to peer at the scars.

John looked at his reflection, ran a finger along one of the slashes. This had never happened to him before. He didn't remember the crash at all; the scars had just always been there. Now they looked, and felt, like molten lava. The mirror was old, and the silvery backing had peeled off here and there – was that why there seemed to be a faint silver glow around him? He turned round, looked back. It had to be some trick of the light. He reached up to scrub some of the dust off, and quickly jerked his hand back as what felt like a stab of electricity leaped through his fingers. And then, weirdly, the surface of the mirror *changed*, rippled somehow. His reflection disappeared, replaced for a millisecond with a silvery *glow*.

'John?'

He jumped, startled, looked at Mr Patel and then back at the mirror. It was just a plain old rubbishy mirror.

'I think you should sit down.' Mr Patel took hold of John's arm, pulled him gently over to a chair. That done, he went back to the sink and poured a glass of water. 'Here, drink this.'

'Thanks,' said John, glugging the water in the hope it would put out the fire in his face.

'Have you become allergic to something?' The old man was crouched on his haunches, concern etched into every line on his face. 'The papers can wait, you know. Go home. You might be coming down with something.'

'Nah, it's OK. It looks a bit r-r-red and s-s-stuff, but I f-feel fine. I reckon it's s-something to do with c-coming in from the c-c-cold – the ch-ch-change in temperature? It's just a bit of a headache. It'll s-s-stop when I go back out, you w-w-watch.'

'I don't think so, my boy. I can't send you out like this. What if something happened to you? I would never forgive myself.'

'It's just . . . w-well, nothing really. I *f-f-feel* fine.'

'Are you sure? It looks very raw to me.'

'Really, I'm good. Honest.'

Mr Patel wasn't convinced – John knew that from the way he kept shaking his head and muttering – but he busied himself with the day's deliveries.

John got up and went back to the mirror – which was just a *mirror*. And John Creed was looking back at him.

If it wasn't for the scars, he thought, he would have been quite good looking. Well, passable anyway. Fyre certainly didn't seem to mind. He'd seen her looking at him, but had always thought she was fascinated by the scars like the rest of them. If she saw him now . . . He blushed at the thought, and the rush of blood to his head set off the throbbing again. Was this what turning thirteen was like? If it was, they could keep it.

'I'm g-g-going to risk it, Mr P-P-Patel,' said John to the old man, who looked him in the eye.

'If you are sure. You don't have to, you know. The customers will complain, but that's what customers do. I will tell them that I cannot have my best paperboy dying of the flu just so they can read their horoscopes or be told what they already know – that it is snowing.'

'It's OK, really.' John could only smile at the naked concern in those dark, soulful eyes. He didn't know what it was about the old man, but whenever he was around him, John felt safe. He felt wanted. He felt . . . *loved*.

'My dear boy, just . . . just take it easy, OK? Please? Oh, before you go, how is the writing coming along?'

'Oh, yeah, I n-nearly f-forgot.' John reached into his jacket pocket and pulled out a crumpled sheaf of paper. 'Here. The t-t-teacher reckoned it was p-p-pretty g-good.'

Patel took the papers – John's latest essay – gently, as if they were ancient scrolls of crumbling parchment. He held them to his chest and gazed up with his usual beaming smile.

'Thank you. I will read it this very day. Now, off you go. And be careful, OK?'

John's newspaper round wasn't difficult. Norton Folgate was a rabbit warren of unlovely tower blocks in council estates where the entrance to most buildings was controlled by an access card. No way anyone was going to deliver papers *there*. No way. But there were little pockets of posh – Victorian or Georgian houses arranged around a patch of grass – and they wanted their papers come what may.

One of these, a pretty square surrounded by three-storey white houses, was part of John's round, and today there were the usual twenty or so deliveries. He loaded them into the special rucksack that his grandfather had made for him, swung it over one shoulder and headed out into the snow. Hood up, shoulders hunched against the cold, head down and rucksack swaying heavily in time with his footsteps, he could have been an explorer making his way across the Arctic Circle. Again, he wondered why his scars had flared up this morning. Testosterone perhaps? They learned all about that stuff in Biology, but he didn't think it happened just like that – turn thirteen and *pow*? If it happened that quickly, then chances were he'd wake up with a beard tomorrow.

He'd been delivering papersalmost on autopilot, but

that stopped as he got to the Colonel's house. He had the paper (addressed to *Mr B. Christmas*) ready in his hand when he stopped dead in his tracks.

In the front garden, ankle deep in snow, was Colonel Christmas's brother: the school rumours of the mad twin were true, but John, who knew what it was like to be the butt of jokes, had kept it to himself, despite the currency such information would have had in the playground.

The first time he had found the brother out in the street, he had thought it was his teacher, so identical were they. But then the Colonel had pulled an embarrassed John to one side at school and thanked him for helping his 'unfortunate brother' back inside the house.

Of course, they weren't *exactly* identical. The mad brother looked like his teacher after a bad night on the town. A *really* bad night. His hair resembled a haystack after a thunderstorm, and in the side of his mouth perched a half-smoked cigarette. A set of burnished dog-tags jangled around his neck and he wore scuffed boots and an old green army shirt, the sleeves rolled up to reveal thin, saggy forearms decorated with faded blue tattoos. He was as slouched as his brother was upright. It was as if he wanted to be the very opposite of his sibling, with his military bearing and spit-polished shoes. But this was nothing compared to his left eye, which seemed to have come loose from its moorings and floated around in his eye socket without a clue which way to go next. His right eye would be looking at John, but the left one – so milky it was almost white – was looking everywhere else: up, down, left, right. It was like the eye of some huge deep-sea fish, and it made John a little seasick just to look at it.

And there he was again, the other Mr Christmas, glassy-eyed in the front garden. In baggy green army shorts. In what was essentially a *blizzard*. His head was cocked to one side as if straining to hear something faint and far away. In his right hand he held an ornate wrought-iron birdcage – tiny, but with a real live bird in it: a sparrow that twitched with the cold and kept ruffling its feathers up to keep warm.

'Mr Christmas?' shouted John.

He mouthed something that John couldn't quite catch. What was the mad old sod doing out here in this weather? He'd catch his death. John unlatched the front gate and went in, wondering why his brother didn't take better care of him.

'Can you hear it?' said the man.

'You should go back inside. Where's your brother?'

John trotted up the steps and shouted into the house through the half-open front door. 'Mr Christmas? Your brother's out again!'

He went back and gently coaxed the man into his home.

'Can't you hear them?' the old man asked again, this time almost angry with John. 'They're *through*.'

And with that he coughed, sniffed backwards as if his life depended on it and spat a blob of thick yellow mucus into the snow outside the front door. He looked at the emission for a moment, and then grinned as his eyeball rotated wildly in its socket.

7
MANY HAPPY RETURNS

At school later, John sought out Fyre. It was a new sensation for him, this need for company. After years of weaning himself off other people, he now looked forward to seeing her. He told himself that it was to thank her again for intervening the previous evening. It wasn't, though. It was simply that she made him feel less like . . . well, less like *himself*. He was glad his scars had calmed down – what was that all about? – and he didn't look so much like a comic book villain.

She was sitting in a far corner of the playground with a group of girls, under an eave that sheltered a few bench seats from the snow. There were still a few minutes before the bell went, and kids ran around shrieking and laughing and shouting and throwing snowballs at each other.

John was acutely aware that Caspar and his gang were

hanging around off to the right, just at the edge of his vision. He knew Caspar wouldn't be happy that his ambush had failed, and would be looking for an opportunity to try again. However, they seemed not to have seen him yet, and were content with pushing younger kids over in the snow, despite dire warnings from Mr Christmas, who had drawn the short straw of playground duty.

He took a few steps in Fyre's direction, trying to attract her attention by . . . what? Osmosis? Telepathy? He sighed angrily at himself. She liked him; he knew that. But then one of her friends – Toni? Tracey? Twinkle? – looked up from her phone long enough to notice him. Her face changed – a subtle purse of the lips; a bored roll of the eyes – and she said something that John couldn't catch but which made the others glance in his direction and giggle.

That did it: he felt his neck muscles contract, making it impossible for him to get a word out. It was like getting cramp all the way from his jaw down to his collarbone. And for the first time in years he felt like bursting into tears at the frustration of it. Then Fyre looked up, saw him, and gave him a smile so genuine that all his hesitation and fears dropped away. He felt the cramps ease up, felt his confidence coming back. What was it about this girl that— He saw something else flare in Fyre's eyes. She half raised a hand, as if bestowing a benediction upon him, and he *knew*. Caspar! Out of the corner of his eye he saw him hurling a rock-hard, compacted-ice snowball at his head.

He couldn't miss . . .

And yet he did.

John instinctively bent down, swivelling round to his left. The snowball hurtled past his right ear, close enough for him to feel the breeze. It continued for another few metres before smashing against the school wall and exploding in a shower of icy shards.

Wow, thought John. *That would have sunk the* Titanic.

It certainly sank Caspar Locke who, in his haste to attack Creed, had lost his footing; after windmilling his arms comically for a few seconds, he fell flat on his back in the snow.

Fyre started giggling and John went over to her.

In the meantime, Caspar, covered in snow, had struggled to his knees. Baz, Aziz and Cem were fussing around him.

'You all right, Cas?'

'Yeah, what happened, man? How did you miss? I was sure—'

'Leave me alone! Get away!' Caspar shrugged them off and stood up. He was livid now, beyond anger, his hands clenched into tight fists that radiated hurt and violence. John had made him look a fool – again. And this time it wasn't just in front of Aziz and the rest; this time almost the whole school was looking on – and that sort of thing just didn't happen to Caspar Locke. Oh no.

'Mr Locke!' It was the Colonel, striding towards them. 'I saw that, Mr Locke. A bit of snowball fun is all very well, but *that*' – he pointed at the icy starburst that his missile had left on the wall – 'could have hurt that boy quite badly. See me after assembly and I'll find something more useful for you to do in your lunch break.'

Caspar's reply was drowned out by the school bell. Which was just as well; John couldn't read lips, but he could read the expression on the boy's face.

He turned to find that Fyre had sidled up and taken hold of his arm, a simple act which sent her friends into paroxysms of giggles.

'How did you avoid that snowball?' she asked as they walked towards the school. 'I was so sure . . .'

'No idea,' he confessed. 'I s-s-saw your hand g-go up, and I . . . sort of *knew*. Look, I d-ducked and he m-m-m-missed. I reckon he must have m-messed up his aim when he slipped. Just lucky, I guess.'

'Yeah, probably. Oh, by the way, happy birthday!' She handed him an envelope.

'What's this?'

'A birthday card, you dooley. What else?'

'Thanks.' He took it and quickly stuffed it into his bag. 'I'll open it later, if you don't mind.'

'Sure. So, what did you get? Anything good?'

Which, he groaned inwardly, was precisely why he kept quiet about his birthday. People just asked questions and he didn't want to lie. What was he going to say? Oh, yes, a lovely new bike, an Xbox and a trip to Disneyland . . . Or the truth: a crappy card and a five-pound note. 'Ah, well, we d-d-don't really do much in our house, birthday-wise. My grandpa's not so . . . he c-can't afford a lot, so we . . .'

'It's OK, I'm sorry,' said Fyre, realizing she'd embarrassed him.

'Mr Creed!'

They froze as they headed for the assembly hall. The voice had come from right behind them – a bellow that echoed along the corridors and disappeared up into the great atrium. It was the Colonel, stooping down from his great height to talk to him.

'I'll see you later,' said Fyre, and slipped away into the crowd.

'Sir?' said John.

'I'd like to thank you, John,' said Mr Christmas, his voice softening as the corridor cleared of children, 'for helping my brother again. He gets confused, you see – never been the same since . . . Well, you get the idea. I can't be with him every minute of the day, and I can't bear the idea of him going into a home. You understand . . .'

'I d–do, sir, yes. It's n–n–not a problem. I hope he's OK, sir. It's p–pretty c–cold out there.'

'Yes, yes, yes, he's fine now.' The Colonel paused and peered at him. At least, John thought he did; with those oversized glasses he could have been looking anywhere. He felt like a microbe looking back up the lens of a microscope. 'Again, thank you.'

'That's all right, sir. He had a b–b–bird with him this morning, though; a s–s–sparrow. Does he like s–sparrows, sir?'

'Not really . . . That's why it's in a cage. And a damnably small one at that. Hates them, it seems. No idea why; it's a recent obsession, to be honest.' He paused, seemingly puzzled. Then the moment passed. 'Still, off to assembly with you. Chop-chop!'

The headmaster, a rotund, grey-suited man with short grey hair and jowls that sat heavily on many chins, had already started assembly by the time John slipped quietly into the hall.

'. . . latest reports say that the snow will continue for most of the weekend. Already, several train services and tube lines have been suspended, and there's chaos on the M1, M3 and M5. Scotland seems to have had the worst of it, but according to the latest forecast, the storm will make its way south over the next week or so. If this continues, we may well have to close the school . . . Yes, yes, yes, very funny! Calm down! Please keep an eye on the website for news. We will also be sending texts to your parents with updates.'

Humph − not to Grandpa Mordecai, you won't, John thought to himself. *Carrier pigeon might just about do it.*

'And for those of you without mobile phones, there's always the school hotline. That's all for now, but please, as you leave, take one of the newsletters that Mr Hammond is handing out; it contains all the contact details.'

With Caspar stuck in a classroom with the Colonel, John's lunch break was uneventful. Because of the cold and the falling snow the teachers decreed that nobody *had* to go outside. A few did − it wasn't often that they had this much snow down south, and they wanted to make the most of it − but John sat with Fyre in an empty classroom on the second floor. They talked − *talked* − about school mostly: the teachers, friends, enemies. It was the most fun John had had at school since . . . *ever*. After swearing her to secrecy, he made her laugh with the story of how his grandfather was determined to teach him an eastern European gypsy language that nobody spoke any more. 'It's even more useless than Latin,' he groaned. 'And more complicated.'

'So tell him no?' suggested Fyre.

'Argh – I can't. It's, like, really important to him for some reason. Something to do with my mum and d–dad, I think. They died in a car crash. Long t–time ago. I only just s–s–survived; that's wh–where the s–s–s–scars c–came from.'

'I heard it was a dog attack.' Fyre frowned, feeling stupid for listening to the gossip and repeating it. 'Well, that was the rumour.'

'Looks l–like it, I know,' said John, absent-mindedly fingering the raised edges of the scars. 'But it was the accident. I was the only one to survive. I was about s–six months old – l–lucky to be alive. Grandpa's brought me up. The stupid l–lessons are the least I can do for him, but it's like reading Shakespeare in Klingon. So wh–what's your story?'

'Oh, nothing as interesting. Just me and Mum. Dad . . . well, he's a bit of a mystery. Mum never liked to talk about him. We're as boring as hell. Oh, apart from the, er, albino thing. You might have noticed.'

He laughed, surprised at how relaxed he felt with this girl. 'Now you come to m–mention it, I see it. Yeah. Wow.'

'I know, I'm easily overlooked.'

'Not with a name like F-F-Fyre, you're not.'

'Yeah, about that . . .' She rolled her eyes in mock exasperation, hoping to get another smile from this strange boy; he was oddly handsome when he smiled, even with the scars. 'Mum said – *says* – that when I was born she wasn't expecting, well, *me*, if you know what I mean. And then I burst into tears and turned bright red – *As if you were on fire*, she said. And that was that.'

'Well' – John grinned – 'it's m-more interesting than John.'

'I'd be happy with Mary, or Jane or Christine, trust me. Fyre . . . Seriously, who calls their kid Fyre? Especially when they look like *this*. My mum's called Rose – what's wrong with that? Why stick me with bloody Fyre?'

'I think it's a c-cool name,' John said with new confidence. 'I think *you* look c-cool.'

'Thank you, birthday boy . . .' She hesitated. 'You know, Caspar's not going to let it go . . . He doesn't like being laughed at. Trust me, I know from experience.'

'You w-w-went out with him, r-right?'

'Yeah, well, we went to the movies a few times, that's all. But not for long. He's, like . . . madly jealous like you wouldn't believe. Still thinks he *owns* me. And us . . . like this . . . talking – he wouldn't like it at all, not at *all*.'

'Yeah. M-m-maybe I should just have it out with him – you know, g-get it over with. Can't keep running away, can I?' John smiled shyly. 'After all, you w-won't always be there to rescue me.'

But Fyre was annoyed. 'What's his problem? Why is he such a hater?'

'He's angry.'

'I know that. But at what? He's like one person on the outside and another on the inside. You've lost parents; my dad might just as well be Batman, for all I know: what right does he have to be so . . . so . . . *pissed off* at the world?'

'Well, he was a lot older than us wh-when his mum disappeared. I mean, we've n-never known anything else, right? It's not like either of us remember them. Our . . . *scars* have healed. C-Caspar's haven't.' He shrugged, and immediately cursed himself for it.

'You know, that's one of the reasons I like you.'

'Wh-what?'

'You're so nice. Everyone else seems to have something nasty to say about somebody, but you . . .'

'I c-c-can't s-s-s-say *anything* – n-n-n-nasty or otherw-w-w-wise,' laughed John, exaggerating his stammer.

'Fool.' Fyre grinned and jabbed him with her elbow. 'You know what I mean. Caspar's all fun and games and charm on the outside, but on the inside . . .'

'Yeah, I know. Jekyll and Hyde, that's what the Colonel called him.'

'Yeah. It's freaky.'

'Too much Hyde and not enough J-Jekyll, that's his problem. Hyde *was* the bad one, wasn't he?'

They were still laughing when one of the prefects, a gangly boy with acne so bad his face looked like a cheese and tomato pizza, poked his head into the room.

'Hey, you two, school's out. The head's given everyone the afternoon off because of the snow. Forecast isn't good. Back on Monday unless . . . well . . .'

Fyre and John were gathering up their stuff when the bell sounded – three long blasts, as if to say, *Hurry up, hurry up, begone!*

'Let's get out of here before Caspar appears. You can decide what to do about him later,' said Fyre.

John agreed. It felt like running away – again – but after such a nice day, he couldn't face Caspar.

But they were too late. Baz, Aziz and Cem were hanging about in the corridor, no doubt waiting for Caspar. Baz's deep *yuk-yuk-yuk* laugh echoed everywhere and mixed with Cem's whiny cackle.

'Shit!' whispered John.

'They haven't seen us,' hissed Fyre. 'Let's just wait for

a while. Over here, where they can't see us. It won't be long— John?'

But John wasn't listening. He was rooted to the spot. The snow was a fluffy white backdrop outside the windows, making the faint reflections of the three boys flicker like a faulty television set. But there was something else: their reflections were weirdly distorted. As they wrestled and pushed and shoved each other, John could have sworn that their faces had changed. They looked like dogs; puppies flopping over each other, dressed as schoolboys.

'John?'

'Am I s-seeing things?'

'What? Come on,' she hissed, and tugged at his jacket. 'They'll see us!'

'Look! Look at their reflections! What do you see?'

'Idiots.'

'No, no, be serious. D-don't you s-s-see?'

'See what?'

John closed his eyes, rubbed them hard. His head throbbed and his scars hurt again. What was *wrong* with him? He looked again. Baz, Cem, Aziz . . . no animals, no dogs. Just ordinary schoolboys. He sighed.

'Nothing,' he muttered, and allowed Fyre to lead him back into the classroom. 'I could have sworn . . .'

8
A THOUGHTFUL MAN

Rajesh Patel was a thoughtful man. He wondered about the world and the people in it. Indeed, these days he was more of a thinker and watcher than a doer. He knew that. Back in India, struggling to keep his head above water – economically and actually – he'd done enough 'doing' to last any person a lifetime. Now he was content to run his newsagent's, to talk to his customers (or not, if they didn't care to) and just, well, be.

His wife had passed away peacefully several years previously, and his son had . . . Well, suffice to say, Patel was alone in the world. He looked up from John's essay – the one about the boy who dreamed of wolves and one-eyed carrion crows – and gazed out of the shop window. Still snowing! The path he'd shovelled out that morning was gone – and it certainly wasn't worth clearing it again, not in the semi-dark. The shop had been as busy as usual during the day, but you could see it in people's faces: they were already starting to find the weather irritating, especially all those commuters trapped at Tube stations, and the motorists stuck in traffic jams. The radio news was full of breathless stories of elderly people or young couples with children being rescued from stranded cars or remote houses.

And it looked like it was going to continue: the whole of the country was covered in snow clouds – and there was no sign of a let-up. A once-in-a-lifetime extreme event, they were saying. Planes turned away from airports, flights cancelled.

Through the window the old man saw John Creed stop at the park across the road. Even before the boy had reached into his pocket, the air around him was filled with little brown specks as a large flock of sparrows dropped out of the sky. He was a good-hearted boy, that John. A good writer too. Reminded him of his own son. Perhaps a little too much . . . Patel was nothing if not self-aware; he knew how much his affection for John Creed was a hankering to replace his own son, who had died when he was about John's age. So what? Did it matter in the great scheme of things? The boy was kind, pleasant, respectful and – surprise, surprise – for once not alone. Another boy, tall and thin and dressed almost identically in black school trousers and a hoodie, had emerged from the snow next to him. This was both unusual and, in Patel's eyes, a change for the better: a boy needed a friend, this boy more than most. And certainly a friend who wasn't a seventy-year-old grandfather or a sparrow.

In his younger days Patel had been surrounded by brothers, sisters, cousins, aunts, uncles and grandparents. That time, when he forced himself to think about it, was full of happy memories. Mostly. Unfortunately, they inevitably dredged up what had happened to Ranjeev, his son. He pushed the thought aside. They were all gone now.

And then there were John's scars. You stopped noticing them after a while, but if they were caused by a car accident, then he, Rajesh Winston Patel, was a banana. He'd grown up in a rural part of India where tiger attacks were not uncommon, and he'd seen marks like those on the thighs and backs of those who'd survived to tell their tales. Or on those, like Ranjeev, who hadn't. No, John Creed might believe they were from a car crash, might have been told so by that oddly gruff grandfather of his, but *he* knew better: whatever had made those marks was—

'Hi, Mr Patel.'

John's cheery greeting mingled with the tinkle of the doorbell and brought him out of his reverie.

'John, John, John, how are you? Come for your money, yes?'

'Sure, if it's n-not too m-much t-trouble.'

'Not at all, not at all – it's here . . . somewhere. Come in, come in, both of you. Warm yourself up while I find that envelope.'

He busied himself rifling through drawers. He knew exactly where the envelope was, but wanted time to find out about the boy's new friend.

'I read your essay.'

'Yeah? And?'

'Excellent, John, most excellent. Very dark and very sad.' He laughed. 'What goes on in that head of yours, eh? So, how was school? They didn't cancel, I take it?'

'Well, yes and no. W-w-we just did the m-m-morning and then they let us go early. Well, the rest did; we sort of got s-stuck behind for a while. Long s-story.'

'Ah! Here we are! Hiding right in front of me the whole time.' He handed over the plain brown envelope. 'A long story, eh? I am intrigued. What keeps two boys from leaving school as soon as possible? Certainly when I was a young man, I couldn't leave fast enough!'

'What? Oh no . . . um . . . this is . . . You s-see, this is . . . m-m-m . . .'

Patel frowned in confusion. John had gone red to the

very roots of his hair, making his scars stand out like the finger bones of some skeletal hand. And then all was revealed: the other boy took his hands – beautiful, tapered, elegant hands – out of his pockets and pushed the sweatshirt hood back from his face.

It was a girl!

A white girl . . . a *really* white girl, translucent even. Hair, skin, eyelashes – and disconcertingly pale eyes.

She was smiling knowingly at him, and he realized he was staring.

'Oh, I'm so sorry, miss, I thought . . .'

''S all right,' she laughed. 'I get that a lot. I'm Fyre. With a Y.'

'Fyre? A very nice name, for sure. And I'm Rajesh, please. None of this "Mr Patel" I get from *Mr* Creed. It is *so* nice to meet you.'

'We should g-g-go,' muttered John without looking at anyone. He seemed suddenly inordinately interested in a rack of birthday cards.

'And to make it a happier birthday, there's a little something extra in there for you, John.'

'Oh, right. You d-d-didn't need to, Mr Patel.'

'I know, I know, but isn't that the point? You are a good boy, John, and you deserve it.' He looked at Fyre, who was smiling shyly at her friend. 'I have had many boys and girls come through here, but John is the best of all. Conscientious, hard-working . . . handsome.' He laughed at his own wit. 'Indeed, I am doing him a dis-service by turning a birthday treat into a business bonus. I am a very bad man, Fyre.'

Fyre laughed, and again looked sideways at John, who glanced at her and then quickly looked away. Patel smiled at them both, but at Fyre in particular. She was fascinating: like a character in a fairy tale.

'Well, thanks again, Mr Patel,' said John with a smile. 'Yeah. So, er, wh-wh-what time in the m-m-morning?'

'Looking at this weather, and listening to the forecasts this afternoon, John, I would say we can dispense with your services tomorrow. Have a sleep-in for once. It was very nice to meet you, Fyre. Come in any time, eh? Just for a chat? We can talk about John behind his back.'

'Mr Patel! G-give it a rest!'

When they were gone, Patel went to stand at the front window. He watched as the two figures, their hoods up, shoulders hunched, gradually disappeared into the snow. He might just as well have been looking at two adventurers in Antarctica. And yet, for all that, he felt a warm glow inside. And also an odd sense of loss. His son would never find a girlfriend and walk off into the world with her. As usual, snapping at the heels of memory came the snarling jaws of regret. If only, if only, if only—

And just then a solitary sparrow flopped down out of the whiteness, as if it had been shot. It landed in a heap, shook itself, ruffling its feathers until it looked like a little fluffy ball of wool, and cocked one eye in Patel's direction.

It was then joined by another. And another. It was snowing snow and raining sparrows at the same time.

Kama, the Indian god of love, thought Patel, carried a bow and arrow and flew about on the back of a sparrow! It was a good omen. And also a sign . . . yes, a sign that the magazines out the back wouldn't put themselves on the shelves! But first, perhaps some bread for the sparrows? Maybe some karma would come from feeding Kama? He smiled sadly to himself and shook his head. Rajesh Winston Patel, you are a fool . . . If only the world were as simple as that.

Outside, the snow continued to fall.

9
ENTER THE KITTEN TAPPER

Detective Sergeant Siimon 'Tapper' Locke had been leaning back, bored, in his squeaky office chair when the call came in about someone breaking into a building site in north London. It wasn't his patch, but this particular fate of crimes had started in the Folgate, so all calls on the matter were being routed through to him.

He had been idly watching his screensaver send rainbow-coloured bubbles hither and thither, bouncing off each other. He knew how they felt: the snow had driven everyone inside, all was quiet, and he was bouncing off the walls doing nothing. His office window looked down onto the main road outside the police station. He had stared out, growling quietly to himself. A few desolate, hunched figures stumbled through the snow, which was still falling steadily. Scumbag City had been replaced by Winter Wonderland. It didn't bode well for the weekend. A few oldies would drop dead, no doubt, and there'd be a lot more car crashes, though most of those would just be boring little 'bingles'. Minor accidents, that is. He remembered when he'd first used the word and everyone had looked at him like he was mad. He'd been a woodentop himself then, a fresh-faced policeman newly arrived from Australia. 'It was just a bingle,' he'd said, to blank faces.

Tapper let his feet fall off the desk with a bang and the momentum swung the rest of him upright as he leaned forward to answer the phone.

'*Yes?* Yes, this is Locke, yeah. G'day, George. What can I do for you, mate?'

In his hand, the telephone looked like a toy, for Tapper Locke was huge. He had wiry black hair that stood out from his head like a haystack in a tornado, and continued down the back of his neck to disappear into his shirt collar. He also had big bushy sideburns, and his coarse, pudgy features were adorned with a matching handlebar moustache. It looked like the pelt of a medium-sized stoat had been draped over his top lip and down the sides of his face. Even the backs of his hands were hairy.

What could be seen of his face wasn't pretty: acne-scarred cheeks, a nose like a blighted potato, and bags under his eyes that could carry home the week's shopping. The eyes themselves were wide, wild and bulbous, with scarily pale-blue irises that glistened wetly, as if he were permanently on the verge of tears. Imagine the Wolfman with freshly peeled lychees for eyeballs and you wouldn't be far wrong, the chief inspector had said when asked to describe the Australian.

In the early days, when he had first arrived from Down Under, Locke had been invited to the house of David Evans, a slightly older PC who was now a chief superintendent somewhere up north, and talked about his upbringing in a small town in the Australian Outback. Dave Evans's wife and two oldest children – eight and eleven at the time – had been fascinated by this oversized presence from another world, and the tales he told of kangaroos, koalas, drought and locust plagues. Their eyes widened even more when he explained that on his father's cattle farm they had had sixteen working dogs. As city kids, they were fascinated by these stories of far-off country life, but . . . *sixteen* dogs?

'Ah, yeah, well, you need 'em to round up the cattle, right? Of course, they were never allowed in the house. We had one dog in the house – the house dog – but the others all stayed out in the kennels. Working dogs, ya see? Can't have them getting too familiar or they don't know who's boss. Mind you, we did have one lovely kelpie called Croc; what a terrific dog she was—'

'What about cats?' interrupted Eva, a dark-haired little girl with a serious expression. She had been agitating for a kitten and felt sure there was some advantage in bringing them into every conversation.

'Yeah, we had a few, but not too many. See, in Australia, cats are pests. There were no cats there before you Poms arrived. Did you know that?'

'No cats?' Even Dave Evans's wife, Polly, was surprised at that.

'Nah, none. People still have them, of course, but they can be a problem, especially in country areas where they go feral – you know, wild. Eat all the birdlife. We got around that by tapping them.' He made a little motion with his hand, like a priest conferring a blessing.

'Tapping?' Polly Evans was puzzled, and waited for the explanation.

'For sure. When our cat Lily had a litter – there were about a dozen of them, I reckon – we just tapped them.'

Again, just puzzled looks. It was the bingle incident all over again. Wasn't it obvious?

'You know, tapped the kittens. On the head. With a hammer. Doesn't take much when they're that small. Skulls are like chicken bones really. Little whack and that's it, job done.'

'You mean you . . . smash their heads in with a

hammer?' said Polly incredulously, trying to get her head around the idea. Her children just sat on the sofa next to her with their mouths wide open. 'Why? Why didn't you just get the cat sterilized?'

'And spend eighty bucks at the vet when a hammer's free?' Locke laughed. He fell silent, though, when both the girls burst into tears and dashed out of the room, followed quickly by their mother. Though not before she threw the dirtiest of looks at him.

Locke looked up at his host in confusion.

'Did you have to?'

'What? It's just what we do in the bush. It's just . . . life.'

'In future, Siimon, I'd keep the kitten-tapping stories to yourself.'

'Too right, mate. Jeez, I'm glad I didn't get to what happened to Croc.'

'Which was?' asked Dave, knowing he was going to regret it.

'I had to shoot her.'

'Had to?'

'Yeah. Lovely dog, she was: even-tempered, sweet personality, but a rubbish cattle-dog. Can't be having that, can ya? That was hard, mate, very hard. Harder than tapping a few kittens, that's for sure.'

Within days the story of Locke the Kitten Tapper had

spread like wildfire. It had all happened twenty years ago, but the legend loomed large and the nickname stuck. There was even a rumour that he kept a hammer hidden in a secret pocket of his voluminous jacket for use on recalcitrant crims – a rumour he neither confirmed nor denied.

DS Locke growled silently to himself. Well, he *thought* it was silent; around him, the other policemen looked at each other and rolled their eyes. Tapper was at it again. It was a sound they knew all too well, a throaty purr that eventually grew into an angry rumble. It meant that Tapper wasn't a happy bunny.

There were four of them – two plainclothes and two uniformed – hiding behind the rubbish bins opposite a building site. The road was in a posher part of the city, a street of Georgian houses with little front gardens and classic stone steps leading up to the front doors. Streetlamps threw puddles of orangey light every few metres.

Even to Tapper, it looked quite beautiful in the snow – and quite empty, like one of those films where the hero is the only person left alive but everything looks like people just up and left ten minutes ago. The lights were on, but nobody was home – a description, thought Locke, of most of the idiots he worked with.

It was true: Locke *wasn't* a happy man. He had a splitting headache and he was thinking, This was it? This was what he had left Australia for? Left his home in the sweltering, sunny Outback for *this*? If only he'd known before he got here! Crouching behind a smelly dustbin to catch a couple of petty crims. How sad was *that*?

And, of course, when he'd approached the guv'nor for permission to check a gun or two out of the armoury, they'd laughed at him. 'You can't go armed to a job like this, Locke,' Detective Chief Inspector Collett had said with a sarcastic grin. 'This isn't Australia, you know.'

No, no, it wasn't, thought Locke, closing his eyes against the pain in his head – weird, short, sharp bursts like someone jabbing him over the right eye with an icicle. *Jab! Jab! Jab!* He ignored it. No, this wasn't Australia – far from it. Back there, coppers were armed all the time. No wishy-washy truncheon stuff. Not for the first time he thought about going back, but there was Caspar to think of. He'd have gone back years ago, but there was Caspar . . . The kid was a bloody millstone tied around his neck. Still, five more years and he'd be eighteen and on his own.

Jeez, though, you had to look on the bright side. The idea that someone somewhere was doing something they shouldn't – and that he was close enough to put a stop to it — was enough to cheer him up, if only temporarily. It was as if the snow and freezing wind had disappeared, replaced by the warm glow of anticipation of catching a criminal in the act. Now, if only this headache would ease up. *Throb throb throb.*

There was a noise then, a short metallic screech from the other side of the hoarding around the building site. One of the other woodentops shifted backwards and stepped on a tin can that had escaped the recycling bin. Locke threw him a look that would have peeled paint off a door.

They heard voices now too. Locke peered through the snow to where two planks had been pulled free and then loosely replaced. He smiled wolfishly; all they had to do was wait for the perpetrators to come out with their ill-gotten gains. Copper pipes, a few tools, perhaps? Well, he had a tool too. And he wasn't afraid to use it. *Tap, tap, tap! Here, kitty-kitty! Come to Uncle Locke.* And still the snow fell. And with it came a large black bird that fluttered down out of the darkness like a black bin liner, landing on the garden wall a few metres away from the crouching policemen.

Caw! Caw! Caw!

Tapper shook his head. The bloody bird was screeching in time to the pain in his head. Whatever it was, it was driving him crazy.

Tap, tap, tap.
Caw, caw, caw.

One of his team made a quick snowball and threw it at the bird, which took off in an indignant flurry before settling on top of a nearby streetlamp, where it sat and watched them. There was something odd about the way it did so, thought Locke. But what? He closed his eyes; thought about his son. Maybe he'd take the brat to the movies. Funny how all that had panned out. Him of all people, a father. Not that it was much of a hardship now that the kid was a teenager. He could pretty much look after himself, especially after the incident with the Davis kid and Caspar's lunch box. A chip off the old block, there! It had taken some doing, but with a few well-aimed threats at Davis and his family he'd been able to keep it out of the courts.

Suddenly the loose wooden planks in the fence were pulled aside and a small dark hooded head popped through the gap. Locke waited until the head vanished back inside before turning to his men.

'Stay here until I signal you, OK?'

'What are you going to do?' asked one.

'Just. Stay. Here.'

The men shrugged in unison. It was no skin off their noses – and maybe this would be the day when Tapper Locke went too far and they could get rid of him at last.

They shifted to get a better view as he moved swiftly across the street and crouched down behind a big skip.

Fee fi fo fum . . . this was going to be so much fun!

But then his elation turned to disappointment. The first figure to squeeze out through the gap was a boy. It was a fat kid, no older than, what, twelve or thirteen – about Caspar's age. It was as if someone was trying to squeeze a marshmallow through the slot of a money-box. When he finally managed to get his stomach out, he dropped like a stone into the snow. Locke hoped that the kid was just an accomplice, and that whoever else was in there was over eighteen and built like a rhino – it was so much more fun cutting the big ones down to size. But no: next came another kid – a skinny one this time, who hissed at his fat buddy to get up, and then began taking armfuls of piping through the gap and laying them in the snow.

Locke groaned. What a waste of time. Even getting this lot arrested would mean acres of red tape, admin-istration, forms, reports, and at the end of it all there'd be reports and talks with the parents, and that would be it. Until the next time he nicked them. He stood up just as a third kid flopped through the hole and then whispered 'All clear!' back through the hole; blimey, how many of them were in there? A whole school?

When they saw the massive snow-covered yeti

creature that emerged from behind the skip, the three boys let out strangled shrieks and sped off down the street. The copper pipes were forgotten – as were however many of their accomplices remained behind.

Locke didn't bother chasing them. One would be enough – he could reel the others in later. Whoever was left would give them up soon enough when confronted by the Kitten Tapper. So he just watched and waited. Soon enough, a large bag of assorted tools was pushed through the gap in the fence, thudding into the snowdrift below with a muffled metallic jangle.

'Baz? Cem? You there?' said a high-pitched voice in a strangled whisper. Locke froze. Surely not? He *knew* that voice. 'Stop messing about. Aziz?'

He waited next to the hole until, inevitably, a head poked out. Before there was even time to register that the others were missing, Locke used both hands to grab it round the neck and pull. Given the size of his hands, he looked like a gorilla trying to pull a particularly stubborn coconut off a palm tree.

'Ow! Ow! *OWWW!* Gerroff! *HELP!*'

It was a struggle to begin with, but finally his prey allowed himself to be hauled through, if only to prevent his head coming off in the monster's hands. Locke pulled the boy upright and slammed him into the fence, holding him so that his toes only just touched the ground. 'Let me go or I'll get the Old Bill on you, you pervert,' snarled the boy in a voice made deep and hoarse by Locke's hold on his windpipe. His eyes fixed on Locke's for a second, taking in the great hairy face and the stacks of unruly hair.

'Dad . . . ?'

Locke dropped the boy to the ground. 'Run,' he hissed.

Caspar didn't need telling twice. He turned and shot off down the street as if the hounds of hell were on his heels. He looked back only once, to see four men emerge from an alley and converge on his father. Two of them looked as if they might give chase, but they soon realized he was too far away. At the top of the road Caspar turned right and fled.

'Well, well, well,' said one of the uniformed police-men, 'I never thought I'd see the day when Siimon Locke would let someone get away that easily.'

'What happened?' asked a plainclothes detective.

'Dunno,' snarled Locke. 'My fingers must have been frozen from all that waiting around. He just wriggled out of my grasp. Fast too, the little bugger.'

'Well, he's long gone by now.' The first speaker shrugged, smiled condescendingly, and chanced a quick look at the bear-like DS behind them. 'Bit of a waste of time, all in all. Hours in the freezing cold and not one collar to show for it. Still, plenty of overtime, eh, lads?'

He was still laughing when the huge hand grabbed him by the back of the neck and threw him up against the fence. Before he knew what was happening, Locke had him by the throat.

'I am fed up to the back teeth with you and your stupid comments,' growled Tapper, his face just centimetres away from his victim's nose. 'Keep it *shut* or I will *bite* your face off, no worries.'

The copper, who didn't doubt that the DS was completely mad (like everybody else, he'd heard the stories about the kittens and the hidden hammer), just nodded mutely in agreement. Yes, yes, his eyes wordlessly promised, he would keep his stupid comments to himself.

At that, Locke dropped him like he used to drop the bags of dead kittens into the old mine workings out the back of his father's property in Australia. But where the kittens just fell into the darkness, the policeman dropped back onto the ice-covered pavement, where he slipped and fell heavily on his bum. He cursed loudly, but Tapper was gone, striding away up the street, a dark giant silhouetted for a moment against the dancing snow but quickly swallowed up. The other policemen helped their companion to his feet, brushing him down and finding his helmet.

'You OK, Phil?' asked one.

'I hate him,' muttered Phil as he struggled to clean himself up. 'He's an animal.'

Tapper Locke, meanwhile, was confused. He realized he had to get away from the others or risk hurting them. They were all so *stupid*. And the *tap-tap-tap* rhythm was still beating maddeningly against the inside of his skull, driving him crazy. And now, it seemed, his simple-minded son was a Bad Guy. How do you deal with that?

A young couple struggling past in the snow gave the madman a wide berth.

'Can't you hear it?' he whispered at their retreating backs. '*Tap-tap-tap.*'

Locke shook his head as if to clear it, and then noticed another large bird – surely not the same one? – settle on top of a nearby wall with a papery rustle of its big black wings. As he watched, it let loose a long, nonchalant stream of guano that looked like a messed-up snowflake.

Caw! Caw! CAAAWWW! it shouted in triumph.

Locke, angry beyond reason – with himself, with his son, with the general lack of guns in his life – whipped out the hammer from his pocket and hurled it at the bird like a boomerang. The crow saw the missile only at the last second; its flapping wings stilled as, with a dry crunch, its neck broke.

The bird and the hammer flew backwards a few more metres and then dropped like stones into the ankle-deep snow. Locke went over to retrieve his weapon, but as he bent down, he noticed something odd about the bird. That was it! That's what he had noticed earlier. Unlike other birds, this one hadn't cocked its head to one side or the other to look at him.

Because this one only had *one eye,* right in the middle of its forehead.

10
BIRDS OF A FEATHER

Fyre had found it hard to hide her disappointment when John explained that he couldn't see her over the weekend because he was visiting cousins. Unlike her, he was a bad liar. He didn't have any cousins – at least none that he was visiting that weekend. No, there was something else. And that just made her even more intrigued. Not that she had pressed him about it; she'd get it out of him eventually. After all, he wasn't the only one with a secret or two.

After going to pick up John's wages, they'd walked around talking until the cold had seeped into their bones and they were forced to take shelter in McDonald's, shining like some warm, bright beacon on the high road. Mary and Trace were there as usual; they had waved and giggled at them from the far corner. John bought Fyre an ice cream and they sat in the big

120

front window watching the world trudge by and marvelling at the snow. He'd told her about seeing Baz and the rest with dogs' heads.

'It had to be the glass or something like that,' she had suggested. 'You know how old and distorted it is. Dickens looked through that glass, it's that old.'

'Yeah, I suppose so,' John had finally agreed without enthusiasm.

'Though you described them pretty well; Baz is a bit of a labradoodle at times.'

'No, I said he l–looked—'

'Joking?'

'Yeah, right, s–sorry. Sorry. I wonder . . . Hey, look at the time. I gotta go – Grandpa's bum will be m–making buttons by now.'

'Making buttons?' she'd snorted. 'With his bum? *What?*'

'You know – impatient like. Pacing the f–f–floor. It comes from . . . Well, I d–don't know. No idea.'

'I like it, though,' she'd said. 'It's, er, different. Do you have to go?'

'Yeah. Bloody g–gobbledygook time again. *Krishna kroshna krik-krak!*'

'What does that mean?'

'No idea, I just m–made it up. Klingon?'

'You twit!' She'd laughed, and slapped him on the

arm. It felt good to laugh. She hadn't done enough of it recently, and John seemed to know exactly what to say to make her smile.

'So wh–what about you?' he'd asked. 'You d–doing anything exciting tonight?'

'No, just some homework and then the telly, I s'pose. Maybe ring me later?'

'Wish I could, but no phone – remember? Grandpa says there are more important things to spend our money on.'

She'd smiled. 'Like ice cream?'

'Shhh – that's our secret, OK?'

And that had been that. They'd struggled back into their sweatshirts and jackets and plunged into the cold, snowy maelstrom outside where, almost immediately – and much to Fyre's annoyance – a bus had loomed up out of the darkness. The 385! Her bus! It rolled to a slow, controlled halt right outside the McDonalds, the driver taking no chances on the packed snow, and the doors wheezed open.

'Go on,' John had shouted over the wind. 'I'll see you on Monday!'

She'd wanted to hug him, but instead satisfied herself with a squeeze of his arm before stepping into the fluorescent interior of the bus. By the time she'd found her card and squeezed through the crush of wet bodies and dripping umbrellas, John had gone. At least, she'd thought, he'd had the good grace to sound disappointed at not seeing her again till Monday.

Now, as the bus approached her stop and she rang the bell, she found herself burning to know what John was doing over the weekend that was so important. Whatever *he* was hiding couldn't in a million years be as bad as what *she* was hiding.

The bus stop was just a short stroll from the block where she lived. On the way she bought a chicken kebab from the shop next to the old pub that was now a sari warehouse. As she turned the corner, the kebab tucked into a side pocket of her rucksack, the lights came on in the kitchen of her flat on the twelfth floor. She looked at her watch: bang on. The timer was working perfectly.

The flats were made of ageing concrete, brutal and soulless. Even the snow, which was imbuing even the most mundane objects with a bit of glitz, failed to help. Some bright spark had decided to build even bigger towers on three sides of the original and link them all up with grey walkways. It was like living in some perverse modern interpretation of a medieval castle. When she'd read *The Lord of the Rings*, she'd thought, *I live in Mordor!*

Upstairs – thankfully the elevators were working –

she crunched across several centimetres of snow. This high up, the wind was howling noisily, whipping the snowflakes back and forth and creating little eddies. Normally, despite the location, the view across the city was pretty spectacular, but tonight it was just a confusing, whirling mix of darkness and wild snow. There were a few lights on in the other flats, but all the kitchen windows, which looked out onto the long landing, were covered by curtains or blinds.

As Fyre slipped the key into the lock, an excited whimpering began behind the door where her dog, Oscar, slept while she was at school. One of her first chores when she got home was to take the poor thing for a walk. He was a good dog, rarely making a mess in the house, but by the time she got home he was always busting to relieve himself. Today, though, there was no way either of them was going back out. He would have to do his business on the back balcony.

'Hello, boy, hello, boy,' she crooned, leaning down to ruffle the ears of the small black-and-tan mongrel as he threw himself around in excited circles. 'Yes, yes, yes, I love you too. Yes, I do.'

You had to laugh; even his eyeballs looked fit to burst.

'Yes, boy, OK, calm down. Out the back now; here we go.'

She dropped her bags on the floor in the little hall-way and strode through to the lounge, turning on lamps as she went. Oscar danced behind her, his long thin tail whipping around and threatening to knock stuff off every flat surface he passed. The door to the small rear balcony was in the lounge, which was cluttered with old-fashioned but comfortable furniture. Fyre unlocked the door, wondering why she bothered to secure the door to a balcony twelve floors up. Who was she worried about? Spider-Man?

The dog jammed his nose against the gap as soon as the door began to open, exploding out into the virgin snow like a mad thing and immediately cocking his leg to take the pressure off his bladder, and his eyeballs.

Meanwhile Fyre went across to a tall upright freezer standing against the right-hand wall of the balcony. It was kept shut by a large chain and a heavy brass padlock. She fumbled with her keychain and then opened the padlock. The chains fell away and she opened the door. All the shelves had been taken out to create one big open space inside, in order to accommodate the body of a woman in a pale blue nightdress. She was frozen solid, and there was white, frosty rime on her lips and hair. In life she had been pale and pigment-free, like Fyre. In death she was more so, her eyes wide open, opaque, like milky marbles. She had been wedged in sideways and now rested there, half standing, half kneeling, looking awkward.

'Hello, Mum,' whispered Fyre as Oscar peed heavily and noisily into the snow behind her. 'How was your day?'

On Saturday morning, Fyre was sitting upstairs on the edge of her mother's bed, puzzling yet again over a series of photographs she'd found on her mother's camera. There were about fifteen of them, and they were *all* of John Creed, taken when she and John first joined the school, before her mother was in a wheelchair with the wasting disease that had eventually killed her.

What *had* her mother been thinking? She frowned. She had assumed her mother was taking photographs of *her*. But in the background of *every* photograph, there was John Creed. Why? What was so special about *him*? She looked up and addressed the room as if her mother were actually there. 'Eh, Mum? Answer me that.'

Eventually she went downstairs. On the front balcony of the flats she swept the layer of snow off the ledge, leaned her elbows on it and looked out over the city. Behind her, Oscar whimpered excitedly at the prospect of a walk, but was also intimidated by all this cold white stuff. He kept sticking his snout in it, sniffing, and then sneezing when it got up his nostrils. When she turned to look at him, he stared back with a look of almost human incomprehension on his little greying face: *What is this?*

'You are a stupid dog. You know that, don't you?'

As far as the eye could see, the city was covered. Today, though, the falling snow wasn't so much feathery as suspiciously solid, somewhere between rain and hail. Above, the grey-white clouds that covered most of the country didn't seem to be moving at all; it was like being under the sea and looking up to find the surface covered in dirty polystyrene.

The streets were calm; not deserted, but certainly quiet for a market day. Hushed. Like a breath drawn in but not let out. Perhaps that was the sense of anticipation she felt. Or was she just trying to blame the snow? The feeling that something bad was going to happen had been there ever since her mother had—

'Come on, then, buster,' she said to the dog, who raced along the landing towards the lifts, almost knocking over a large, ruddy-faced woman who emerged from one of the flats at the same time.

'Whoa! Watch it there, Oscar!' The woman, Mrs Malchar, was holding a stiff broom and grinning widely. 'Hello, Fyre. Terrible weather. Mind you don't lose that dog in a snowdrift.'

'I won't, Mrs M,' muttered Fyre as she slipped past, hoping to avoid a conversation. It wasn't to be.

'So, how's your mum? I haven't seen her for a while. She OK?' Mrs Malchar was the twelfth-floor busybody. Any noise, and she was out and sticking her nose in. Fyre suspected she lived her whole life glued to the letterbox, and had taken to creeping past her door.

'She's OK. Got a bit of a cold so she's staying inside.' Which, thought Fyre, wasn't strictly a lie.

'Should I take her something? I've got a lovely chicken soup on the go inside. My Albert used to say it would cure cancer, my chicken soup. God rest his soul.'

'No!' Fyre felt panic rising in her throat. *Christ, don't be sick; vomit is not going to help the situation.* 'Thanks, but she's got to get as much sleep as she can – lots of rest. According to the doctor.'

'You are a good girl, Fyre. It must have been a nightmare getting that wheelchair to the doctor's in all this snow. I don't know how you do it. She's lucky to have you, is your mum. Tell you what, stop by on your way back and I'll give you a big bowl of my soup to take in. After all, that's what neighbours are for, eh?'

'I will, Mrs M, thanks.' Fyre smiled. Sweet! That was dinner sorted for a day or two. She knew, though, that she was going to have to come up with a better story sooner or later. Nobody else seemed to give a hoot, but

Mrs M was a problem. Why couldn't she live on the tenth floor?

As she waited for the lift, it came to her that maybe she could tell Mrs M the truth. *Hello, Mrs M – can I call you Edna? Well, it's like this, Edna: I came home from school one day six months ago and my poor housebound, wheelchair-trapped mother had just, well, died. No, I have no idea: heart attack, pneumonia (she had an awful cold at the time), brain thingy – aneurysm? All of the above?*

What did I do? Isn't it obvious? I put her in the freezer on the balcony and have been pretending she's alive ever since. I know her bank card number, I can forge her signature; her pension and everything else goes straight into the bank and . . . Well, that's it really. Why? Because I'm an only child, because I'm an albino, because I don't want to be sent to some children's home where I'm the new freak . . . And maybe because I don't want my mum to go? Not yet. And most of all because of John. You see, my mum was adamant that I befriend him. He needs all the friends he can get, she said. And, despite all that, I like him.

So what do you reckon, Mrs M? she thought as the lift doors rattled open and Oscar leaped in. *Gonna help me?*

No. Fyre smiled grimly as she thumbed the ground-floor button and the doors closed. *I thought not.*

Nobody was going to help her. Nobody.

11
DOG EAT DOG

John had slept fitfully, haunted by images of snow and wolves and boys with dog heads. It was seven a.m. when he woke – early for most people on a Saturday, but a lie-in for him. He had a sneaking suspicion that it was also part of his birthday 'present'. Maybe Mr Patel knew that he wouldn't have kept any of the extra money for himself; it had, as usual, all gone to his grandfather and the Duchess, whose arthritis stopped her doing much. Between them, with his grandfather's early morning shift at the café, they managed to keep their heads above water. *Just.*

He dressed, made toast and ate it in silence while slurping down the bitter brown tea that his grandfather had left stewing in the pot. Mordecai would have already been to the café to prepare for the day and would now be downstairs drinking tea with the

Duchess. It was an unchanging ritual, much like that of the previous evening: home from school, the bloody language lessons, homework, dinner, listen to the radio (or read) and then bed. The only break in the monotony was the home-made cake that the Duchess had made for his birthday. They had pushed the work to one side and stuffed themselves until they all felt sick. It wasn't brilliant, but it was better than nothing. He wondered if he should have invited Fyre. Would Grandpa Mordecai have approved? Did it matter? And then there was the question of the weekends: Fyre had wanted to hang out and he'd had to lie to her; told her some story about his cousins. Not that he had any – well, *any* family his own age, for that matter. And no friends other than Davey Leonard. It hadn't been easy, lying to her, but it had to be done: if she found out what he really did at the weekends, she'd probably never speak to him again.

He went into the bathroom and peered at himself in the tiny mirror above the sink. This was something new too: he suddenly seemed to *care* what he looked like. And look at him! He resembled a wild man from some lost Amazonian tribe that hadn't invented the comb. Well, the parts of himself he could see, anyway. The mirror was so small he had to keep moving his head this way and that to get the full picture.

Mirror, mirror on the wall . . . Or should that be '*tiny*' *mirror on the wall*? The place was bereft of any mirrors bigger than his hand, thanks to his grandfather. *Eisoptrophobia*. He'd looked it up: a fear of mirrors. Who knew this stuff existed? Fear of spiders, fear of the dentist, fear of being put on the spot and asked a question at school – *these* were all well-founded fears. But *mirrors*? Mind you, what if it was hereditary? That weird stuff with the mirror in Mr Patel's place had got him thinking. Maybe whatever had happened to Grandpa Mordecai was now happening to him.

He took a bite of toast and thought about all the things they didn't have thanks to his grandfather's . . . what was the word? Idiosyncrasies? Idiocy? A bit of both?

Number one: no money. Two: no credit cards. Three: no phones. Four: as little official ID as possible. As far as was possible in the twenty-first century, they lived off the grid. Grandpa Mordecai put it down to coming from eastern Europe and growing up in societies where people were, as he put it, 'filed, stamped, indexed, numbered . . . and slaughtered'.

John had tried to talk to the Duchess about it, but she, he was surprised to find, was as adamant as his grandfather: they should live as anonymously as possible; in the shadows, between the cracks. It was a gigantic pain in the butt, but the look on their faces when he spoke of it was enough to make him back down. And it wasn't just anger – *that* he could have dealt with; it was the fear in their eyes.

The Duchess didn't only have four Dobermans; she had six cats too.

Whenever anybody knocked on the door, or farted three streets away, the dogs would erupt in a frenzy of barking; this set off the cats, which would shoot up the curtains. Anywhere else and the Duchess would have been thrown out on her ear; here, though, she knew everyone and everyone knew her. When not at home, Mordecai was invariably taking tea with the Duchess, and Sarah Hunter was in and out all day making sure the old lady had everything she needed.

The Duchess herself looked like the Queen. Only smaller. And living in a council house. She had a little wrinkly, smiley face, and short white permed hair that framed her head like a halo. For her age – anything from sixty-six to a hundred and eighty-six – she was pretty nimble. She could, for instance, still touch her toes. Though this had much to do with bending down to pick up the piles of poo the dogs left in her tiny garden and the evil-smelling black coils the cats left in the litter tray in the bathroom.

The place was filled with scavenged and second-hand furniture, all of it slightly down-at-heel. Mordecai looked at her as she returned from taking a particularly noxious 'poo parcel' to the bin in the tiny garden. He was sitting sipping from a china cup that, in his hands, looked like part of a kid's tea set.

'You listen to news this morning?' he asked her as she eased herself into an upright wooden chair opposite him. Was it the chair or his sister that creaked the most? 'The snow? Places in Scotland – *Scotland*, Duchess – completely isolated. Just helicopters getting in. Nobody going nowhere today, that's for sure.'

'Anywhere. Nobody is going *anywhere*. How many years have we been here? Honestly, Mordecai—'

'You think it's *them*?' he interrupted. 'I think it's them. Do you? I think they found us.'

'You can't know that, Mordecai. It could easily just be snow. Perhaps it's just snow. It's been a long time.'

'I can *feel* them.'

'No, you can't, you silly old fool. No more than you could then. The boy, though . . . The boy might. They used to say this is when the Change happens, if it's going to. Manhood. Adolescence. His scars seem . . . deeper? More prominent? Do you think we're already seeing it in his face?'

'Possibly. I don't know. Gods, I wish they'd caught

his leg, an arm maybe. You can amputate arm—'

'Ssssh, you mad old fool. Has he said anything?'

'Is quiet, you know. Too quiet maybe.' A pause. 'I know he's friendly with girl. Saw them. Outside.'

'That's a good thing, isn't it? Better than mooning over Sarah, eh? He's a good boy, Mordecai. Thanks to you.'

'Thanks to *us*. All of us. But . . . if it is *them*?' He looked wistfully out of the window: the garden was now just a lumpy white eiderdown. Even the four piles of fresh Doberman dung – that morning's efforts – already looked like little white pyramids. The grit trucks wouldn't be out today; not when it was this bad.

Was it *them*? Were they here, bringing winter with them? Mordecai had to know before it was too late.

'I'll send—' he said, just as the doorbell rang and the whole place exploded with noise and movement. It was all Mordecai could do to stop his tea spilling as the dogs fell over themselves to get to the door and the cats raced vertically up anything to get out of their way.

'That'll be John,' said the Duchess. 'We'll talk about this later.'

As soon as the door opened, the four dogs burst past the Duchess's legs and through to the wrought-iron security gate, but once they realized it was John, the little stubs of their docked tails began wagging like busted metronomes, and they snuffled and whined at the bars as if they hadn't seen him only yesterday.

'Morning, Duchess,' he said as she slipped a big iron key into the lock and let him in. He waded through the sinuous black bodies as they milled around him, leaping up, licking his hands and letting out little yelps of excitement. He stroked an ear here, tickled a belly there.

'Morning, John, darling. Kiss?'

He smiled and leaned down to peck her on the cheek. 'Grandpa here?' he asked, knowing the answer.

'Yes, dear, in the lounge. Go on through. Nice cup of tea?'

It was the first question the Duchess asked when anyone came into the flat. As if tea were the answer to all life's problems. Having trouble paying the rent? Nice cup of tea will sort that out. School bully making your life a misery? Cup of tea. Touch of cancer? Lovely cup of tea. Seeing odd things in the school windows? Nothing a nice cup of tea won't cure.

'No thanks. Had one upstairs.'

'Oh, dear – not that muck Mordecai makes? It's like drinking glue.'

'I heard that,' growled a deep voice from the other room.

The Duchess poked her tongue out in his direction and made a face.

'I heard that too.'

She ignored him. '*Another* cup of tea, Mordecai?'

'Love one, thanks, Duchess. John?'

The Duchess headed for the kitchen while John wandered into the living room and flung himself down into a soft, thick armchair that had seen better days.

'You OK?' asked his grandfather. 'You seemed distracted last night.'

John shook his head and picked at a fraying edge of the armrest. 'Just t-tired, I guess. Long w-w-week, with the snow and that.'

'Nothing you need to tell me?'

His grandfather was sitting stiff-backed, chin up, shoulders square, like a proud tin soldier. He looked a lot like Mr Christmas, John thought: upright, soldierly somehow.

'I'm g-good, Grandpa,' he said. 'Thinking about s-s-schoolwork, that's all. Bit hungry, I s'pose.'

'And *I* heard *that*,' shouted the Duchess from the kitchen. 'One bacon sandwich coming right up.'

'What about you, G-G-Grandpa?' John didn't like where the questioning was going. Was he ready to talk about Fyre? About the mirrors? No, they had enough on their minds already. Best to change the subject. 'Are *you* all right?'

'Me?' Mordecai Creed took in a huge breath, puffing out his not inconsiderable chest, then made a fist and curled his arm in the classic bodybuilder pose. 'See that?'

'Yes,' laughed John, who had seen this exhibition before. 'Looking g-good, Grandpa. Looking good.'

The doorbell rang again, sparking the barking and madness. John jumped up to let Davey in; he was sporting his usual bobble hat and a magnificent black and purple eye from the encounter with Aziz.

'Morning, all,' he chirruped. ''Allo, Duchess.'

'Cup of tea, Davey?' The Duchess poked her head round the kitchen door.

'That'd be great.'

'Oh, Davey, what have you done to your face?'

'Well, *I* didn't do it, Duchess,' he said, 'but you should see the other bloke.'

'What happened?'

'School happened. It's nuffin'. I'll live.'

'Bacon sandwich, then? I'm making John one.'

'Please, Duchess.'

It was Davey who was John's partner in the job that kept him from seeing Fyre. They finished their sandwiches, said goodbye to Mordecai, and looked in on the Duchess, who was washing up in the kitchen.

'OK, boys?' She smiled, wiping her hands on a tea towel so threadbare it was almost see-through. 'I know it's cold out there, but it's a good day for it, right?'

'Right, Duchess,' chorused the boys.

'So, remember: nobody young, nobody poor, nobody who can chase you down.'

'Yes, Duchess.'

'This snow, boys, is just what the doctor ordered. All those rich people falling over and needing to be helped up. All that ice – so slippery under foot . . . Who knows when people will need a hand from a couple of sweet boys? Right?'

'Right, Duchess.'

This was something Mordecai and the Duchess had started in order to make ends meet – until old age had crept up on them and arthritis had ruined their joints: pickpocketing. Now it was John's 'job', with a little help from Davey. They didn't take much, they didn't take chances, and John hated every second of it. But he also knew that, given his grandfather's bizarre way of life, it was the only way they could survive. So no, he thought, as he struggled into his heavy second-hand overcoat, there was no way Fyre could 'hang out' with him at weekends. Not this weekend, not the next weekend. Not ever.

John had teamed up with Davey after he had seen the kid steal a turkey from the supermarket by stuffing it down the baggy rap-boy jeans he had been wearing and swinging it beneath his crotch. It was brazen and crazy, but it had worked and they had become friends.

They headed out, crunching carefully through the snowdrifts. Well, John did; Davey scampered ahead, ran in circles, fell behind when something caught his eye. In his layers of frayed hand-me-down clothes, he was like some sort of urban tumbleweed, pushed to and fro by the wind. He slowed enough to walk beside John and looked up at him with undisguised admiration.

'Hey,' John said. 'Where are your g-gloves? You must be f-freezing.'

'Bruvver took 'em. Least, I fink he was me bruvver. One of them anyway. He certainly lives in the house. Ha-ha-ha! Nah, I'll be all right, honest.'

'Here, take m-mine,' said John, tugging at his own gloves.

'Nah, I'm sorted, I'm sorted. Fanks anyway.'

They were in Norton Folgate high street, where the roads had been gritted and most of the shopkeepers had shovelled the snow away from their doorways. It was still a surprise, though, to see the Saturday market in full swing. The stalls were out, many with fairy lights strung up to combat the gloom. And with the snow still falling quite heavily, it looked a bit like Christmas – until you looked closely, of course, and saw that the stalls were still selling cheap ordinary rubbish instead of cheap Christmas rubbish. The stallholders, puffed up in their padded jackets, stamped their feet and told people how you couldn't do without a rhinestone mobile phone cover, love! Or how a china tea set for a fiver was a bargain – you'd never forgive yourself for missing out an such an opportunity.

John trudged on towards the Underground station at the end of the street, knowing that Davey would catch up when he was good and ready. Suddenly there was a shout from behind him – a loud, belligerent and offended cry of '*STOP HIM!*'

He turned, but a small dark figure knocked him off his feet. It was Davey, running away from the owner of the clothes stall outside KFC. John lay on his back and stared up at the sky, which seemed far too murky and far too close.

'Are you all right?' said a concerned voice. It was the stallholder, who had obviously decided that giving chase and leaving his stall unattended wasn't a good idea. Of Davey there was no sign.

The man helped him to his feet and brushed some snow off his shoulders.

'I'm, I'm . . . OK, I g-g-guess. Wh-wh-what happened?'

'Some little thief,' explained the man. 'Blatant as anything! Walked past and nicked a pair of gloves, just like that. Look – you OK?'

'Yeah, yeah,' said John, trying not to smile. 'Thanks.'

He headed off again in the direction of the station, where he knew he would find Davey lounging around as if nothing had happened. He was like the Artful Dodger and Oliver Twist all rolled into one, thought John. If it wasn't nailed down, Davey would liberate it.

As expected, Davey was downstairs, ostentatiously reading the network map. He grinned cockily from ear to ear when John walked up.

'See? Told ya I didn't need no gloves.'

'Yeah, w-w-well,' whispered John, 'next time you might w-w-want to nick something more your s-s-size. Those things are b-b-bigger than your head.'

'Shit.' Davey examined the gloves and frowned; he looked like a little old man, one with a dirt-streaked face and ears that could pick up signals from outer space. 'So,' he said after some thought, 'wanna buy a pair of gloves?'

John laughed and cuffed him lightly round the head. 'You muppet. Come on, let's go.'

And with that they validated their Oyster cards – themselves previously liberated from stolen wallets – and made their way to the platform that would take them towards the rich pickings of Mayfair and Bond Street. John sighed quietly. His heart had never been in his grandfather's little sideline, but now . . . Well, now he kept seeing Fyre's face alongside Mr Patel's and Mr Christmas's in his Gallery of Guilt. If they found out, how would he ever face them again? Just the thought of it made him blush. Fyre especially. He was still thinking of her when they squeezed onto a packed train. Hopefully, Davey wouldn't pick anyone's pockets before they got up west.

They emerged from Marble Arch tube station and drifted apart. They didn't talk; it wouldn't do to show they knew each other. And whatever else the snow had done, it had not stopped people shopping. Women emerged from the big department stores laden with expensive carrier bags, and Davey was there to 'accidentally' bump into them or to 'slip' on the ice in front of them. At which point John would scoot up and relieve them of their valuables.

It was after one of these encounters – John had relieved a fur-covered woman of a bulging purse – that it happened. They were opposite a department store – one of the ones with huge plate-glass windows – and John was lounging against a street sign pretending to read a newspaper, when he looked up and his breath caught in his throat.

In the window display there was a large mirror, and in the mirror he could see the reflections of all the passers-by. He was a long way off, for sure, and the view was constantly interrupted by passing trucks and buses, but he saw that some of the passers-by had . . . *dogs' heads*.

That woman in the fur was a poodle; the man in the posh suit looked like he had the head of a wolf – no, an Irish wolfhound. Most people were unchanged, but *there* – that man in the bulky overcoat had the head of a Doberman. He stood there, feeling sick and knowing that any sudden movement would make him vomit. The visions didn't go away, as they had yesterday; he could only watch as people went about their business, hurrying this way and that, all looking like ordinary people in real-life but with some sort of dog- or wolf-like reflection.

He had to get away. He threw his newspaper in a bin and headed towards Davey. He tried to walk normally, even though his legs were turning to jelly, and as he approached he opened his eyes wide, as if he'd seen a ghost, begging the boy to look in his direction and realize that something was wrong.

Too late: Davey had spotted another mark, and was moving in for the kill. He didn't even look in John's direction, knowing from experience that his friend would be there to back him up. Only this time he wasn't; freaked out, feeling sick, John had completely mistimed his approach.

Davey had walked out in front of a shopper whose

expensive clothes, flashy watch and self-satisfied air put him squarely on their radar. It was perfectly done. If John hadn't known better, he would have said the punter wasn't watching where he was going and had plunged headlong into that poor little boy.

There was nothing for it but to keep going, but John was still unnerved by the reflections in the mirror. He saw Davey grasp the man's hand and pull himself to his feet. There went the watch. John skipped round behind them, slipped a hand into the man's coat. What he hadn't seen, in his distracted state, was the man's wife standing on the kerb. She spotted John's hand emerge with her husband's wallet in it.

'Thief!' she shouted. 'Andy! He's got your wallet!'

John pushed the mark away from Davey and grabbed his friend's arm. 'Run!' he hissed.

Two security guards had emerged from the store and were now following them. Just a few metres away, a policeman, hearing the shouts, looked up and joined the chase. *Just our luck*, thought John.

They darted down the first side street they came to and ran as fast as they could.

'Coppers?' puffed Davey.

'One. And two s-security guards. J-just keep r-r-running. Here, this w-way.'

They turned again, into an alleyway that John knew

led into the small courtyard behind an Italian restaurant; in summer, there were tables and chairs outside, but, more importantly, the courtyard had three exits. Behind them they could hear the huffing and puffing of their pursuers.

'Go r-r-right,' ordered John. 'I'll go l-l-left. S-see you at home.'

'OK.' Davey seemed to be enjoying himself. 'See ya later.'

The men burst into the snowy courtyard just in time to see the boys split up.

'Over there!' shouted the policeman. 'I've got the big one.'

John almost slipped over as he emerged from the alleyway. Had the men gone after Davey? He hoped they had; Davey wasn't carrying any booty, so they couldn't prove anything, while *his* pockets were full of valuables.

'Oi, you! Stop!'

He chanced a quick look back. The copper was gaining on him, and had now been joined by two others. It spurred him on, and he found an extra reserve of wind. There – up ahead! An alley between what looked like two disused warehouses: if he could reach it before they saw him, he could disappear. But no! The snow! He was leaving footprints; they could follow him for ever unless he got back in amongst the crowds.

He reached the alley, only to find that it ended in a four-metre-high wire fence. The windows on either side were boarded or bricked up. A large rubbish bin stood against the wall at the far end; somebody had dumped old bits of carpet beside it.

It was a dead end.

He was trapped. There was no way he could get over the fence before they caught up with him.

But if you didn't try . . .

With the sounds of his pursuers in his ears, John ran at full tilt and leaped as high as he could, half expecting a hand to grab his ankle and haul him in like some sad fish gasping in a net.

Instead, his hands and feet barely touched the top of the fence as he flew over it, and he found himself landing softly on all fours on the other side. He hid behind a stack of pallets, and tried to quiet his gasping breaths. He looked through the pallets to where the policemen had come stumbling into the alleyway.

The first one stopped and looked around, puzzled when he saw that John's footprints seemed to just *stop*. He pulled at the discarded carpets, obviously expecting John to come tumbling out. He peered into the big rubbish bin: nothing. He kicked out at it.

'He can't have disappeared into thin air.'

The two other policemen shrugged and began searching the alleyway inch by inch. John closed his eyes and held his breath. Snow settled softly on his shoulders but he dared not move. Finally the men gave up. As they turned and wandered back the way they had come, John peered round at them again.

In the flesh they were just three policemen, but their reflections told another story. In the broken glass of the windows he saw that two of them had the heads of jackals!

When they had gone, he stayed rooted to the spot. Something impossible had just happened, and he was scared.

No, not just scared; he was terrified. This was way beyond the thing with Caspar and the snowball. It was the same feeling – a massive rush of adrenaline – but bigger, more out of control. Then his legs started wobbling so much that he fell to his knees. He waited a minute or two, trying to control the shaking. An onlooker would have thought he was shivering from some drug problem.

He edged quietly away from the pallets, away from the high fence, and vomited into the snow.

What in God's name was happening to him?

12
LET IT SNOW, LET IT SNOW, LET IT SNOW...

Rajesh Patel yawned and stretched. God, he was tired. He was sitting behind the counter in his shop, reading a book about Dublin in the 1950s. Next to him was a well-thumbed dictionary. He liked the author but, really, some of the words he used! At the top of his stretch he broke into a wry smile. *Pandiculation*, he thought. Not a word you see very often, but one he had looked up only minutes before. *Pandiculation: the act of yawning and stretching at the same time.* Who knew such a word existed, or that there was even a need for such a thing? What a wonderful language it was, this English. He'd loved it all those years ago; tried so very hard to inculcate it into his own son . . . *Inculcate* – see? There was another one!

Pandiculation – he rolled it around his mouth and wondered if perhaps the word operated on much the same principle as yawns; that it was somehow, like yawns, catching. You see someone yawn; you yawn. You read the word *pandiculation* and you . . . pandiculate?

Why was he so drowsy? He'd only just got up, and here he was, ready for bed. He reached up and turned off one of the bars on the electric heater. Perhaps it was too hot. And maybe a voice or two might help. He jabbed at the 'on' button on the old radio, twiddled the knobs and found a news station.

'. . . *while some supermarkets in remote areas have reported panic buying, the biggest queues so far have been at the petrol pumps as people stock up . . .*'

As the newsreader began to recount tales of people coming to blows over food – two men and an elderly woman were in hospital already – Rajesh tutted. Only yesterday he had seen two women in the supermarket fighting over the last packet of nappies. Nappies! Who fought over nappies? The world was going mad. How thin, he thought, was the veneer of civilization. *Are we all just animals waiting to burst out of our skins at the first sign of trouble?*

He thought again of John Creed, and of Ranjeev, and of the violence that had claimed his son's life. Why? Why was *he* coming back to haunt him after all these years?

Yes, yes, he knew: he should have *been* there. The two of them might have been able to escape, to fight the tiger off. Instead he, Rajesh, too busy at work, had failed to meet up with his son, and the boy had died. Alone. Or maybe they would both be dead now. It was not something he could resolve . . . not in this lifetime anyway.

'. . . *and in other news, reports are coming in from the north of a series of animal attacks in which a number of cows have been savagely killed. The storm is making communication with outlying districts difficult, but our reporter did manage to talk to one farmer who . . .*'

Rajesh sighed and leaned forward so that his forehead rested on the counter.

'. . . *blood everywhere . . . never seen anything like it . . . If I didn't know better, I'd say it was a wolf or something . . .*'

He remembered how the villagers had brought the little bundle of rags that was Ranjeev back to the village. How devastated, how grief-stricken, he'd felt. How guilty.

Never again.

He closed his eyes. See? That was so much better. He'd just rest for a minute.

And when he finally opened them again, it was to find himself peering through someone else's eyes. There was no transition, no panic, just acceptance that, instead of seeing the shelves of his shop, he was high up in the air, looking down on a landscape drowned in powdery snow. There were farmhouses, barns, the black wiggly lines of hedges, and stark, bare trees that marked the boundaries of snow-covered fields.

He was flying!

He was speeding across the countryside, wheeling this way and that on the wings of the cold, cold wind.

A train line cut across his vision from right to left, a straight black line like a rip in a piece of paper.

He was flying!

And he wasn't alone.

He looked sideways to find that he was surrounded by dozens – hundreds – thousands of . . . sparrows. They were swooping and tumbling and chattering and search-ing for something. It was bizarre and frightening and vertigo-inducing and . . . oddly heart-warming. He was not alone any more; he was welcomed, accepted, part of a family.

Down below them, in the frozen wastes, something was coming nearer; something ancient and relentless and evil.

And then he saw them: seven enormous wolves – six black and one white – moving through a forest off to their left. As one, they wheeled round and dived towards the ground. As they did so, the wolves looked up into the sky and growled menacingly. They leaped into the air as the flock zipped past. One or two of the sparrows disappeared with dry crunches as the wolves' slashing teeth and paws reached their mark.

This was madness – they could never—

He woke with a sleepy spasm as a gust of wind rattled the front door. The radio still droned on:

'. . . *while the opposition were demanding answers, a government spokesman warned that, according to the forecasters, the worst is yet to come.*'

Rajesh yawned again, stretched. *Pandiculation.* What was wrong with him?

Great gouts of scarlet blood spurted up the wall – was that a bit of greyish brain matter in there? – as Caspar buried the machete in the man's head and immediately yanked it out before the second attacker could get too close. A step to the right, another swing, and an arm went flying through the air, spinning end over end and spewing more blood everywhere, but despite switching to a handgun, he was soon overwhelmed.

He threw the controller down on the bed. On screen his avatar was disappearing under a horde of rampaging, Hawaiian-shirt clad zombies, his health bar going as red as the blood that was smeared over the faces of his killers.

START AGAIN Y/N? asked the computer.

He ignored it for now, too wound up to do it justice. *You just stuff it up if you're too angry. You need to calm down, wait, then do it again.* His hands were sweaty and aching from gripping the controller too tightly. He leaned back on the bed, stared at the ceiling. From downstairs came the muffled sound of his father laughing at something on the television.

At least he *was* laughing now. When Caspar had finally arrived home the previous night – after seriously thinking about *not* going home at all – his father, not the most loving or caring man in the world at the best of times, had been red-faced with anger, his words flecked with spittle as he screamed at his son.

Caspar tried to sleep, but his mind kept racing back to the moment his father had grabbed his arms and pulled him off his feet. It was like being attacked by a huge enraged bear. He pulled up the sleeves of his T-shirt and examined the bruises. Blue, red, sickly yellow, black . . . His arms looked like they'd been beaten with an iron pipe.

'What did you think you were *doing*?' Siimon had roared. 'I'm a *policeman*, ya little drongo! I *catch* people like you and *put them in jail*!'

'Dad, I'm sorry, it's just . . . just . . .' Caspar had felt tears welling, but fought them back.

'Just what? Just *what*? Are you as stupid as your bloody mother was? I thought you had some brains – but *this*? This takes the biscuit. Nicking copper from a building site? Why?'

'Az-zz-Aziz . . .' Caspar had heard his voice catching and stuttering like bloody John Creed. 'Aziz – well, his older brother, he knows these guys and—'

'I didn't ask who, I asked *why*!'

'Why?' Caspar had finally had enough. He pushed his father in the chest – a pointless move – and screamed back. '*Why?* Why *not*? Ever since Mum left you haven't taken *any* notice of *ME*. It's all Old Bill this and Old Bill that. You can't think about anything else, can you? Well, you've noticed me *now*, haven't you? I wish I'd gone *with* her. I wish she'd loved me enough to take me with her rather than leave me here with *you*! *I hate you!*'

'*Good!*' his father had bellowed back at him, his prominent eyeballs red with rage. '*Good!* It's about time you grew some balls and stopped whingeing all the bloody time. You make me sick. And now *this*?'

'What a pity you didn't do us all a favour and "tap" me when I was born, eh?' Caspar had grown up on his father's tales of the Outback, and the 'tapping' of the kittens had been a firm favourite when he was younger.

'Don't think it didn't cross my mind!'

'Do it!'

'*What?*'

'Do it!' Caspar goaded him. 'Do it now; put me out of my misery. I'd rather be dead than live here with you. Maybe that's what Mum did; maybe she chucked herself in the Thames rather than put up with you.'

His father had raised one great hairy fist at that, pulled it right back behind his head like Thor's hammer. Caspar flinched and closed his eyes. It was one thing to demand death, but it was something else to have that demand met.

Instead . . . nothing. He had opened his eyes to find the room empty. He stood there for a while, unsure what to do. And then came the faint sound of voices from the lounge as his father turned on the television.

DS Locke wasn't watching the television. He was sitting there with the television on, but he was *watching* the inside of his head. He just couldn't get rid of the image of the one-eyed crow he'd killed. It was a dilemma. He was a policeman, and yet he was a killer. Sometimes he wasn't sure which side he was on any more. It was like some great monster had been merely 'wearing' him all these years, and was now stretching and yawning and struggling to get out of the too-tight skin.

He shook his head in a vain attempt to stop the throb-throb-throbbing. Closed his eyes. There it was again – the one-eyed crow – but this time it had Caspar's face. 'Go on! *Do* it!' it said.

And he very nearly had. He knew that he had come within an inch of killing his son.

Caw! Caw! Caw!

Tap! Tap! Tap!

He leaned forward, squeezed his aching head between his hands and gritted his teeth. How long would it be before he lost it completely? Again.

Perhaps he should talk to Caspar properly, man to man. When everything had calmed down.

G'day, Caspar. I'm thinking we should head off back to Australia, son. Whaddya think? Yeah, that'd do it. *It's too bloody cold here*, he'd say, *and the cops won't let you have guns. I mean, how are you goin' to stop the bad guys if they won't let you kill them? I'm fed up with trying to catch bad guys with one hand tied behind my back, you know?*

The kid had been through a lot, after all. As much as he ever could, Tapper Locke felt bad about that. She had been screaming her head off at him, going red in the face about something or other – just like Caspar earlier – only *her* breath had been reeking of gin. And that's when he found he was holding his trusty hammer . . . and, well, it was just a small tap – hardly anything at all really, just to make her stop hollering. And then she'd dropped down dead there and then. Did it on purpose, she did.

Tap!

Crash!

Down she had gone, those blue eyes staring back up at him, unblinking, slightly surprised. One of these days he would dig her out of the bedroom wall and get rid of her properly. Maybe persuade Caspar to go on one of the school trips again, get him out of the way.

Upstairs he could hear Caspar killing zombies.

Outside, on their fifth-floor balcony, there was a muffled sound.

He got up, opened the door and stepped out into the icy cold night air; the wind had whipped the snow into a snarling frenzy. And there, standing brazenly on the snow-laden balcony wall, was the biggest crow he had ever seen.

Caw! Caw! Caw! it went, in a voice that sounded like a baby crying.

Locke felt the throbbing in his head ease for the first time all day.

And this time, the one staring eye didn't seem quite so bizarre.

13
SUNDAY BLOODY SUNDAY

Sunday was a strange day for John Creed. He and Davey had explained to the Duchess and Grandpa Mordecai some of what had happened, but John had left out everything about the bizarre reflections and his miraculous escape from the policemen. He also kept quiet about the shimmering mirror at Mr Patel's. Why? He didn't really know. Initially he thought it was to spare Mordecai the worry that his grandson might be a bit strange in the head. But the more he brooded over it, the more he worried. He imagined it was like finding a zit or something on a private part of your anatomy; you're not going to show your grandfather, are you?

And something else was going on. His grandfather seemed anxious – but not about how badly things had gone wrong on Saturday. It was as if his mind were elsewhere. The Duchess was different as well. She had seemed relieved that he and Davey had escaped arrest, but again, it was almost as an afterthought.

'I think you should be on your guard for a while, John,' she had said while putting the kettle on for yet another cup of tea.

'What f-for?' John was puzzled; the chances of him running across the same coppers were one in ten million, weren't they? They were from central London; he was hardly going to bump into them in the scummy concrete canyons of the Folgate over to the east.

'Just to be on the safe side. There can't be too many teenagers in London with scars like yours.'

'I was w-wearing my hoodie the whole t-t-time. They w-w-wouldn't know me in a m-m-million years.'

'It's true enough,' piped up Davey through a mouthful of the Duchess's carrot cake. 'They never saw our faces. Got a good look at our bums racing away, though.'

The Duchess frowned at him briefly and then turned straight back to John. 'Just be careful, John. Please? Indulge an old lady?'

Mordecai had chimed in too. He had been visiting old Mr Glass opposite, but had come back when John and Davey had tumbled in through the front security door. He stood by the kitchen door, feet apart, his muscular arms crossed over his bull-like chest, chin thrust forward belligerently. 'You just need to tell us if you see anything unusual. *Anything*. OK? John?'

'Yes, yes, OK, Grandpa. Anyone w–w–would think the d–d–devil was after us.' He peered at his grandfather just a little bit longer than necessary. What wasn't he telling him?

'*Anything* unusual,' echoed the Duchess. 'You tell us, right?'

Davey grunted around a mouth full of cake and tea, but John only nodded in reply, not trusting himself not to blurt out something he might regret.

Like seeing things in people's reflections?

Like being able to scale a four-metre fence with ease?

Like suddenly being scared of sparkling mirrors?

Like going completely and utterly bonkers?

Stuff like that . . . ?

It was about three a.m. – in a lucid moment between worrying dreams of wolves and ravens and mirrors – when it hit him. He couldn't talk to his family, but he *could* talk to Fyre. He knew where she lived, and that she walked her dog in the park every day. Or no, maybe not. Maybe he'd wait until school. But would there be school on Monday? He'd have to go, thanks to his grandfather's insistence on living in the Stone Age, but Fyre wouldn't.

He got up late, had breakfast – Mordecai was nowhere to be seen – and was on his way down the stairs when he heard raised voices coming from the Hunters' flat. Was his grandfather's one of them? It was hard to tell, and he felt awkward eavesdropping, so he hurried past. There was silence from the Duchess's flat. Not so much as a peep from the dogs.

Nothing much had changed outside – unless you counted an extra six or seven centimetres of snow. He headed off towards the little park. He had half a loaf of stale bread with him, but what he found there stopped him dead. The number of sparrows had been increasing every day, but this was . . . surprising, to say the least. The trees in the park, naked of leaves, gnarled branches reaching up into the feathery deluge falling around them, were covered in sparrows. Hundreds of them – no, more like thousands: every twig was laden. And where they couldn't find a perch, they spilled over onto nearby houses and the tops of lampposts.

And if that wasn't freaky enough, the little birds were completely, eerily silent and unmoving. Their usual jostling and twittering was gone; they just sat there in their thousands, watching him. It seemed a bit egotistical, but deep down John knew this was so: they were watching *him*. It should have been frightening, this bizarre, silent flock, but it wasn't. He took out the bread and began to crumble it on top of the snow.

A few individual birds hopped down from the trees to peck at the offering, but the effort was half-hearted. *They must be getting fed somewhere else*, John thought indignantly as a large raven swept down out of nowhere and chased them away. The raven – or was it a crow; he could never tell the difference – flapped its wings self-importantly, looked in John's direction – and froze.

John gasped.

It only had *one eye*. Right in the middle of its head.

But that was impossible.

The eye, beady yet glazed, swivelled oddly in its socket. John thought he could even hear a faint, gluggy noise, like a worm turning in on itself and disappearing down into its hole. He even had the unsettling sensation that, like the wolf in his dreams, the bird *recognized* him.

He started to back away, but then the bird gave a triumphantly raucous cry and flew off.

It didn't get very far. Most of the assembled sparrows took flight and swooped down on it like an arrow. John stumbled backwards, shocked by the fierceness of the attack, and fell into the snow. He watched in astonishment, crawling away, and trying to quell the sick feeling the one-eyed crow had brought on. He watched as it struggled up through the thick cloud of sparrows, its wings beating in wild panic, making sad papery sounds. With a heroic effort, it managed to rise about four metres into the air, but then, as one, the flock of sparrows plunged downwards. It didn't stand a chance; it was hammered into the snow with a thud, its wings strange black origami shapes sticking out of the whiteness, before it disappeared beneath a mass of little brown bodies.

Just seconds later, the sparrows lifted off again and wheeled away into the sky, a massive brown orb that seemed to throb with glee at what it had done.

The crow/raven thing was *gone*. Only an indentation and a red smear in the snow remained. A few black feathers quickly blew away in the wind.

John jumped up, turned tail and fled, expecting the murderous flock to fall upon him, leaving only a big red stain and a few tufts of hair. At the main road he half walked, half ran behind a bus that was slowly edging its way towards the Underground station. It seemed to him even more important now to find Fyre. He had to talk to someone. Or go mad. He caught up with the bus at the next stop. It might not have been faster, but it was certainly warmer. He didn't notice the small hooded figure that slipped in as the doors closed, then sat down and pulled out a mobile phone.

'Hello? Caspar?' whispered Cem as he settled down

at the front of the bus. 'Guess who I just seen? Yeah. He's on the thirty-eight. You bet. I'll let you know when he gets off.'

Fyre was huddled inside her big white parka, watching Oscar take a very large dump in the snow. Where was it all coming from? It was almost as big as the dog itself. She looked around the white expanse of the park: there was a woman way over the other side with what looked like a poodle, and some kids had braved the cold to make a snowman, but she and Oscar were alone in this little corner. Ordinarily she would have felt obliged to pick up her dog's 'doings', but today . . . she used her boot to cover it up with snow.

She smiled at that; all her guilty little secrets were being *put on ice*. Hiding dog doo was one thing, but how long did she think she was going to get away with pretending her mother was still alive? The teachers had been fooled by the forged signatures on the notes sent back to school – and her mother had never encouraged visits from friends – but it wouldn't last for ever. Maybe it was time to confess? *No*. She would maintain the pretence for as long as possible. The longer she kept herself out of a children's home, the better.

'Fyre!'

The sound of her name made her jump. Talk about a

guilty conscience! She peeked out from the confines of her white hood, and felt Oscar drift back to her side.

'Fyre?'

She peeked out even more; felt her heart beat a little faster. It was John.

'It *is* you.' He sounded pleased to see her, but the expression on his poor, scarred face was worried.

'Hi.' She smiled. 'What are you doing here? Oh, be careful where you—'

It was too late. He glanced down as his boot squished something that, he knew immediately, wasn't snow.

'Oops,' said Fyre, not sure whether to laugh or not.

John lifted his leg and looked at the mess stuck to the underneath of his boot. 'N-n-nice.'

'It's good luck, isn't it?'

'L-luck like that I can d-d-do w-without,' he said as he scraped it off on the snow.

They fell into step and began walking slowly around the perimeter of the park.

He looked at her sideways. 'I like the sunglasses,' he said awkwardly.

'It's all this snow,' explained Fyre, her alabaster skin turning pink. She touched the glasses, which were matt black with leather side shields to block peripheral light. With the white hooded parka John thought she looked like she was about to tackle Everest. 'All the white hurts my eyes after a while. I know it looks stupid.'

'No, no, no; I m-mean it. They look good. Really. Cross m-my heart and all that.'

'So you couldn't stay away, eh?'

'Seems not.'

'How are your cousins?'

'Who?'

'The cousins you were visiting yesterday.'

'Oh, them.' John felt his stomach contract. What an idiot! 'Yes . . .yeah. They're f-fine. Good. Yeah.'

'Good.'

Rather than face any more questioning from Fyre, John scooped up some snow, made a ball and threw it out across the park. The dog, thinking it was a game, raced after it and sniffed frantically in the snow where it had fallen, digging here and there in an effort to find it. John and Fyre watched him, laughing. Eventually he came back to them and barked: *Do it again, do it again.* John did it again. And again, Oscar went off searching before coming back for more.

'You are the s-s-stupidest d-dog in the world.'

'Don't call my dog stupid. He's just . . . confused, that's all.'

'Aren't we all,' muttered John gloomily.

'Are you OK?' Fyre stopped. 'What's happened?'

'It's hard to know wh-where to s-start.' He shrugged.

He wanted to tell her *everything*, but when it came down to it, wouldn't talking about it – his weird life – make it *real*? And then you *couldn't* ignore it any more. Keep quiet and it would all go away, wouldn't it?

'Well, for a start you didn't go to visit your cousins yesterday, did you?'

'No,' he admitted. 'No, I d–didn't. It's just that, all this w–weird stuff has been happening. I mean, like, w–weirder than normal. And I don't know where to b–begin. You're g–going to think I'm crazy.'

'I think you're crazy already. It can't get any worse.'

'It c–can.'

'Tell me. I won't think you're crazy,' she insisted seriously. After all, what could be weirder than keeping your dead mother in the freezer? John stared at her with such a strange, haunted look that she felt the need to repeat herself. 'I won't think you're crazy, I promise.'

'OK.' He reached down, threw another snowball and watched Oscar belt off after it, as if he didn't want to say anything in front of the dog. 'Well, for a start, this morning I saw a flock of sparrows murder a one-eyed raven. Or a crow. I never know which is which.'

Fyre looked at him impassively. She knew better than to laugh. '*That*,' she said, 'I *wasn't* expecting.'

And so he told her: about the mirrors, how he kept

seeing the reflections she had scoffed at; about his dreams of the wolf; about his escape from the policemen. With the wind sending snowflakes whirling around them, Fyre felt like she was caught up in some bizarre parallel world, cut off from reality by an icy wall, a cold circular prison that held just her, John Creed and her dog.

Finally, when he had finished, they stood in silence. It was all very bizarre, but was it any stranger than keeping your mum on ice? Or being asked to befriend the boy with 'the face'? Maybe she should tell him. She'd feel better, wouldn't she? A secret shared?

'John, I—'

'Creed!' shouted a voice from afar, a voice she, with a deep feeling of dread, recognized. 'John Creed!'

It was Caspar and his gang, coming across the empty park. In their heavy puffa jackets they looked like a posse of evil balloons blown up by a crazy clown at a funfair.

What John saw, though, and what Fyre initially missed, was that one of Caspar's arms seemed longer than the other.

'We need to get out of here,' he urged. 'Caspar means business this time. Real business.'

'Business?'

'He's got s-something – a piece of w-wood . . . iron;

something up his sleeve. That's for me – it must be. We've got to go.'

Fyre put Oscar back on the leash and they edged nonchalantly out of the gate as if they hadn't heard Caspar's shout.

'Hey!'

They increased their pace, not looking back.

'Hey! Stop!'

Hearing this last cry, they realized that their pursuers had started to run after them. They kept walking until the corner of the next street, trying to stay calm. As they rounded the corner, John grabbed Fyre's arm.

'Run!'

And they did. Across the road in a slip-sliding diagonal that took them out of sight of the park. With luck, thought John, they would reach the cover of the railway arches before Caspar could see where they'd gone. It wouldn't stop the pursuit, but it would gain them a few precious seconds. What he hadn't foreseen was that Caspar would send Cem and Aziz diagonally across the park to head them off. There was no gate over there, but the railings were low enough to climb over. John and Fyre were almost at the railway arch when another shout alerted them to Caspar's ruse.

'Caspar! They're over here. At the arches, innit!' It was Aziz, pointing them out.

The road and the pavement under the old Victorian arches were free of snow. It was dark and wet, with curtains of drips falling through the brickwork here and there, but the snow stopped on either side of the arch. On this side, snowbound Folgate; on the other, snowbound Whitechapel; in the middle, a shadowy, dryish netherworld. It was like they had stepped from Narnia into the wardrobe instead of the other way round.

Fyre stopped. 'Wait,' she whispered.

'What?'

Yes, *what*? Fyre thought for a moment, looked around. She remembered how much she liked it here – the wonderful combination of twenty-first-century trains passing over the old Victorian arches. And here and there, stunted trees and bushes had pushed their way through the crumbling brickwork. Over on the other side of the borough a blackberry bush grew out of the wall of some arches, producing the most succulent berries she had ever tasted. It was nature refusing to lie down and be bullied.

She took John's hand.

'What?' He wasn't sure whether to look at Fyre or at the four figures who had entered the tunnel.

'We – *you* – can't keep running away. I don't know what Caspar's problem is, but . . . it's got to stop.'

'But—' John came to a halt. She was right. It was amazing how clear-headed, how much stronger, he felt around Fyre. It was like she breathed confidence into him. He could only stand and admire her as she pushed her sunglasses up onto her forehead and turned to face Caspar and the rest.

'No,' said John. 'Go. Get out of here. I can d-do this.'

She grinned. 'And miss all the fun?'

With the glasses stuck up on her forehead, he thought she looked like some glorious white warrior ant with bulbous black eyes. She shrugged off her hood, and John's jaw dropped. Fyre's beautiful pale hair had been chopped across at the front to create a fringe; the sides of her head had been shaved down to stubble.

'You've cut your hair,' he said.

'Yeah, do you like it? I did it myself.'

'That's pretty obvious,' muttered John with a smile.

'I'll ignore that. I reckon the back might be a bit of a mess, though.'

'I like it,' he said, and turned to face their pursuers. He was, he found, eerily calm. At his side, Fyre ushered her dog forward. 'I do. The haircut. I like it,' John repeated. 'It's awesome. Very, um, punk.'

Oscar growled quietly at the newcomers. It was enough to stop three of the boys, but Caspar had other ideas. He let what he was holding slide out of his sleeve.

It was a long piece of iron piping. His face was a curious mixture of joy and hatred. 'That dog comes near me, Fyre,' he snarled, showing his teeth, 'I'll bash its brains all over the wall.'

As he spoke, he swung the pipe back and forth in front of him like a divining rod that couldn't decide where the water was: Oscar, Fyre, John, Fyre, Oscar . . .

'What *is* your p-problem?' demanded John. 'I've never d-d-done anything to you, Caspar. N-nothing.'

Caspar, who had decided to take his father's advice – stop whingeing and *do* something – smiled. It was the easy smile of someone with a weight taken off their shoulders.

Fyre had the awful feeling that, this time, she wouldn't be able to talk them out of trouble. Caspar was determined to inflict pain, no matter what she said or did.

'I just don't *like* you, Creed. You're ugly. How's that for a start?'

'So's Cem, but I don't see you hassling him,' snapped Fyre.

'Oi!' blustered Cem, insulted but too scared of the dog to do anything about it. Despite their fear, the boys had formed a semicircle around their prey.

'I don't like your face,' growled Caspar, ignoring Fyre completely, 'with its stupid scars, I don't like your stupid s-s-stutter and I don't like the g-g-goody-two-shoes act – how's that? It's not *logical*, you moron, it just is.'

'*You're* the idiot,' snapped Fyre. She turned to give John a supportive smile, only to find that he had gone. Well, not *gone* as such; just glided silently away from the curving archway walls into the middle of the street.

'So,' he whispered, 'let's g-get this over and done with. You wanna go f-first, Caspar?' He paused and, with a disdainful curl of his lips, turned to the rest of them. 'You, Baz? Aziz?'

In a silence broken only by the ragged breathing of the other boys, Caspar advanced slowly, the iron bar held aloft like a samurai sword. Fyre noticed that he positioned himself carefully behind his friends – the coward. He was going to wait until the others distracted John and then bring the bar down with a bone-cracking swipe. Coward.

What happened next was over so quickly that it made no sense. Cem and Aziz seemed to make a joint decision and leaped forward simultaneously, throwing wild looping punches and kicks that were designed not to hurt but to confuse. It was like two out-of-control windmills had come loose from their foundations. Baz, never one to exert himself, bounced around on the periphery, waiting for his chance to attack.

But suddenly, out of the melee, came John Creed. Fyre couldn't work out if he was moving at lightning speed or if the others were moving in slow motion. He seemed to avoid the welter of blows as if they weren't there; within seconds he had twisted between Cem and Aziz, not even trying to hit back at them, and whirled round in a circle that brought him right in front of a shocked Baz.

And then he seemed to slow down. It was as if the effort had exhausted him – a toy car that had used up its batteries in a wild dash across the floor. It was the chance that Caspar was looking for, and he brought his weapon down in a vicious swing that started from far above his head.

Fyre's shriek of 'John!' mingled with the crunch of bones shattering, and was followed almost immediately by a keening cry of pain that went on and on and on. She had covered her eyes with her hands when the bar started its descent, and was now surprised to find them yanked away. It was John.

'Quick!' he snapped. 'We have to go. Now.' He pulled her away, back towards the snowy Wonderland outside the arches.

'But . . .'

Her words were drowned out by a series of horrific screams.

'Don't look back,' ordered John, but she couldn't help herself. There, in the semi-darkness, she saw Baz on his knees, screaming, his left arm held out in front of him. He was holding it with his right hand and look-ing at it as if he'd never seen it before. And he hadn't, not in that state. Arms were never meant to bend like that; not halfway up the forearm. And they weren't meant to hang down and swing in the wind like that either.

Baz's screams followed them all the way back to the park before the wind swallowed them up.

'So, Mum . . .' said Fyre, much later, after John had gone home. He'd wanted to come back to her place but she had made some excuse. Something about not wanting to disturb her sick mother. Well, it was sort of true.

'So, Mum, about that boy . . .'

She had discarded her outer arctic-weather gear and was standing on the balcony, dressed only in jeans and a long-sleeved T-shirt. From where she stood she could see the arches where John Creed had moved like a wild animal; where he'd somehow manoeuvred Caspar into striking poor Baz. Even through the storm she could see the flashing lights of the ambulance under the railway line.

'So, that boy, right . . . Well, it's all a bit odd. And

getting odder by the day. And the thing is, right – well, I don't care. But you know that, don't you? Knew that. Sorry.'

She waited. Silence.

'Are you sulking?'

'I like your hair.'

'Do you? Not too, um, severe?'

'No. Well, yes. But it suits you.'

'Good.'

Fyre turned away from the view, such as it was, and stared at the freezer. *It's official*, she thought. *I'm mad. I'm imagining a conversation with my dead mother while the mother of all blizzards descends on us.*

'So, the boy. Is he good? Is he good, this boy? Was I right?'

'Yes, I think so, Mum.'

'You should *know* so, darling.'

'I *know*.'

A movement at the edge of her vision made Fyre turn round; it was a solitary sparrow, hopping along the balcony rail, making its way towards an almost identical sparrow made of ice. Where did that come from? It was perfect, amazingly detailed, *carved* from ice. She stared at it in astonishment.

'Who the—?'

The sparrow – the real one – shivered with cold and

cocked an eye in her direction before spreading its wings and giving itself over to the wind. It tumbled away like a piece of screwed-up brown paper, not so much flying as allowing itself to be thrown away.

Yup, it's official, thought Fyre, still unable to take her eyes off the ice sparrow – the one that only *she* could have made. *I am crazy, and the world's going to hell.*

14
WHITEOUT

Monday morning dawned big and bright and blue, the air clean and clear. The radio news was full of stories of survival and disaster: of people trapped in their cars surviving on cheese and crackers and melted snow, and of elderly people who'd frozen to death in their homes.

'We must tell him.'

It was early morning, and Mordecai was sitting in his usual place on the Duchess's sofa. He was balancing a mug of tea on his knee, but it was tepid, forgotten.

'I think you might be right,' replied the Duchess. 'Did you listen to the news this morning? We need to be one hundred per cent sure, but those reports are worrying, I agree.'

'We should know soon. Sarah will find out for sure.'

'Good. The waiting is killing me.' A pause. 'Do you think he'll believe us?'

'Would you?'

'Depends.'

'On what?'

'On what it is *he's* not telling *us*.'

'Something, for sure. Perhaps is just the girl. Boys are shy about such things.'

'Well, we'll know soon enough. Perhaps when he gets back from school?'

She reached out and cupped a hand around his. It was a tender gesture that almost broke his heart. He looked at their hands, so gnarled, so wrinkled – if rhinos had hands, they would look like his; hers reminded him more of bird claws.

'Are we too old, Duchess? Did we wait too long to tell him?'

'No, and no. Yes, a few more years would have been better, to strengthen him up, hone his skill, but as it is . . .' She shrugged.

'Yes.' Mordecai got up and strode over to the window. 'Will be difficult, but he knows Old Language now, knows the *spells*, even if he doesn't know he knows.'

The Duchess smiled at his back as he stood there, tall, straight and powerful. Her brother had always blossomed under pressure. In the twelve years since they had passed over, he had mellowed, become an old man,

peering up through the murky depths at a fisherman.

'Are you OK?' shouted John. 'Want m-m-me to d-dig you out?' He pointed at the snow and mimed shovelling. The old man shook his head. He obviously wasn't up to shouting, so he just gestured to indicate that he was using the back entrance and would come round to dig himself out later. He then used both hands to signal a bit more shovelling – of food, into his mouth.

'Breakfast f-first?' John smiled. He waved goodbye and let himself slide back down the snowdrift to the pavement. With any luck, school would be snowed in like Mr Patel and he could hang out with Fyre. Above him, unseen and silent, a mass of sparrows swept across the blue sky, whirling to and fro.

John trudged through the knee-deep snow like a sleepwalker, his mind on what had happened the previous day. He had no idea how he'd done what he'd done, but it scared him. The dreams, the mirrors – they were bad enough, but at least nobody got hurt. He wasn't even sure that Baz's broken arm had been the accident it seemed to be. Looking back, he recalled a moment of absolute clarity in which he 'saw' exactly what was going to happen. It was only a few seconds, but he knew what the outcome would be when he fooled Caspar into swinging that pipe in Baz's direction. It was as if he could see the tension in their muscles, know which way they would turn, which fist would be thrown, who would step right and who left; not a 'vision' exactly, but a sort of animal instinct.

And what was worse, he hadn't *cared*.

Didn't care.

Quite the opposite, in fact.

He had *enjoyed* it, had *relished* the crunch of metal on bone. And part of him still did.

And that made him sick to his stomach. Not *revolted* sick like the crow had made him feel, but a deep-down disgust with the very essence of himself, of what made him *him*. What would his grandfather say? The Duchess? It wasn't how they had brought him up. And what about Mr Patel, who thought John was Good with a capital G?

School was mostly empty. Anyone living too far away had been excused because all the trains were cancelled. Which meant most of the kids had decided that wherever they lived was too far away. There was only a skeleton staff. Mr Rabin was there in his tracksuit; Ms Holles too, looking like the Eskimo version of a bag lady. The Colonel was around somewhere, if John was right about the clipped martial voice he heard echoing in the distance.

But even though there were a few teachers about, nobody was expecting to learn anything. The staff had obviously decided it was pointless trying to educate half a school, and lessons became 'free' periods, or trivia quizzes or movie marathons. John found Fyre in the main hall, where she was helping to set up a large portable TV screen. He ushered her to one side.

'Have you s–seen Baz or Caspar or any of them?'

'No,' she whispered. 'I asked around – nobody's seen them. But you don't expect that lot to come to school if they don't have to, do you?'

'No, but I j–just thought . . .' He shrugged half-heartedly. 'Well, after yesterday . . .'

Fyre pulled him out of the hall – to much knowing tittering from her friends – and paused at the bottom of the main staircase.

'And talking of yesterday,' she whispered, 'what *did* happen? You left so quickly afterwards. I've never seen anyone move so fast. How did you do it? Seriously, John, this isn't funny. That was freaky.'

'I don't know. It didn't f–feel like I was moving fast at all; it felt like the others were j–just moving really slowly. It's like what happened with the p–p–policemen. I'm scared, Fyre. What's happening to me?'

'And Baz?'

'Wh–what?' John frowned at her. 'What about him?'

'Did you do it on purpose?'

'Me? I didn't d–do anything!'

'Keep your voice down,' hissed Fyre. She looked

around and then pulled him up the stairs towards the first floor. 'No, you know what I mean: did you trick Caspar into hitting Baz with that pipe?'

'No,' he said. 'Well, I d-don't think so. No, I didn't. It all happened so f-f-fast. It was like I w-wasn't thinking at all.'

'I think you did. You slowed down just long enough for Caspar to get a good swing. You don't have to lie to me, John.'

'Would you p-prefer it if I let him hit me? Or you?' John's voice rose, although he wasn't sure who he was angry at: Fyre for doubting him; Fyre for putting her finger on the truth; or himself for . . . what? For lying to Fyre? For simply not caring? Wasn't it nice to be top dog, just for once?

'No, you know that's not what I'm saying.'

They had reached the second floor and Fyre was heading down one of the old, beige-painted corridors.

'Where are we g-going?' asked John.

'To the Art room.'

'Why? Ms Holles is downstairs doing trivia in the dining hall.'

'Which means her room is empty. And she's got a huge mirror in there.'

John felt his stomach turn.

'And I want to *see* what you told me about yesterday.'

'I d–don't know about that. It's . . . you know . . .'

'No, I don't. You want to know if it's real or if you're crazy, right?'

The room was dominated by a collection of old-fashioned easels, set out in a circle. In the middle, plonked on a spread of paint-spattered newspapers, was a large chest. On that sat a vase of dead roses, the dry petals scattered around the base. Beyond them, half-painted papier-mâché puppet heads lay waiting for their finishing touches. One of them, John noticed, had three disfiguring scars running along one side of its face; even here he couldn't get away from Caspar Locke. The room smelled strongly of turpentine.

'I hate that smell,' he said. 'It gives me a headache.'

Fyre scooted over to one corner and came back pushing a full-length oval mirror on a stand with wheels.

'Ms Holles uses it in her lessons sometimes – mirror images and all that. But really I think she has it here to put her make-up on straight. Epic fail *there*.'

'Now what?'

'Now, you do your thing,' said Fyre, and took a few steps back.

John pursed his lips: was she stepping back to get a better view, or was she edging towards the door to get away from him? There was something else, though;

something in her voice. She didn't entirely believe him, and yet the bit of her that did believe was more than a little frightened. Well, that was OK; so was he.

'You know, I d–don't really know how it happens. If it happens. It m–might not.'

'Just try. Please?'

John shrugged, as if to say, *Don't blame me if this doesn't work. Or does* work *– that might be the worst thing.* He moved round to the side of the mirror – he had no wish to see his mutilated face, thank you very much – and gingerly extended his right arm. Fyre was standing right in front of the mirror, and saw her own reflection staring back at her. She watched as John's hand crept closer and closer to the mirror, and then stopped just millimetres from the surface.

Nothing. Just John's hand and herself behind it, watching and waiting. She realized she was holding her breath. She let it out smoothly and silently. It was a sigh of . . . relief? Yes, relief. It meant that the world was as it should be and, apart from her mother's corpse in the freezer and mysterious, beautifully carved ice sparrows, things weren't all topsy-turvy.

And then John's forefinger touched the surface of the mirror. Just lightly, a feather-light brush, and the surface shimmered. It was like the ripples you sometimes see when a breeze passes over the surface of a pond. No

– *ripple* was too harsh a word. A shiver. As if something huge and invisible had breathed on it from the other side and caused a hundred million tiny stars to start twinkling.

John winced as an intense cramp surged through his arm. It hurt like hell! It felt like his hand wanted to curl in on itself, to turn into a claw. He fought the urge to pull it away.

He looked at Fyre, who had taken an involuntary step backwards. He could see shock and fear and awe written on her face. So it was *true*.

'Oh, John,' she whispered hoarsely as amazement won over fear. 'It's beautiful. Can you—?'

'Johnny! Johnny!' It was Davey Leonard, who had dashed along the corridor at full speed and used the door handle to swing into the room with a crash. 'Johnny!'

John jerked his hand away from the mirror. The spell, Fyre saw, was broken, and it was once again just a mirror. She and John turned round guiltily. Davey, who as usual looked like he had dressed in the dark with one hand tied behind his back, was puzzled.

''Allo, Fyre. Watcha doin?'

'Nothing,' said Fyre and John simultaneously.

'Yeah, sure.'

'Well?' growled John, oddly upset at being interrupted.

'Ms Holles wants to see you.'

'Wh-why?'

'How should I know? What am I, a mind-reader?'

'C-come on, Davey. What's happening?'

'I don't know, honest. She's downstairs with Caspar and Cem and Aziz. Oh, and Baz – you should see him: got a great big plaster cast. Looks like he's done a right number on himself. Right up his arm, it goes. I bet that hurt. And there's a big geezer with them – looks a bit like Wolverine. But fatter. I think it's Caspar's dad. Ain't he a copper? I bet it *is* him; you can smell 'em a mile off.'

'Oh, c-c-crap,' whispered John. 'We should have known C-Caspar wouldn't let s-something like this go. What's the b-b-betting he told his dad that *I* b-b-broke B-B-Baz's arm?'

'You broke Baz's arm?' Davey smiled at John with undisguised admiration. 'Cool. Why?'

'No, I didn't. Caspar did. Fyre? Fyre . . . ? Are you OK? You look ill.'

'I'm fine,' she snapped; she had her own reasons for not wanting to get involved with the police. 'We'll just have to tell them what happened.'

'They w-won't l-listen. It's the two of us against the f-f-four of them. And we'd end up having to go the p-police station, which would mean Grandpa

Mordecai and your mum being d–dragged down there.'

'What do we do then?' Fyre was indignant, angry. 'Getting my mum down there might be difficult.'

'Yeah, we're m–munted.'

'Tell you something else: whoever he is, he looks like a bulldog chewing a wasp. He's not happy; not happy at all,' Davey offered.

'We've got to get out of here,' said Fyre.

'You can't.' Davey gestured downwards. 'They're with old Mother Holles right at the bottom of the stairs. You'd never get past them.'

John looked at the door, as if the policeman and Caspar were about to walk through it, and then dashed across to the windows.

'John?' Fyre guessed what he was thinking. 'We're two floors up. You *can't.*'

He ignored her and tugged at the old-fashioned sash window. It slid up with an alarming screech. He looked out, and down. It was a big drop, but the snow that had gathered at the base of the wall looked soft and deep. Maybe . . .

Fyre thought he was actually going to do it; she grabbed him by the arm and pulled him back. 'Don't be stupid. You'll kill yourself. There's got to be a better way. *Think.*'

In the end it was easier than they thought. Certainly

easier than throwing yourself out of a window. Fyre and John went out onto the second-floor landing and leaned over, glancing down. Baz, they noticed, looked pallid, drawn and, above all, miserable, as he clasped his arm protectively. They stood there, chatting nonchalantly. It took a few seconds, but eventually Caspar looked up and saw them. He tugged at his father's sleeve and pointed upwards.

John and Fyre gasped. The policeman was like a bear in a suit. And not the Yogi kind either. In other times this might have been funny, but now . . .

It was as if everything had fallen into place, Locke thought; as if during the past few days he had been holding the last three parts of a massive jigsaw puzzle and he had finally found where they went.

The constant *tap-tap-tap* in his brain stopped.

Caw! Caw! Caw!

Three lines, three beats, three scars . . .

He knew now what the one-eyed raven-thing had been trying to tell him. The boy! Caspar had said he was scarred, but . . . that face! The three scars! Suddenly it all made sense. *They* were looking for this boy, and he, Siimon Locke, had found him. And once he took the kid back to the station and got his hands around his throat, all would become clear.

Tap-tap-tap!

Caspar, redundantly now, spoke up. 'It's him! That's who attacked Baz!'

It was as if his words had broken a spell that had set everyone in aspic for a few seconds. Fyre and John disappeared from view and began dashing up the stairs, their footsteps echoing around the atrium, hands pulling at the banisters on they made their way up to the top floor.

Locke, Caspar, Cem, Aziz and Ms Holles dashed after them, leaving Baz cradling his arm at the bottom.

'They're trapped, Dad,' shouted Caspar as they rushed up the stairs. 'There's no way out up there. Unless they jump out of a third-floor window.'

'Don't be silly, Caspar,' wheezed Ms Holles, who was by no means sure of John Creed's guilt. 'I can't believe this. John always seemed like such a nice, quiet boy.' She looked up at the mountainous policeman. 'Very shy,' she added, as if this explained something important.

They continued upwards, past the first floor, past the second floor. Above them somewhere, a door slammed shut on raised voices. Fyre and Creed arguing as the net closed in, thought Caspar, grinning. He was enjoying himself: finally Creed would get what was coming to him. Oh, he was going to enjoy this.

But as they turned the corner of the last flight, they

failed to see a hooded figure detach itself from the shadows in the second-floor corridor and hurry down.

John skipped down the stairs as quietly as possible, one ear listening to the fracas above him. As he approached the bottom, he came face to face with Baz. He froze, wondering what to do. Baz had been through enough already, and the idea of pushing past him made John feel sick. If Fyre was right, then – subconsciously or not – he'd caused him agony. On the other hand, if Baz decided to shout a warning . . .

'Baz, I—' he began.

'Go,' said Baz quietly, and moved to one side to let him past. 'Before they get back.'

There was such a sad look in his eyes, and the smile that briefly touched his lips turned down at each end; John felt like stopping and giving him a hug. Instead he rushed down the rest of the stairs. It wouldn't be long before Caspar and his dad realized they had been deceived; but where to go next? Would there be other policemen waiting out the front? Would it be better to use the back gates? It was while he was contemplating this that he heard a long-drawn-out hiss, like air escaping from an over-inflated tyre.

'*Pssssst*. John.'

It was coming from the room they used to give

career advice to sixth formers. The inside of the panelled windows was covered with brown wrapping paper – the school's high-tech solution to the need for privacy. The door was partly open, and through the gap poked the oversized dark glasses and nose of Mr B. Christmas.

'In here, boy,' he said, beckoning.

John slipped through the gap, which closed with a quiet click behind him. 'S-sir?'

'You seem to be in some sort of trouble, John.'

'Yessir. The thing is—'

The Colonel held up a hand. 'No need. Mr Locke seems to be at the bottom of it, and I suspect he's up to no good. That about the size of it?'

'Well, y-yes, you s-see—'

Again the hand came up. It had, John noticed, a long squiggly black blot like a tattoo down the side, thanks to the Colonel's insistence on using fountain pens.

'Bringing a policeman onto the premises and making false accusations against a fellow student – I assume they're false, as Master Pickering seems far from certain who broke his arm – is beyond the pale. Also, I'm indebted to you for the kindness you've shown my brother. I'll deal with Mr Locke later, but in the meantime, stay here until the coast is clear.'

'Yessir,' said John. Maybe this was going to be all right after all. 'But, sir, wh-wh-what about F-Fyre? She . . .

well, she might be in t-trouble too. She's the only other person who saw wh-what r-really happened.'

The Colonel sighed, as if the news was yet another irritant to spoil his day. He adjusted his tie, pulled his shirt cuffs into military order, and yanked the door open. 'Stay here.' He closed the door and locked it behind him.

John sat down at one of the desks. He rested his head in his hands, closed his eyes and let out a defeated sigh. Crikey – when was it he'd stopped breathing?

It seemed like only seconds later that the door opened and Fyre crept in. Behind her, the door was hurriedly pulled to and they heard the key turn in the lock.

'Are you OK?' John whispered.

'Yes. What about the Colonel, eh?'

'Yeah.'

'He says he owes you.'

'Yeah. Long story.'

She sank into a chair next to him. 'I'm exhausted.'

'What happened up there? It worked, obviously.'

'Like a dream. That Davey's a bit mad, isn't he? When Caspar and that big man came crashing into the class-room, he was standing on a desk reciting "The boy stood on the burning deck".'

'He wh-what?'

'I know,' Fyre giggled. 'He'd just got to the bit about sticking his head between his legs and whistling up his—'

'Yeah, I get the p-picture.'

'You should have seen their faces; now *that* was a picture. Caspar just looked confused, but his father . . . Ooh, he was angry. He knew what had happened right away. Talk about looking daggers.'

'And then?'

'Well, Ms Holles asked me where you were and I told her I didn't know. Davey was funny – he just stood there on the desk. Eventually he said, "Do you mind? I'm working here." And then, when Ms Holles told him to get down, he said, "If I fail English, I'm blaming the Wolfman here." I nearly choked myself laughing.'

'And?' asked John, whose sense of humour had deserted him.

'And then they all rushed out again. After that, me and Davey sat there until the Colonel came in. He threw Davey out and explained where you were.'

'Thanks for helping me b-back there.'

'What else was I going to do? If they arrest you, I go back to being boring old Fyre King. At least with you I'm boring old Fyre King with the crackpot friend with the magic mirror fingertips.'

'Thanks a bunch.'

'What was that – that thing with the mirror? That was spooky stuff, John.'

'I d-don't know, I really don't know. It's just m-mad. If you hadn't seen it as well, I'd think I was losing my m-mind.'

'I think you need to talk to your grandfather about it. Didn't you say he has a thing about mirrors? So he's got to know what's happening, right? We're never going to make sense of it on our own.'

'Yeah, you're right. We'll head s-straight back there when the c-coast is c-clear. You'll get to m-meet my family at last.'

Fyre smiled at that, and made a decision. 'John? You're not the only one with weird things happening to them.'

'I'm n-not?'

'No. Yesterday, after you went home, I—'

Fyre was interrupted by the door swinging open to reveal the Colonel.

'The coast is clear,' he whispered conspiratorially. 'Master Locke and his father have left. I suggest you go straight home, John. You too, Fyre. I'll try to get to the bottom of this from here.'

'Thank you, s-sir,' said John. 'I didn't hurt Baz – honestly I didn't.'

'I believe you,' said the Colonel. 'Something very odd is going on around here, and I intend to find out what it is. Now, be off with you. Go out through the science labs. Fewer people, and you'll be under cover most of the way.'

'Thanks again, sir,' said John.

'Yes, thanks, Mr Christmas,' added Fyre as they made their way to the door and peeked out. The coast was clear and they slipped along the deserted corridors to the new annexes, and emerged through the back door of the gym. They checked for policemen and finally, hesitantly, crept away into the back streets behind the school grounds.

The sky was still blue and clear, but something had changed. There was a sepia cast to the air: the sort of light that appears before a storm when one part of the sky suddenly glows with malevolence while the other is bright and shiny.

In the distance they saw the enormous bulb of a bluish-white thundercloud, like a massive radioactive cauliflower, unfolding and bubbling and expanding; a harbinger of weather even worse than they'd already experienced.

'Wow,' muttered Fyre.

'Come on,' said John, hurrying her across the road as the wind picked up. They could already feel something between rain-spit and tiny icicles in the air. 'I wouldn't want to get caught out in what's coming . . . Fyre?'

Fyre wasn't listening. She had stopped in the middle of the road and was staring at the oncoming storm with something approaching joy in her pale eyes. She held one white hand up as if she could touch it.

'It's beautiful,' she whispered to herself.

'Fyre?'

She didn't get the chance to answer, because at that moment a red car came skidding round the corner and slid to a halt next to them. The passenger door opened and the Colonel leaned across to shout at them.

'That policeman is coming back. Get in. We don't have much time.'

John didn't hesitate; he grabbed Fyre's arm and pushed her into the front seat before getting in the back. No sooner had the doors closed than the Colonel had taken off again.

'Get down!' he said as they cruised past the school.

Crouching on the floor, John could see nothing but blue sky. Three dark shapes crossed his field of vision – three ravens, he thought – pursued by a flock of sparrows.

In the well of the front seat, Fyre shivered, but not with the cold. 'Where are we going?' she whispered.

'My place,' said the Colonel. 'You'll be safe there. DS Locke has already sent people round to John's house. And yours too, probably. Don't worry. We'll get this mess sorted out.'

The Colonel parked the car haphazardly outside his house, looked around furtively before opening the doors and ushering Fyre and John into the little front garden and up the stairs to the front door.

'Welcome to my humble abode,' he said quietly.

15
ALL YOUR CHRISTMASES

The house had grown organically over the years, the Colonel explained, as he and his brother acquired the buildings on either side and had built, torn down, rebuilt, added connecting passages and redesigned at whim. From the front it still looked like an ordinary house; only from the inside was the extent of the changes apparent. It was like some huge enchanted castle.

First impressions were misleading, though, because the houses had been parcelled up into smaller sections. John and Fyre found themselves in a hallway just large enough to hold the three of them. It was like meeting up in a wardrobe.

'Sorry about this,' said the Colonel. 'It's Joringel, my brother. He keeps moving the walls.'

John and Fyre stared at him. Did they hear him correctly? *Moving the walls?*

'Jingle bell?' asked John.

'Joringel.' It obviously wasn't the first time he'd had to explain his brother's name.

'And he moves the walls?'

The Colonel twirled a finger next to his temple. 'Yes. Very annoying. They're all on wheels. Well, not the retaining walls, of course. But he keeps changing his mind. Mad as a hatter – as you know, John – but harmless enough if you don't mind waking up to find your lounge has lost fifty centimetres in the night.'

'I can see how that might be irritating . . .' Fyre kept her voice neutral just in case he wasn't joking.

Meanwhile John turned purple as he fought back a laugh. 'How long have you l-l-lived here, Mr Christmas?'

'For ever.' He laughed mirthlessly. 'Well, it seems like it sometimes. Come on through.'

The next room wasn't very big either, but it was crammed from floor to ceiling with packing cases, bookcases and makeshift wooden shelves on which rested relics, tokens and keepsakes from the Christmas brothers' long army careers. There was a cabinet devoted to old hand-grenades; another to bayonets, badges, berets and folded flags.

John frowned at the guns that hung like a deadly

daisy-chain around the walls. Some looked ancient, while others were more modern. It was a sudden insight into the Colonel's life that John didn't quite like. Obsessed or what?

'Where d–d–did you g–get all these, sir?'

'Oh, just picked them up here and there over the years.' Christmas waved at them dismissively. 'My brother and I joined the army at sixteen – lied about our age. It's a good life.'

'You said you would sort out this problem with Caspar and his dad. How?' said Fyre, changing the subject. She didn't know why, but something about Christmas worried her.

'As soon as we've had some tea and cake, eh? An army marches on its stomach – it's been an exhausting day and you must both be famished.'

'Yes.' As soon as he mentioned food, Fyre realized she was starving. 'Yes. Thanks.'

John, who'd been taking an unhealthy (to Fyre at least) interest in a collection of hand–grenades, agreed. 'Yeah, that would be g–great, sir.'

'Good for you. Tea and cake coming right up.'

The next room was so different to the previous two that it might have been in another house. The Colonel, still wearing his ridiculous oversized sunglasses, strode into the middle and turned to face them. He looked like a soldier on his first kit inspection, beaming with pride that he had passed muster.

'Again, welcome to my humble home.'

Fyre looked around: the room was exactly what she would have expected of a former soldier who marched everywhere as if he were still on the parade ground. There was a deep burgundy leather sofa and a long, low coffee table on which lay a few artfully placed magazines. Mr Christmas would have received top marks in a kit inspection: the place was as neat as a pin.

'I'll get the tea,' he said, heading for a second door. 'Make yourself at home.'

After he had gone, Fyre and John examined the black-and-white photographs that hung on a wall – a visual record of the Christmas brothers' careers. Here, looking much, much younger but still easily recognizable thanks to that nose, was a radiant Private B. Christmas, and next to him in the line of grinning, over-enthusiastic young men in ill-fitting uniforms was . . . exactly the same face. Same hair, same eyes, same nose.

'R-remember I told you I s-s-saw him the other day?' said John. 'They're identical, but not identical. If that m-makes sense.'

The photographs continued in the same vein: the two brothers always next to each other, always grinning, always indistinguishable from each other. There they were in some bomb-damaged town, side by side, mirror images of each other, both with a rifle looped lazily over the crook of an arm. There they were in the desert, tanned, leaning cockily on a battered old jeep, squinting against the sun. Another showed them all in white against a snowy backdrop that echoed the weather outside. Next came a jungle scene, this time with half a dozen other men, wearing baggy shorts and sweat-stained singlets.

'Hey, check this out,' said John. He was pointing at a picture further along the wall: here, the two brothers were finally distinguishable; with the pyramids at Giza in the background, they affected much the same heroic poses as before, but this time one of them had a cigarette stuck in his mouth and one arm in a sling. 'That'd help to tell them apart.'

'Yeah, but can you?' asked Fyre before lowering her voice to a whisper. 'John, you know what I was going to tell you earlier? It's—'

'Sssh, he's back.'

The Colonel re-entered the room carrying a tray with three mugs of tea and a selection of cupcakes.

'Jor is the one smoking,' he explained curtly as he transferred his load to the coffee table. 'Filthy habit. He picked it up in Egypt while convalescing from that broken arm. Slipped and snapped it clean across while crouching over one of those hole-in-the-ground toilets. Not very soldierly. Had to wipe his bottom left-handed for weeks. Just don't tell him I told you. It was fifty years ago but he's still a bit sensitive about it.'

'Will I get to meet him?' asked Fyre.

'Later, perhaps,' said the Colonel, pouring tea. 'He's not too sociable these days. Getting old and cranky. Right. Tea all round? Good. Tuck in, soldiers.'

The tea was hot and the cakes delicious, but no sooner had they finished than the Colonel jumped up and began clearing away.

'That was lovely, Mr Christmas,' said Fyre. Outwardly she was politeness itself, but something stirred inside her. The Colonel seemed to have forgotten *why* they were there. 'Thank you.'

'Yeah, thanks, s-sir,' agreed John, though he too was beginning to wonder what was going on.

'Back in a tick,' said the Colonel, and swept away into the next room.

'I wish he'd go and talk to your grandfather,' whispered Fyre. 'Aren't you worried?'

'Y-yeah, we need to g-get him back on t-t-track. He's gone up the garden path, like in Geography.'

Fyre got up and went to look at the photographs again. Here, they were in – where? Another jungle.

Joringel still had a cigarette in his mouth. They were standing in some kind of flat-bottomed boat. Next to that was a photograph that didn't feature both brothers, the details difficult to make out. And then, suddenly, the picture cleared, like one of those 3D puzzles that you have to unfocus your eyes to see. It was one of the Christmas brothers all right, but which one? Whoever it was, he glowered at the camera, his uniform dirty and torn.

In one hand he held a vicious-looking machete.

In the other, a severed human head.

'Urgh.'

'What?'

Fyre stepped to one side. 'There – the last photograph on the right.'

'It's a bit blurred.' John stepped up close. 'It's just . . . Oh.'

'Yes, "oh". But which one is it?'

'Who cares? Let's g-get out of here. This is getting too weird.'

'Excuse me!'

The voice startled them so much that John jerked round and dislodged the final picture from the wall. He caught it inches from the floor after a clattering, heart-stopping fumble. Fyre took a step backwards, bumped into John and then stared in undisguised horror at the newcomer. Well, at his head. In a ghastly echo of the photograph, only the man's head stuck out through the open door that led back to the trophy room. It was Joringel Christmas.

'Come,' he whispered. 'Come on. Come on. Before Barbary gets back.'

Fyre was rooted to the spot, unable *not* to look at the roving eyeball as it swivelled around in its socket. Finally its owner came into the room with a theatrical flourish.

'Joringel Christmas at your service,' he declared with a nod in Fyre's direction. 'Now come along. Come along.' He seemed agitated, looking at the door Barbary had disappeared through. 'He'll be back soon, and then you'll be in trouble.'

'No,' said Fyre. She didn't like this man at all.

'No?'

'Why should we?'

'Because Barbary isn't going to help you. Haven't you guessed that yet? He's going to keep you for *them*. There's a reward out for him – for John. Have you seen the picture yet? Oh yes, I see you have.' He grinned at them and flicked the ash from his cigarette in their direction. 'He did that. In the war. Some war somewhere. And much more. Come with me. I can get you out. Come on, before he gets back. You've seen what he's capable of . . .'

For all his idiosyncrasies, Joringel seemed harmless. Eccentric, yes; scruffy, yes – but *dangerous*? Even so, John and Fyre backed way, edging towards the far door. John opened it and peeped through. It was indeed the kitchen, but there was no sign of their teacher. 'Mr C-C-Christmas?' he shouted.

'See?' The other Christmas brother grinned. 'Don't you see? He's gone to get *them*. He's going to collect the reward himself.' He drew on his cigarette and inhaled deeply before pointing it at John. 'You,' he said with great emphasis. 'Not her. They don't want *her*. They want *you*.'

'Who,' asked John, 'are *they*?'

'The wolf, silly boy. The *white wolf*.'

John felt the blood draining from his face.

Fyre turned to look at him. 'That's in the dream you told me about! John?'

Joringel grinned and waved his hands around about his head, trying to imitate something. Cigarette ash flew everywhere. 'The birds, John; the birds have been whispering, chatting . . . *spying*. They're here, you see, and they're looking for you and your kindred.'

'Kindred? You mean my *family*? Why?' What was this madman talking about? How did he know about the dream? John felt the world dropping away beneath his feet. 'No. No. This is impossible.'

'But it all makes some kind of sense, John, don't you see?' Fyre looked at him with something like triumph in her eyes. '*Something*'s been happening, right? Something weird. All your life you've dreamed about this white wolf, and now—'

'She's here? What does that even *mean*? C-come on, Fyre! That's just n-n-nutty.'

'Any nuttier than what happened to Baz? The mirror? Even I—'

'Wh-What?' John grabbed Fyre's hand. 'Even you *what*?'

'The snow. With me it's the snow. I think I can *do* things with it . . . Oh, it doesn't matter now.'

'You need to come with me. Now!' growled Joringel.

John and Fyre took stock of him again. He was as slouched as his brother was upright. He pulled out another cigarette and lit it with an old-fashioned silver cigarette lighter, which he flicked open with practised ease. On one side it was decorated with a Nazi swastika. He saw John looking at it.

'Took it from an enemy soldier. Very reliable. The lighter, not the soldier. Always lights first time. Are you coming?'

John squeezed Fyre's hand, his eyes flashing a warning. But he wasn't looking at the lighter – he was looking at Joringel's hand.

'We need to g-go,' he said. 'Thanks, Mr Christmas, b-b-but we really n-need to get home. That storm will be here soon.' He turned to Fyre. 'We really should g-go.'

But Joringel had other ideas. From a pocket of his baggy shorts he produced a black revolver and pointed it nonchalantly at them. 'I'm so sorry about this, John,' he said. 'I like you, really I do, but they're coming. Things are going to change; and it's time to pick sides.'

He forced them through a bewildering series of rooms. The Christmas house, it seemed to them, had been chopped and changed around so much that it was impossible to identify the boundaries of the original houses.

'Where are we g-going?' asked John.

'Want to show you something. Can't say. Official Secrets and all that. Up here! Not far now.'

The staircase they were climbing was dark, narrow and enclosed on both sides. It ended at a large oak door. Joringel produced a bunch of keys and shook them.

'Open the door,' he ordered Fyre, picking one out and passing it to her.

'What's that noise?' asked John. 'C-can you hear that?'

Fyre strained to hear above the jangling of the keys as she tried to turn it in the lock. Yes, there it was: a faint noise coming from inside. Finally the tumblers clicked and the door swung open.

'Oh,' said Fyre. 'What's that smell?'

Joringel pushed them into the room, his gun still pointing at them. It was obviously three attics joined together, and was filled to the rafters with birdcages. They hung from the ceiling, lined the walls on shelves or just sat on the floor. They were square, round and rectangular; they were tall and short and squat; made of wire, iron and bamboo in styles as simple as a hamster cage through to exotic Russian cupolas.

It was an astonishing collection.

But that wasn't the worst of it.

Oh no.

The worst of it was that every cage was occupied.

By sparrows. Hundreds of them. Sometimes ten or fifteen to a cage.

When they entered, the noise that John had heard earlier rose to a crescendo as they all began twittering mournfully. He knew that his mouth had dropped open; there was a wet sloshing in the pit of his stomach and he had to fight the urge to vomit. This was wrong; very, very wrong. It was almost as if he could *feel* their suffering.

'They're normally pretty quiet,' grumbled Joringel.

'I should think s–so,' muttered John as he approached

the birds. 'I w-wouldn't find m-much to sing about, l-locked up like this.'

'It's your dream again,' whispered Fyre to John, who could only nod in agreement. 'Why?' she asked Joringel.

'Because they're vermin. Filthy little spying, whispering, feathered *fiends*.'

'So why keep them?' Fyre's voice quivered a little at his vehemence.

'Yeah, wh-why?' repeated John, making his way through the cages, ducking to avoid the hanging ones. 'It must cost a fortune to feed them.'

'Oh, we don't feed them.' Joringel grinned evilly. He looked like a troll who had just swallowed a particularly pleasant peasant.

'You don't?' Fyre stayed near the door while John moved across to a set of three round windows.

'That would be pointless. No, we just imprison them. It's so much more fun to watch when there are several in a cage and they get hungry . . .' He paused to snort back a hanging globule of snot the colour of faded grass and the consistency of a rotten oyster. When it had vanished in a gluggy gulp he went on: 'They eat their dead, see?'

Fyre did see then. The base of many of the cages on the floor contained a disgusting mixture of guano and sparrow corpses, some old and dry and bony, others plump and fresh. As she looked, a maggot crawled out of one bird's eye. She closed her eyes and grabbed hold of the door frame.

John looked out through one of the windows. He saw that the storm was now upon them: the snow was coming down faster than ever, but through it all he could see a sloping roof and, below that, an overgrown expanse of garden. The snow had built up, pristine, white and deep, between the high fences. It was like looking out of a castle keep – a castle plunged into some snowbound fairy-tale nightmare.

John shivered and looked back at the caged birds. 'This is r-r-revolting,' he said grimly.

He spun round just in time to see Joringel perform a smart about-face and head off through the doorway.

'Why are you doing this?' cried Fyre.

'Our f-friends will be looking for us!' shouted John. 'They'll f-f-find us.'

Joringel turned back to face them. 'Oh, I think not. Number one, you don't *have* any friends, John; I know that. And number two, even of you did, they wouldn't be out looking for you in this weather. You're just a couple of teenagers who vanished in the snow. And soon it won't matter. *She'll* be here.'

'This wolf? Mr Christmas, this is crazy.'

'Foolish boy! Can't you hear the huffing and the

puffing? You'll find out soon enough.' And with that he slammed and locked the door.

Fyre looked around their prison, took in the cages, the suddenly silent birds, and burst into tears. She threw her arms tightly around John, buried her face in the crook of his neck and sobbed. Finally she let go; John, she saw, had been crying too. The hands they used to wipe red-rimmed eyes were trembling.

'Is he going to kill us?' she asked.

'I don't think so,' said John unconvincingly. He turned to examine the windows and felt a spike of panic in his throat. *Keep calm – keep calm, John*, he thought. He looked over at Fyre. She, too, seemed to be trying to stop panic turning into full-blown hysteria.

'I can't b-believe he'd do that – you know, after everything he d-d-did for me.' John stared at the door as if he could see through it to the man who had mentored him, encouraged him, treated him with kindness . . . What had happened?

Fyre looked at him oddly. 'John, that's not our teacher; that's not Mr Christmas. You're getting them mixed up. That's Joringel.'

'No,' said John with a certainty that surprised her. 'It's not. I've been thinking about it. Didn't you notice that he's g-got exactly the s-s-same ink s-stain on his hand as the Colonel had at the school.'

'Anyone can have ink on their hands!'

'N–not in exactly the s–same place and exactly the s–same shape. I think Barbary and J–Joringel are the same p–person.'

'*What?*'

'Yeah. Mad, right? Think about it! I've never s–s–seen them both at the s–same time. Ever. And that ink s–stain proves it. I reckon those big g–glasses "our" Christmas wears are to disguise his wobbly eye.'

'But why? There were two of them in those photographs; where's the other one?'

'Dead? Gone? They'd be, like, ninety or s–s–something, wouldn't they? And the one that's l–left is like that J–Jekyll and Hyde s–story we were talking about the other day. You know: two people in one body? I think Barbary w–wants to help us, while Joringel wants to . . . wh–wh–whatever.'

'But why?'

'I d–don't know. Who knows wh–wh–what's happening? I know one thing, though.'

'What?'

'We n–n–need to get out of here before Joringel gets back.'

'If you're right, maybe he'll come back as Barbary: he helped us to get away from Caspar and his dad,' said Fyre hopefully. She tugged her jacket tight around herself as if it could protect her from the world.

'You want to b–b–bet your l–l–life on it?' asked John.

'No.'

'Then let's l–look for a w–way out.'

Apart from the caged birds there was nothing much in the attic except some packing cases and cardboard boxes stacked in a dark corner. John wandered over, poking a finger into the occasional cage as he went and whispering to the captive sparrows. How could he have ever thought they were . . . what? Evil?

He was so absorbed that he didn't notice the skeleton until he was almost on top of it.

'*Yeow!*' He jumped backwards, tripped over and fell in a heap. 'Fyre!'

'What? *What?* Oh my God!'

John got up and looked back at the skeleton – a white ghost grinning in the shadows. They edged closer, squinting in the half-light.

'L–l–look at the arm,' he gasped. 'Snapped right across. Remember Barbary saying that his b–brother broke his arm?'

'You don't think . . .'

'I do. I think we've f–found Joringel Christmas.'

'Oh, that's gross. Do you think the Colonel killed him?'

'Could be. Or maybe he just d–died. It makes s–sense.

Well, as m–much as anything makes sense at the moment.'

'But how do you end up keeping your brother's skeleton in the attic?'

'I d–d–don't think I want to know. We need t–to g–g–get out of here in case—' He stopped short, but Fyre realized immediately what he was going to say.

'In case we end up like *that* . . .'

They searched the attic frantically, but apart from the locked door there was, they realized, only one way out. John pointed at the windows. Fyre stared out into the garden three storeys below.

'You *are* joking,' she said.

'No, I'm n–not. I'd rather take my ch–ch–chances out there than with a m–m–maniac with a gun. And that snow's got to be two metres deep. We'll be f–f–fine.'

'Unless we land on a fence or something just under the surface and break our backs. There's got to be another way . . .' whispered Fyre. She leaned past him and gave the window latch a tug. 'And these are stuck fast; we'd have to break the glass.'

'Then we b–break the glass.' John grimaced. 'But first . . .'

'What?'

'Well, we're n–not the only ones imprisoned up here,' he said with a grin. 'It's only f–fair.'

Fyre grinned too. Even with the scars John was cute when he smiled like that, she thought; so happy, so confident.

'Let's do it,' she said.

They dashed from cage to cage, opening the doors and releasing the sparrows. Some flew out immediately, swooping up to land in the eaves. Others, from weakness or fear, eyed the open doors tentatively before hopping over and peering out. Gradually their song increased to a happy crescendo and, one by one, they began to take to the air. Within minutes the room was a wild, thrashing whirligig of wings.

'This is so *cool*,' laughed Fyre as she stood, amazed, in the middle of it all.

'It is, isn't it?' said John. He was waiting by the window, holding a thigh bone from the skeleton he had dismantled. 'Now, l-l-let's get out of here.'

And with that, he lifted the bone high above his head and brought it down against the glass, which shattered with an ear-splitting crash. A mighty blast of freezing air blew in. It didn't stop the sparrows, though; they gathered together in the middle of the room, a squawking, chirping, screeching ball of beak and feather. And then, like a swarm of bees, they swept out through the window and disappeared.

John turned to Fyre. 'Let's g-go,' he said.

* * *

Just minutes later, attracted by the noise, Barbary/
Joringel Christmas burst into the room. He was still
wearing his skimpy army fatigues and shorts, gun held
out in front of him. He took one look at the empty
cages and the broken window and lowered his gun.

'*NOOOOOOOOOOOOOO!*'

He dashed across the room and leaned out gingerly.
Below him a section of the snow on the sloping roof
had been disturbed, a slippery escape chute.

'*NOOOOOOOOO!*' he roared again into the howling wind. And then he noticed, caught in the gutter –
bone-white against the snow – a skull grinning back up
at him. 'What in heaven's name . . . ?'

Behind him, John and Fyre crept out from behind
the big oak door and slipped out of the room. As Fyre
crept down the stairs, John pulled the door closed and
turned the big iron jailor's key in the lock.

'Come on, come on,' hissed Fyre. 'He's still got the
gun, remember?'

Downstairs, in the front hallway, they pulled up their
hoods and zipped their jackets. Fyre put her heavy black
sunglasses back over her eyes.

'Ready?' asked John. 'We've got to be c-careful –
Caspar and his d-dad are out there somewhere.'

'Do we have a choice?' said Fyre.

John turned the door handle, only to have it ripped out of his grasp. For a moment he thought someone had pulled it open, but it was just the storm, now a screaming hurricane-force whiteout. They couldn't see more than a metre in front of them, but going back wasn't an option, especially when they heard gunfire and the splintering of wood.

Without a word they plunged into the teeth of the freezing maelstrom.

16
ONCE UPON A TIME . . .

It was a world frozen in time. Everything had ground to a halt. From overflow pipes and windowsills and garden hosepipes sprang a forest of sparkling icicles, great curtains of frozen water. The few flowers or leaves that remained were like sculptures, glistening ice versions of themselves.

They stumbled down the steps, slid across the narrow front garden and through the wrought-iron gate into the snow-covered square. Fyre had to pull John close and holler in his ear to be heard above the screaming wind. She felt curiously at home in the ice and the cold and the snow. Even her eyesight, poor at the best of times, had changed. She could see patterns, make out details that John would never notice.

'Follow me! I think I know the way!'

John grabbed her hand and followed her into the

blizzard, hoping she wasn't leading them straight back the way they had come. And the storm wasn't the only thing that had changed. John now knew that, unbelievably, the white wolf was out there somewhere, somehow, hunting, sniffing . . . and she was coming for *him*.

Hello, little sparrow . . . Wasn't that what she said in his dream? *I've been waiting for you.*

Was she? He squinted into the whiteout. Was she out there, just waiting to huff and puff and . . . what?

Eventually the storm began to take its toll. Despite their hoodies and heavy coats they still weren't dressed for these arctic conditions. John's feet were so cold he couldn't feel them. Then, just when he felt like giving up and sitting down to die, Fyre stopped. She leaned towards him and said something that was snatched away by the wind.

'What?'

'We're in the alleyway at the back of the newsagent's.'

John was astonished. How in hell had Fyre found her way so unerringly? She didn't even seem to feel the cold.

'Let's go in,' he said. 'I'm so freezing I c-c-could just go to s-s-sleep right here. And we can see if Mr Patel is all right.'

The alley was almost waist-deep in snow and the

wind shrieked along it. They edged forward and finally found the back door. Only the top half of it was visible, but John dug down into the snow and found the doorknob. Their luck was in: it turned easily, the door swung open and they tumbled gratefully inside.

They pushed their way past several stacks of old newspapers and floor-to-ceiling columns of cigarette and sweet cartons. John turned to look at Fyre: her pale skin was now a shade of iceberg blue – though she wasn't shivering like him.

'Mr Patel?' he shouted. 'Mr Patel?'

There was no reply.

And then he saw why: his employer was fast asleep. He was still on his stool, but slumped over the counter, his grizzled grey head cushioned on crossed arms. The shop was toasty warm, and John began to feel life seep back into his bones. Pins and needles pricked his feet.

'Mr Patel?' he repeated. Something was wrong. Should he wake him up? Fyre seemed to catch some of John's apprehension. The man was a bit *too* asleep.

'Is he dead?' she asked.

It was a thought that hadn't occurred to John, and it jolted him into action. What was the worst that could happen? He gently shook the sleeping man's shoulder.

Nothing.

He shook a little harder.

Nothing.

'Mr Patel?' John leaned closer, and realized that the man's eyes were moving rapidly back and forth. This was a good sign, but why wouldn't he wake up? Perhaps he was in some sort of coma. He shook him again, harder this time. Again, nothing.

Fyre felt his wrist for a pulse. It was very slow. John edged round the other side of the counter and gently lifted the man's head.

'He just w-won't wake up . . . Jesus, Fyre, he w-w-won't wake up. What do we do?'

'I don't know.'

'He's really ill, isn't he? In a coma or something. It's like he's Sleeping Beauty.'

'You could try kissing him . . .'

'Yeah, right.'

'So what do we do?'

'Nothing. There's n-nothing to do. Nothing we can do, is there? Call the police? An ambulance? Nobody's going to come out in this. And we can't take him with us.'

'So we just leave him here?'

'Look, my place is just round the corner. We'll see what my grandfather thinks.' It was more question than statement, and Fyre nodded her agreement: 'Sounds like a plan. Let's go.'

John nodded. 'Can we wait for a minute or two? I don't know about you, but I need to warm up a bit.'

And so they sat there in the warm glow of the three-bar fire, saying nothing about the events in the Christmas house. Instead they rubbed their hands together and stamped their feet to get some life back into them. And they watched the shallow breathing and rapid eye movements of the man who wouldn't wake up.

17
THE WOLF INSIDE

Rajesh Patel wasn't the only one asleep. If Fyre and John had somehow tunnelled their way into the snow-covered bank a few doors down, they would have found sleeping customers leaning against walls and tellers with their heads on desks, faces crushed against pens and paperclips and staplers.

In the police station the sergeant was snoring. In the offices above him and the cells below him, everyone was sleeping.

In offices and shops and cafés and hotels and homes and garages and cars across the land, the populace had simply lain down or leaned against the nearest solid object and nodded off.

Fyre and John didn't know it yet, but Norton Folgate, the city, the entire country was fast asleep, as if a spell had been cast.

Of course, not everyone had been affected.

Fyre and John were awake.

Mordecai Creed and the Duchess were awake, and fretting about John . . .

In a deserted, snowy street to the north of the city, six massive wolves loped along like black missiles in the wake of an even bigger white wolf with golden eyes.

And in a similar street further south, two figures in fur-lined yellow ski suits – one small, one large – made their way north to their destiny. Tapper Locke wasn't entirely sure where he was going or what he'd find when he got there, but he knew it was the right thing to do. After the kid with the scars had evaded them at the school, everything had fallen into place. The three scars were the three lines; the *tap-tap-tap* in his head. It was clear from the voices – no, not voices; more like a constant blast of static that only he could hear, and that had tapped into something deep within him. It was inconsistent and fuzzy, but he knew there was a change coming; he had information that would usher in a brave new world of certainty, of black and white, without the grey stuff in between.

For he knew the location of the boy – the boy the wolf was hunting.

And if he was first with the news that the boy had

been found . . . well, there would be a position for him in this new world. And there would be law. And there would be order. And he would administer it with an iron fist.

'*Information* is the key here, son,' he had told Caspar, 'and I need everything you know about this Creed kid. *Everything*. The truth, the whole truth and nothing but . . .'

Which wasn't quite what he'd told Caspar about his mother, of course, but if all went well, the corpse walled up in his bedroom would become inconsequential, a wisp on the wind of history.

Tap, tap, tippety-tap.

And now Caspar had come up trumps. It was *fate* – those years of waiting, of knowing he was destined for more. All this time Caspar had been feuding with the boy who would turn Locke's life around. *Destiny*. He could feel it unfurling inside him. His mind was like some little boat that had come loose from its moorings – from the dockside of convention - and was now rushing down a churning white-water course, going wherever the currents took it.

And it wasn't hard to see why: it was all down to *her*, whoever *she* was, telling him that he didn't have to hide any more, that he could let his true nature be seen, that he could be proud of it. And so, little by little, he had let loose the monster inside like a dog on one of those long retractable leashes. Oh, happy day!

And, like a dog, he had gone wild, rushing around in his head, sniffing out all the putrid stuff he'd kept hidden at the back of his drawers of respectability and piddling in the corners because, well, because he *could*.

Finally his mind came to a stop when Caspar, his rage and hate and venom for John Creed all played out, finished lamely with: 'I dunno. I just don't like him. He's just so . . . *nice*.'

'Don't worry, son,' Locke had said, getting up. 'He'll get what's coming to him. But first, I've got to head north; meet some . . . *people*. Then things will change around here, believe you me.'

'Can I come?' whined Caspar.

Locke looked at his son – so confident sometimes and such a whingeing brat at others. He seemed so pathetic, so needy, that he almost pulled out his kitten tapper and put him out of his misery there and then. But what if she needed more proof that Creed was the one they were looking for? Maybe the boy would be the final key . . . Yes, the boy could come. Would have to come.

Which was why, a few hours later, they could be found trudging through the snow, heading north. For his part, Caspar Locke was truly happy for the first time in ages. He knew that his father was a man who kept his promises. John Creed had made Caspar look foolish one too many times, and he wanted revenge. And the Lockes were key. Hee-hee. Lockes and key.

And so Caspar bent his head against the wind and forced himself to catch up. He reached out and grabbed his father's huge gloved hand. It was the action of a little boy, not a teenager, but he didn't care. Finally his father liked him, wanted to spend time with him.

It felt good.

It felt safe.

It felt like he was part of a family again.

No, not a family: a *pack*.

In Highgate Cemetery, in a clearing that used to be the meeting place of four paths, stands a massive white wolf. The clearing is a strangely quiet haven from the blizzard. The wolf is as big as a tiger. She has eyes of honey and is half sitting, half lying down, like a sphinx, dignified and calm, those golden eyes flicking lazily back and forth, watching, waiting.

Around her lurk other, smaller black wolves. They slink between the graves like ghosts, stopping every now and then to urinate against them in great disrespectful arcs. In the trees and on the ground, one-eyed ravens perch or hop. They come and go in their hundreds, quarrelling and squawking and telling of sightings of the scarred boy and his family from Land's End to John o' Groats. But the wolf knows; the wolf has a nose for these things – she will know instinctively when the news is right, when the news is *true*.

Now and then a human form approaches the outer edges of the clearing and a raven flutters onto its shoulder to receive news. Men, women and children, some in dressing gowns and pyjamas, come and go, seemingly impervious to the freezing conditions. Many of them will later lose their way, fall asleep and die in the snow, having delivered their news.

When they had found the boy they would use him to force open *all* the mirrors all over the world all at once – a million or more 'rifts' in reality, bridges between her world and this. When that was done, her armies would pour through, a blizzard of teeth and claws, to bring this world to its knees. All they needed was the boy, and then there would be eternal winter; a *very* happy ever after.

Siimon and Caspar Locke stepped into the clearing. And the raven that had perched on the policeman's shoulder flew like a piece of windblown black paper onto the snow in front of the wolf and began whispering . . .

PART TWO

1
BATTLE PLANS

'Once upon a time—'

'Seriously? Once upon a time?' said John. He was sitting alongside Fyre on the battered sofa in the Duchess's lounge. The two of them had left Rajesh Patel and staggered home. Now their coats and hooded tops lay in a discarded heap in the bathtub; it looked as if two people had crawled in fully clothed and then melted away down the plughole.

When they had heaved open the heavy front door, the gate to the Duchess's place had opened almost immediately, the dogs had gone berserk, and the Duchess and Mordecai Creed had rushed out.

'John, where have you—?' they had said in unison, and then stopped when they saw that he wasn't alone.

'Hi, sorry – l-look, you're n-n-never going to believe what happened. Oh, s-s-sorry, this is Fyre. She's—'

And that was as far as he got. Fyre had pulled off her black glasses and thrown back her hood, and the looks of . . . shock, horror, amazement had struck John dumb. The Duchess had clapped her hands to her mouth.

'This happens quite a lot,' said Fyre hesitantly, smiling shyly at John, who was scowling at his family's reaction, 'but not quite to this extent.'

It was Mordecai who recovered first. He held his arms out like a traffic cop at an intersection and shepherded them into the flat. 'Inside, inside – quick. We have much to talk about.'

It wasn't going well, though. John had unburdened himself of everything – the dreams, the mirrors, the animal reflexes, the strange behaviour of the sparrows, the escape from the Christmas house. His grandfather had promised an explanation, but it wasn't exactly what John was expecting.

'You going to listen or you going to talk?' Mordecai was perched on the edge of the glass coffee table as if what he had to say was too important, too urgent, to be told from the comfort of an armchair.

John rubbed his hands together, still trying to work some warmth into them. 'It's j-just that—'

'Where I come from – where *we* come from – *this* is how we start our stories. John, is important you listen and important you *believe*.'

236

'I'd b–believe anything right n–now, Grandpa,' said John. 'But, r–really, *once upon a time*?'

'We're listening, Mr Creed,' said Fyre, elbowing John in the ribs.

From the kitchen came the rattle of mugs and the muted roar of the kettle as the Duchess made tea. They could hear a faint susurration as she muttered to herself.

'OK. So, once upon a time, long, long ago, there was a world of kings, queens, princesses, trolls and, yes, witches and . . . wolves. And it was – *is* – real. As real as aeroplanes and iPods and computers and motorcars.'

'B–but—'

'John, let him finish,' said Fyre.

'Thank you, my dear. I know is hard to take in, John, but is where we came from. We passed through the rift twelve years ago and have been hiding here ever since.'

'The rift?'

'Mirrors, John – the *mirrors* are doors, rifts, to other worlds, other universes, rifts in space and time. Is how we got here.'

'So wh–what you're s–saying is that we're f–f–fairy-tale characters?' John didn't know whether to sit or stand or laugh or cry. His grandfather had gone crazy – that had to be the answer. He fidgeted in his seat, frown-ing, glancing between Mordecai and Fyre. 'This is a j–j–joke, right?'

'Of course not. And is no laughing matter, John. We are all in great danger. You especially.'

'Mr Christmas kept saying something about how "they" were coming.' Fyre wasn't quite so sceptical. 'He said it was wolves.'

'Is true. You dream about them all the time, no?' Mordecai asked his grandson.

'You always s-s-said it was just a b-b-b-bad dream. That I'd g-grow out of it. Why d-d-didn't you tell me the truth?'

'Tell little boy he was from different world and his parents were killed by wolf before they could escape? Think about it, John.' Mordecai's explanation, in such bald terms, stopped the conversation dead.

John bent his head, as if he was thinking about it. Finally he looked his grandfather in the eye. 'So it wasn't a c-car c-crash?'

'No.'

'And these?' John motioned to the scars on his face.

'White wolf. She caught you as we came through. Your parents stayed on other side.' The old man paused. 'We thought you would die. Your poor face was so . . . But thanks to a Scottish lady called Mairie McDougall – we came through into her house – you were saved. She had boy too – Deryk. Good people. Then rift closed. We didn't know for how long, so we saw to wounds as best we could, came south, away from snow.'

'Tea, anyone?' The Duchess appeared in the doorway with tea and biscuits. Fyre nudged John and he jumped up to help with the heavy tray, which was wobbling precariously.

'Thank you, John. So kind,' said the Duchess, smiling at Fyre. She bustled in and plonked herself down in her usual comfy armchair. Mordecai shuffled along the coffee table so that John could put down the tea tray.

'Will you be mother, John?' asked the Duchess.

'Where you get these sayings, Duchess?' growled Mordecai as John poured the tea and added milk.

'Unlike *some*, Mordecai, I have tried to blend in all these years.' She smiled sweetly, and took a mug from John. 'Thank you.'

'Is all this true, Duchess?' asked John, wanting it not to be.

'Yes, John. Your grandfather might be as stubborn as the donkey he rode to school, but he's not delusional. We came from a world parallel to this one.' She sipped her tea and smacked her lips. 'Lovely.'

'Why?' asked Fyre. She seemed to be taking everything in her stride.

'Why?'

'Yes, why did you come here? What was so wrong with your world?'

'The wolves, dear, the wolves. Have you not been listening? You've read your fairy tales, yes? There's always a wolf. *I'll huff and I'll puff,* and all that? Red Riding Hood? The expression *keep the wolf from the door*? You know, I think our people have been coming through in dribs and drabs for centuries, and this world's fairy tales are just versions of our truth – stories told and retold to each generation.'

'So we *are* fairy-tale characters, in a way,' John muttered.

'Yes. Yes, you could look at it that way.'

'But why *did* we come here?'

'Because we were selfish and hateful, John.'

'No, Duchess, is not exactly true,' said Mordecai.

'Oh, yes, it is, and you know it.' The Duchess turned back to John and Fyre. She spoke softly, conjuring up images from her past and weaving them into a story that she was obviously ashamed of. 'We needed land for our crops. We cleared the forests, killing the wolves in the process. We wiped them out without a second thought. We drove them to extinction. Or so we thought. Instead, they slunk away into the frozen Northern Wastes, biding their time. And then one day they returned in their millions, bringing death and snow with them. They wiped out everything in their path – men, women, children. They huffed and they puffed all right. But no matter how many we killed, they just kept coming, driven on by a white wolf with golden eyes. They wanted nothing more than to exterminate us – just as we thought we had exterminated *them*.'

The silence that followed her tale was empty and yet full to bursting at the same time, like some great blood blister. Even the Dobermans, John realized, were mute.

'And they succeeded,' grumbled Mordecai eventually.

'They did, indeed. We were forced further and further away from our homes. The castles, the villages were . . . destroyed. We were facing certain death when your father, John, discovered – rediscovered – a way to open a rift between our worlds. He was from a long bloodline of shamans, but the old spells had been lost over time, replaced by the more practical skills of healing. The tribe thought he was mad at first, poring over old manuscripts and parchments while the rest of the men battled the wolves, but eventually he deciphered them.'

'Not a moment too soon,' Mordecai muttered.

'Yes, there were only a handful of us left, under siege in the ruins of an old castle, when he opened the rift.'

'Wh-what did it l-l-look like?' asked John.

'It was beautiful. There was a huge, ornate mirror in the great hall and he'd been working on it for weeks when, suddenly, it turned to . . . I suppose "liquid diamond" would be the best description.'

'But . . . ?'

'But he was unable to keep it open. We glimpsed *something* in the mirror, but the pain was too great and your father had to pull away. I remember how his hands cramped up. It was unbearable, he said.'

'I know the f-f-feeling,' muttered John, flexing his own hands in sympathy. He had never really thought about his father; a ghostly shadow standing behind the big bulk of Grandpa Mordecai. He wondered if he and his father were alike. And if his father had opened a rift, then maybe . . .

'We didn't know what – if anything – was on the other side, but we had no choice. Even as I massaged healing oils into your father's hands, we heard the sound of fighting outside the castle walls. When he finally got the rift open long enough, the last of us were passing through when the wolves broke through the barricades.'

She came to a smooth halt, like a car running out of petrol and coasting to a standstill.

'I d-d-don't b-b-believe any of this,' said John. But even as he said it, he knew he did.

The Duchess sipped at her tea and smiled sadly at them both. '*You* believe it, don't you, Fyre? Part of you *knows* it's true.'

'I do?' said Fyre.

'You know, we thought it was you John was being secretive about,' said the Duchess, changing the subject.

Fyre blushed.

'And it was, a little, was it not?'

John nodded.

The Duchess went on, looking at him all the while. 'We are known – *were* known – as the Kindred, a loose collection of tribes – Creeds, Hunters, Archers, a few others – and we had lived in harmony with each other for centuries when the wolves started coming back. We ignored all the warning signs, of course; stopped listening to the whisperings of our friends the sparrows; laughed away the reappearance of the *hremmen*, the one-eyed ravens—'

'I s-saw one of those things,' said John in amazement. 'So I w-w-wasn't imagining it?'

'What happened to it?' Mordecai was half out of his seat, suddenly alert. 'The raven, John – did it *see* you?'

'Yes, it s-saw me all right, but then this c-c-cloud of s-sparrows t-tore it apart. I thought the sparrows were . . . Mr Christmas had loads of them caged up. He called them *spies*.'

Mordecai sat back down, mollified by the news of the bird's demise. He laughed a little. 'They are spies, really, my boy. Or rather ours *were*, back then. Here, is not same. The *sparrwen*, sparrows, here are not so intelligent, eh? But instinct is same, I think. Good to see but not so much helpful. Sorry, Duchess, continue.'

'Well, we became complacent, John. And when we finally woke up to the threat, it was too late. The wolves had secretly joined forces with the Ice Queen— Yes, John, don't look so shocked: she really did exist. She ruled over some of the Kindred tribes spread out along the border of the Northern Wastes. Like your father, she was a shaman. Unlike us, though, her people hadn't ignored the old ways. She was powerful; powerful enough to learn to control the weather that far north. And, as the saying in this world goes, *The love of power corrupts.*'

'What did she do?' asked Fyre.

'She brought winter down on us. Eternal winter. She brought snow and ice and darkness in return for her life.'

'So, like it is now? Maybe it's not wolves; maybe it's *her.*'

'Oh, I don't think so. In the end the wolves learned her secrets, and when they did, they turned on her.'

'And the m-mirrors . . . ?' asked John. 'What about the m-mirrors?'

'As your grandfather said, they're *doors. Every* mirror is a potential door. We didn't know if the wolves would

– or could ever – decipher the old texts, but we couldn't take the chance. That's why we never had any big mirrors in the house.'

'And the l-l-language l-lessons?'

'Incantations,' confessed Mordecai. 'Yes, I know. *Magic spells*. They have to do with rifts between worlds. Your father discovered it – only those with right bloodline can open rift. You, John. I hoped you could learn to do same, that maybe something pass from father to son.'

'Wh-why?' John could feel a lava-like glow of anger building up inside him. They'd lied. All of them. He'd been lied to his whole life.

'Is it not obvious? To escape again.'

'And this b-b-business of seeing things? W-wolf heads . . . dog heads in reflections?'

'Could be side effect of wolf injury *and* being your father's son. Not sure. Mirrors were important in our world – windows to soul—'

'Dear me,' interrupted the Duchess, 'you sound like a nutty old fraud, Mordecai. The boy needs *answers*. Remember your fairy tales, John? *Mirror, mirror on the wall?* Well, for some, those with the Gift, mirrors can reveal people's true natures. You seem to have started to develop *that* ability.'

John, finally, had nothing to say. He stared blindly at the floor, dumbfounded. And angry.

'It's all real, John. We think the wolves have used your blood, your DNA, to somehow open the rift again. If so, then the two worlds collided and they have come through. It explains the snow, and the sleeping sickness which you say has taken Mr Patel.'

'Will he be alright?' asked John. 'Mr Patel? Should we go get him?'

'And do what? Is nothing to be done for him now. Is too dangerous to go back. He will survive. Or he will not.'

John, aghast at his grandfather's cold assessment of the situation but realising he was right, kicked out at the wall in frustration.

'What about you?' he demanded. 'How come you're not in a coma too? Any of us, for that matter!'

'We Kindred are immune,' replied Mordecai in an even tone that did nothing to temper the anger John could feel rising through his whole body. 'The sleeping sickness puts the truly kind-hearted to sleep and leaves the rest for *her*.'

'Her?'

'The white wolf. She controls her pack telepathically and looks into our minds and hearts to appeal to the worst in us. Not everyone is as good-hearted as you, John,' explained the Duchess. 'We were often betrayed by people whose bad natures got the better of them. It's as if there's a wolf inside all of us, and we can either keep it locked up or embrace it.'

'Is like some people give in to animal side, yes?' muttered Mordecai, his voice full of bitterness. 'Wolves bring out worst in man, you know. Stuff we keep hidden – secret thoughts, selfishness – is revealed and is . . . is found to be perhaps not so bad after all.'

'Like Mr Christmas?'

'Yes, Fyre.' The Duchess nodded. 'From what you've said, it sounds as if your teacher was a man in two minds to begin with. And then, when he started to hear the wolf's message – *Find John Creed, bring him to me* – he was torn in two mentally, stuck between wanting to help you and wanting to betray you. Poor man.'

'*Poor m-man?*' John looked up, exasperated. 'That p-poor m-man was g-going to—'

'And what about John's reflexes?' asked Fyre. 'His speed? Did he get that from his father?'

'Ah,' growled Mordecai, before the Duchess could answer. 'Not sure. We think is from wolf. To be wounded like that, so badly, at such early age – and survive . . . Unheard of.'

'We believe,' said the Duchess, 'that John was infected with the wolf's *kernhgehist* when we came through.'

'The *what*?'

'In this world you'd call it – what's the word . . . ?

Essence? No. DNA? Yes, DNA. And if it was going to be activated, it would be at his Coming of Age – on his thirteenth birthday.'

'W-wolf DNA?' John was incredulous. 'You m-mean, I could be a w-werewolf?'

'No, no, no . . .' Mordecai laughed a little too loudly. 'You and wolf exchanged flesh. He infect you. But, worse, *you* infect *him*. Is only way they could have forced rift open again.'

As his anger grew, John thought back to the incident with Baz, and how little he had cared. Was he really that heartless? Was there a battle going on inside him? And was the wolf *winning*?

'You r-r-really b-believe they've opened this r-rift?'

'Oh yes,' said the Duchess. 'The snow – the blizzard – the whole country asleep – the ravens . . . It all points to one thing. They're here. And they're coming for you, John.'

'Why?' asked Fyre.

'If they *did* manage to open the rift, it wouldn't stay open for long. Which means they are trapped here – and they need John to reopen it.'

'So let him! Let him do it and they can go back!' Fyre was almost in tears.

'But they won't want to open it just for a short time,

Fyre,' the Duchess said calmly. 'They will want to open it *permanently*. And if they do, millions upon millions of wolves will pour through; eternal winter will descend; the good and the decent will fall prey to the sleep, while the others – those more in touch with their, shall we say, *unconventional* side – will join the wolves. Like your Mr Christmas.'

'And then?'

'Apocalypse,' said the Duchess simply.

'So what do we do?'

The Duchess and Mordecai looked at each other. It was a look that showed part resignation, part determination and part fear.

'We fight, if we have to, but if we can, we run. Again,' said Mordecai. 'Open rift if we can – if *you* can – and disappear.'

John and Fyre could tell from the tone of his voice that this wasn't their preferred option.

'A few more years would be good, no? You would be older, stronger.'

'Great!' John snapped. He didn't like how everything seemed to be landing on *his* shoulders. It wasn't fair. 'And what about Fyre? We've got to get her home – back to her family, her mum.'

'Oh no you don't,' she said defiantly. 'Fyre stays right where she is.'

'Why, Fyre?' The Duchess suddenly looked grim-faced.

'*Why?*' said Fyre in a *what-a-stupid-question* tone.

'Yes. This is a Kindred thing, and you – well, you just don't *belong*, do you?'

John frowned. Where was the Duchess going with this? Fyre looked like a deer caught in headlights. Why was the old lady attacking her like this?

'John's my friend. I want to help him if I can.'

'But why? This – all this – is madness, no?'

'Yes, yes, it is, but—' Fyre began to redden.

'And your mother? Rose, that's her name, right? Is she like *this*? Like *you*? Snow white from head to toe?'

'Yes, she was – I mean, *is*. But I don't see . . . Hang on, how did you know her name?'

'Duchess,' said John, 'what are you d-doing? Take no n-n-notice of her, Fyre, she's gone a bit m-mad. They all have.'

'John, John, John . . .' The Duchess put down her mug, took their hands in hers and looked from one to the other. 'Don't you see? No, of course not, and neither does Fyre. Though she's beginning to suspect. After all, she's still awake, isn't she.'

'See what?' they said in unison.

'Your mother, Fyre – I *know* her; or rather, I *knew*

her. We all did. In our world, though, we knew her as the Ice Queen. And she was Kindred.'

'*WHAT?*' exploded John. He wrenched his hand away. 'What are you talking about?'

'Fyre?' prompted the Duchess.

Fyre frowned. Her mind raced. She felt trapped and liberated all at once.

'Your mother told you to make friends with him, didn't she?'

'Not in so many words, but . . . well, yes; yes, she did.'

John looked at her like she was an alien. 'You've been *s-s-spying* on me?'

'No, no, I haven't. Well, I didn't realize I was. My mother encouraged me to take an interest in you; she said you seemed . . . lonely, that you needed friends. I thought she was just being nice, but then . . .'

'Then?'

'Well, I *liked* trying to make friends with you, even though you didn't make it easy. And she was so tired and frail, and . . . I just didn't have the heart to . . . And I believed her because . . . because . . . Eventually I – you know, John . . .' She shrugged impotently and fell quiet.

John stared at her. He recalled her uncanny ability to find her way in the blizzard. How she didn't seem to feel the cold.

Mordecai finally broke the silence.

'Your mother wasn't welcome among Kindred after wolves turned on her, but when she came to us she had beautiful, bright white baby girl with her, so . . .' He shrugged, as if to say *What could we do?* 'Then, just after she arrived, John's father opened rift and we came through – Ice Queen too. When it closed, she disappeared into snow in Scotland. We never saw her again.'

'And yet it seems the guilt weighed heavily on her – more than we ever imagined,' mused the Duchess. 'She obviously kept an eye on John from afar. She must have suspected this day would come.'

'Fyre . . . is one of y-you?' John whispered.

'One of *us*, John. Think of her name too. *Fyre King? Ice Queen?* Guilt-ridden she might have been, but she's still arrogant enough not to let her title disappear for ever.'

'*Was*,' whispered Fyre, her eyes welling up. 'She was arrogant. She's dead.'

'Dead? When?'

'Five, six months ago? I didn't know what to do!' Fyre broke down and sobbed, and her next words were almost unintelligible. 'I couldn't tell anyone; they would have taken me away, put me into care.'

'What did she die of?' asked Mordecai. John just sat there listening, feeling the anger build up inside.

'She sort of just . . . faded away.'

'Hmmm. Always wondered how long Ice Queen would last in such a warming world. What did you do with body?'

'I . . . I put her in the freezer,' said Fyre before covering her face with her hands.

John got up and walked as far away from the others as the room would allow.

'So there's a b-bunch of w-wolves coming to get me?' he asked after a while. 'And I'm supposed to d-do what? Open a new rift or t-two? I can't d-decline the verb "to be" in Latin, let alone use a l-long d-dead gobbledygook magic b-bloody spell language to open up an effing doorway in space and t-time.'

'We fight, John,' said his grandfather, standing up and puffing out his chest. And as his chest expanded, so did his voice, becoming a defiant growl. 'We *stand* and we *fight* while you try to open rift. You, my boy, are *second* line of defence. Eventually snow, magic, everything else will stop. They cannot keep this up for ever. Magic will fade and wolves will be trapped. After that, imagine how long wolves will last in city? Either captured and caged or shot dead. Finish.'

'Right. So wh-wh-while I'm trying to "open" a shaving mirror,' John shouted, pointing at Fyre, 'Snow White here is g-going to keep spying on me while the Duchess makes yet more t-tea and you . . . What *are* you going to d–do while all this is going on? Tell me some more lies? Throw your tablets at them?'

'John!'

'No, Grandpa, no. *How* are we g–going to f–fight them? *Who* do we f–fight? Do we know how m–many of them there are, at least?'

'Not yet,' admitted his grandfather, 'but soon. And in meantime is probably good idea to meet people who have sworn to protect you.'

'*What?*' Could this get any worse? 'Sworn to protect *me*? Who?'

'Well, you don't think the Hunters upstairs chose name by chance, do you?'

'*What?*'

'John,' said the Duchess reassuringly. 'This whole building is our castle. Every flat is *ours*. We bought them. Even the empty ones.' She let out a little snort of a laugh. 'It's why we never have any money. Everyone who lives *here* in our little enclave came from *there*.'

'Even Sarah?'

'*Especially* Sarah.'

John found himself staring at the Duchess with his mouth wide open. Was there anyone who wasn't in on this secret?

'She's been keeping an eye on you ever since you were old enough to toddle, John.'

'Well, she did a b-b-bang-up job of it t-today when we were f-fighting our way out of Christmas's attic. Where was she then?'

'We sent her out to find out more about the wolves that have been seen in the countryside.'

'You are k-k-kidding, right? And Mr G-Glass too? Tell me he's n-not one of us – a Kindred – too?'

'And Glass, yes,' confirmed Mordecai. 'He is great man, John. All came through rift at same time – thanks to your father and mother, who gave their lives to save us.'

'Even Mr G-Glass?'

'Even Mr Glass.'

Which, thought John, given that Mr Glass looked like a hobbit, wasn't much of a stretch.

The small figure crouching in the cemetery clearing was wearing a black woollen hat and a black cloak which spread out like a tent. Several hours of snow had settled on and around it, making it look like a gravestone. Only the very occasional puff of frozen breath revealed that it was alive. On at least four occasions since it had arrived, unseen, people had passed by close enough to reach out and touch. Some were dressed in flimsy night clothes, while others were in cold weather gear, but all had a glazed look in their eyes, as if they were sleepwalking.

But the figure wasn't interested in them; it was there to hunt and gather. Hunt down the quarry and gather information. The first objective had been achieved; the second was happening right there and then.

In the clearing the white wolf had obviously finished listening to one of the ravens, and got to her feet. She was enormous. The person walking into the clearing was a great bear of a man in a yellow ski suit, but even he looked up at her.

What followed was some sort of bizarre game of charades, in which the man pointed back the way he had come and, with fingers bent like claws, mimed a face with three scars. Then he motioned for a smaller figure to come forward. The message was confirmed with much the same motions.

Unknown to the watcher, Caspar Locke was shaking in his boots as he confronted the beast with the hypnotic golden eyes. He knew that his mouth was running away with him as he told her about John Creed and where he could be found, but he also knew that the words were superfluous. Something had already touched the edges of his mind, like some kind of mental tentacle. It was the wolf.

His thoughts, as usual, were racing – running up blind alleys and coming back again, turning over permutations, accepting some, discarding others. It was like being on a roller-coaster whose brakes had failed. For once, he wished he'd been taking his pills; at least they might have taken the edge off the sick feeling.

But then the tentacle had tried to probe further, and had encountered the whirring blades of his ADHD. Maybe this was why whatever was happening to his dad wasn't happening to him. The look on his father's face was ecstatic. *He* obviously welcomed the probing tentacle.

Tapper Locke even smiled when the wolf sat back on her haunches, lifted one giant paw and reached out to touch the side of his face in a gesture that was gentle . . . *loving*. And then the claws snapped out and tore three straight lines down the flesh of his cheek.

Caspar lunged forward as his father fell to ground with a cry of pain, blood spattering the snow beneath him.

'Dad?' he shouted. 'Dad!'

Locke shrugged Caspar off and, slowly, painfully, stood up. And Caspar saw that he was . . . *smiling*! Blood dribbled down his face, the cold slowing its progress, but he seemed unfazed by the pain. He had just been initiated into his very own wolf pack. He stared down at his son with a faraway look in his eyes.

Caspar thought he had never seen his father so *happy*.

Then, with eerie synchronicity, the six black wolves

that had been patrolling the periphery slunk into the clearing, circled the white wolf, tilted their heads back and began to howl at the night sky. Even to the un-initiated it was obvious what had happened: they knew they had found John Creed. And they had Caspar and his father to thank for it.

Oh no, thought Caspar deep in his subconscious, away from the tentacle, *what have we done?*

With infinite patience and glacial care, Sarah Hunter slipped away, not daring to move faster than a snail until she was beyond the gates. Then she ran like the hounds of hell were following her. She crunched through the deep snow for two blocks until she reached a spot between the tops of two cars where she had left her snowmobile. She got on, stabbed the GPS into life and hit the accelerator. She swerved out into where the main street used to be. If she didn't hit a submerged car or, given the depth of the snow, a post box, she'd be home in less than an hour. The streets, thank God, were empty. After what she'd just seen, she knew that any-body still awake was an acolyte of the wolves. Everyone else was either asleep, or dead.

John, Fyre, Mordecai and the Duchess were crowded into the doorway of flat 19. Mordecai knocked and the door opened almost immediately – just far enough for a face to look out.

'Yes? Can I help you? We've got all the encyclopaedias we need.'

'Kendall, stop messing about,' said the Duchess.

'But we're not buying today. And if you're selling Bibles—'

'Open the door,' bellowed Mordecai. 'Time for games is gone.'

'Spoilsports,' said Kendall as the door opened wide. 'Welcome to Casa Hunter.'

Kendall Hunter was a tall, muscular young man of twenty-five. He had a wide-eyed, open face with a permanent half-smile that, Fyre thought, would make him look smug if you didn't know that this was his normal expression. His hair was a startling thatch of straw, artfully mussed with gel, and he wore loose blue jeans and a black T-shirt. John had nodded 'hi' to him before, but that was about it.

'Hi, John,' he said now. 'Had the lowdown yet?'

John could only nod angrily. He was beyond speech. He found himself trying to distance himself physically from Fyre, unable to look at her but wanting to all the same.

'How freaky is that? Lot to get your head around, I know. Come in.'

They trooped along the hallway after Kendall. The layout was identical to the other flats, with an outside balcony that looked over the front gardens. This lounge, though, was being used as a munitions room. The walls were covered with swords, knives, bows and crossbows, every one of them fully assembled and hanging on hooks for easy access. On the floor were dozens of what looked like umbrella stands with arrows sticking out of them like the backs of giant porcupines.

'Welcome to the war room,' chuckled Kendall as an older, more grizzled version of him turned and nodded seriously, silently, at them. He was clad from head to toe in army camouflage gear, an incongruous blue baseball cap jammed over razor-cut white hair.

'John, you know my dad, Fletcher. Dad, this . . . er, very – er, pale, young lady with him is . . . ?'

'Fyre,' said the Duchess quietly, looking knowingly at Fletcher. 'Fyre King. And she's the Ice Queen's daughter.'

Kendall's head snapped round, and he stared at Fyre with undisguised interest. His father, on the other hand, absorbed the information quietly. The only evidence that this was a shock was a slight tic under one eye.

'*She* here too?'

'No, she's dead.'

'*Good*. And we need to keep an eye on *her*. If she's anything like her mother . . .'

There was an uncomfortable silence until Kendall took a particularly confusing-looking bow down from the wall. It was a dull grey-green colour, and he handled it with a familiarity that spoke of years of practice. 'Cool, isn't?' He grinned. 'It's a Hoyt Carbon Matrix Camo bow – the lightest high-end bow ever made, with a hollow carbon tube riser and only thirty-five inches axle to axle. I wanted laser sights too, but Dad reckons we won't need them when it comes to it.'

Fletcher smiled indulgently at his son. 'He gets carried away. Picked the first one up when he was four. As good as me, possibly.'

'*As good as?* Think again, old man.'

'I'll give you "old man",' grunted Fletcher as he gave his son an affectionate cuff around the head. 'Might be faster, but I'm more accurate.'

John realized he was watching them intensely, a small, lopsided smile on his face. He quickly rearranged his features into the hard, pissed-off grimace. He was, he realized, jealous of the bond between Kendall and his father – a bond he had never experienced. Grandpa Mordecai and Mr Patel – even Mr Christmas – were all very well, but they weren't the real thing. Were they?

'Are we ready?' interrupted Mordecai. He moved through the room with an energy John hadn't seen in him for a long time. He seemed to radiate strength and command. 'Are we ready?'

'Oh, Mordecai,' said the Duchess as she cleared a few stray arrows off a chair and eased herself down. 'Kendall and Fletcher have been ready for years.'

'Thank you, Duchess,' said Fletcher, 'but I understand Mordecai's worry. Never hurts to make the point again. We're about as ready as we'll ever be. Sarah's out scouting, so with any luck we'll find out what we're up against before nightfall.'

John turned to Fyre, who was standing quietly behind him. Under the savage punk haircut she looked confused and scared.

'Sarah is Mr Hunter's d-daughter; K-Kendall's s-sister,' he barked.

'I got that, yes. I'm not stupid.'

'No, you're a s-*spy*. And a g-g-good one. Had me f-f-f-fooled, that's for sure.'

'I was *not* spying on you! I was trying to make friends with you, you moron. God knows, you needed one, stutter boy.'

'Well, you can g-g-get f-f—'

'Now, now, children, let's not fight,' said Kendall in a schoolteacherly tone. He seemed to find them vastly entertaining. 'Let's get back to Sarah, shall we?'

John and Fyre fell silent, embarrassed by their childish spat.

'Good idea.' Fletcher gave an exasperated sigh. 'At the moment, Sarah is our best hope of finding out how much time we've got before . . .' He let the implication hang in the air – but it wasn't left there for long.

'Before,' continued Kendall with a grin, a widening of his eyes and a silly wave of his hands, 'you know . . . Armageddon.'

'Well, *you know*, n-no, I d-d-don't know,' snarled John. 'I have *no idea wh-whatsoever*. I've been k-k-kept in the dark, and all this has been d-d-dumped on me in the l-last half an hour.'

'Suit yourself,' said Kendall with an exaggerated pout.

'Must be confusing.' Fletcher seemed as unperturbed as his son was permanently amused. 'Thought it best. If nothing happened, then you would have just led a normal life.'

'N-normal l-l-life? Living off the g-g-grid? P-picking pockets for a l-living? How was *that* normal? And now I'm the b-b-bloody Special One who's g-going to w-w-wave my magic wand and get us out of here? Harry bloody Potter didn't have this s-sort of crap thrown at him. And he only had *one* pissy little s-scar!'

'Which brings us to Mr Glass,' said the Duchess, ignoring Kendall's snort of laughter.

'Wh-why?' John's top lip curled sarcastically. 'Don't t-tell me he's D–D–Dumbledore?'

'You'll see. Come and meet him.'

Highgate Cemetery was behind them. They were on their way back to the Folgate, and the future. The six wolves, following their white leader, had streaked ahead through the roar of the storm and the empty, eerie streets – a whole city had ground to a halt and was buried under an apocalyptic avalanche of snow and ice. The wolves had raced off like missiles with one thought in mind. And thanks to *him*, thought Tapper Locke, they were now *guided* missiles, with a target and a destination.

Locke, with Caspar in tow like some limpet fish attached to a shark, was leaning into the blizzard, face down to avoid the snow stinging the three fresh wounds on his face.

Behind him a raggedy troop of acolytes followed his footprints. Locke, as the one who had found Creed and brought that information to the wolves, was now the official leader of a small like-minded army; a human wolf pack who had chosen to embrace the dark side of their natures. Yes, the future was looking bright; there would soon be a new regime and he, DS Siimon Locke, would be its enforcer. And if any of the little kittens didn't like it . . . ?

Well, then, the kitten tapper would emerge once more.

Tap! Tap! TAP!

Behind Locke, using his huge bulk as a windbreak, Caspar was shaking. It was partly the bone-crushing, mind-numbing cold, but mostly it was fear. Somehow, somewhere, things had taken an unexpected turn. Giant wolves? Whispering one-eyed ravens? And, from what he had gleaned from his father, the end of civilization? He didn't like Creed, that was for certain, but something deep inside him was resisting. Did he *really* want to hand him over to a bunch of slavering wolves? He hated Creed because he was so bloody *nice* – and because of Fyre – but . . . *this*? This felt *wrong*, and way out of control.

And now here they were, trudging through the snow, yet again. Freezing almost to death, yet again. To his right he noticed a white-haired man dressed only in a pair of flannelette pyjamas and a brown dressing gown stumble over something hidden in the snow and fall to his hands and knees. He was mostly skin and bone and had a face so cadaverous that Caspar guessed he had made his way to the cemetery from his sick bed. Kneeling there he looked like an old, badly-made tent.

'Dad,' he shouted into the storm, tugging his father's sleeve to attract his attention. Locke stopped and looked down at him, though his gaze was a million miles away. Caspar pointed back to the old man, who was now shaking violently. He opened his mouth so wide that Caspar was afraid he was going to throw up his whole skeleton like some kind of human hairball. Instead, in a cough that turned into an explosion of snot and blood, he spewed out his false teeth. They landed a few feet away, grinning as if it was all a very funny joke. The man's pale, watery eyes crinkled in confusion.

'What?' Locke thrust his ear towards Caspar's mouth. 'What?'

'He won't make it back to the Folgate,' screamed Caspar.

'So?'

'Look at them; hardly any of them will. We need to get them out of the storm.'

'No, we keep going.'

'They'll die. Look at him.'

The old man was staring, puzzled, at his own false teeth; then he sighed sadly, the tears in his eyes frozen over, toppled sideways in the snow and lay still.

'I don't care. We have to keep going. The wolves will need us.'

'I know *that*,' said Caspar through gritted teeth, 'but there is another way.'

'What is it?'

Caspar pointed across the road to the faint red circle of an Underground sign: ARCHWAY. 'We take the train,' he said.

They had to dig through the snow that had drifted down the stairs and into the ticket hall, but then it was easy going. The fury of the blizzard above was now just a whistle, like a distant kettle boiling away. All around the ticket hall, people lay where they had fallen, some in awkward positions, some using their bags or coats as pillows.

Locke led the way down the unmoving escalators and onto the platform where a train, doors open, stood waiting for passengers who would never arrive.

He grinned at Caspar and ruffled his hair. 'Goodonya, son.' He grinned. 'This is genius – fair dinkum it is. We'll make good time now.'

They trooped onto the train and began making their way forward to the driver's compartment.

'Mind the gap!' joked Locke as they stepped over and around the dozens of people who had fallen asleep on the train, dropping bags and newspapers and books and iPads as they did so. Towards the front, though, they came across a woman who was sitting upright in her seat, head tilted back, mouth open, breathing heavily. In her lap she held a wicker basket; as they passed by, they heard a tiny noise – something between a squeak and a high-pitched sneeze. Locke stopped so suddenly that Caspar clattered into his back.

'What the—?'

'Shhhh. Listen.'

The noise came again, but this time it was more recognizable. It was the dreamy mew of a kitten.

Locke put a finger to his lips and turned back.

Oh no. Please don't make me watch this, thought Caspar. His father had told him plenty of tales of life in the Outback, but that one . . . that one he hadn't really believed.

'Dad? Please . . .'

It was no use; the Kitten Tapper was reaching for the pet basket with one hand and into his jacket pocket with the other.

Caspar turned away so he wouldn't hear the crunch.

At about the same time, back at the flats, the Duchess, Mordecai, Fyre and John were leaving the Hunters' apartment. John started to go down the stairs, but Mordecai held him back.

'Up, John. We go up.'

'But Mr G–Glass lives d–downstairs.'

'Mr Glass lives downstairs but he *works* upstairs.'

Puzzled, but now ready for almost anything, John followed him up to the flat nobody lived in.

'As the Duchess explained, we bought all flats,' his grandfather explained as they climbed the stairs.

'It's also,' said the Duchess as she wheezed to a stop at the top of the stairs and clung to the railings for support, 'where we keep some of our supplies.'

'*Supplies?*' said Fyre.

'*Some?*' said John.

Any explanation was halted by the appearance of Mr Glass, who popped out as if he had been expecting them. As usual, Glass was wearing what John thought of as old man's clothes – grey trousers, shoes that could do with a good polish, a brown V-neck sweater over an off-white shirt, and a tie with a knot so small and pulled so tight it looked like someone had tried to strangle him. Over all this was the same baggy-elbowed, shapeless black jacket. And each layer was covered in stains, both faint and new, that revealed either a lack of vanity, a fondness for runny eggs or an inability to find his own mouth. Or all of the above.

The only difference today was that the black jacket was missing, and John saw that the V-neck was sleeveless and that the white shirt was short-sleeved. And what this in turn revealed was that this Hobbit lookalike had skinny forearms that ended in hands so tiny they looked like a baby's.

'Mordecai,' he said.

'Mr Glass.'

'Come.'

'He doesn't say much, does he?' whispered Fyre in John's ear. She could sense his whole body vibrating with anger. What she couldn't feel was the inner turmoil, the fight between wanting to curl up into a ball and rip them all limb from limb for deceiving him.

'Just as w-well,' he said tonelessly, trying to keep his anger in check. 'Information overload.'

'John?' It was his grandfather.

'Wh-what's he got in there — a d-d-dragon?'

'Don't joke — it wouldn't surprise me,' said Fyre.

'John!'

'Coming!'

They passed a room stacked from floor to ceiling with perfectly aligned packets of food, toilet paper and other supplies. It was all so neat, so perfect, that Fyre hesitated a moment. Something about it wasn't quite right.

'Wow!' said John from up ahead. She trotted after him.

It wasn't a dragon.

It was something much weirder.

For where the Hunters had turned their home into an arsenal, Mr Glass had created infinity.

All four walls were covered with gigantic mirrors in

ornate wooden frames carved with letters from his grandfather's books – and also with fairy-tale characters such as Little Red Riding Hood, Cinderella, the Goose Girl, trolls, elves . . . wolves.

As they stepped in, so did a million billion trillion Fyres and Johns, reflection after reflection after reflection. It really did make you feel like you were staring into infinity – if only you could get your own fat head out of the way first.

And as if all this wasn't odd enough, in one corner of the room a ginger cat stood on its back legs, facing the mirror. But where its head and front paws should have been, there was nothing – as if they had disappeared through the mirror before getting stuck. Combined with its own reflection, it looked like a piece of bizarre modern sculpture: the Headless Siamese Cat of Norton Folgate.

'My God,' breathed Fyre.

'Yeah,' said John. 'Of course . . . glass. Mr Glass. He's c-called Mr G-Glass.'

'Here, my boy,' said Mordecai. He waved a hand around the room, and a multitude of Mordecais did the same. 'This where you will weave magic, open door to new worlds.'

'Hang on,' said John. 'You w-wouldn't l-l-l-let us have big mirrors in the flat but you had *these*?

You c–could get an army of elephants through this.'

'Notice the frames,' muttered Mr Glass enigmatically. He waited for a moment, seeing the look of bewilderment on John's face. 'The symbols and the carvings mean they can't be opened from the other side.'

'How d–do you know this? Or do you only think you know this? How d–d–do we know that a horde of w–w–wolves isn't going to come c–crashing through at any moment?'

'Your father . . .' The Duchess put a hand on John's shoulder and smiled sadly. 'Your father, John – it always comes back to him. He studied the old books, the ancient texts. He made many, many mirrors with Mr Glass; experimented . . . and failed every time until that very last day, when it mattered most.'

'My father?' John felt a sob welling up from deep inside. He took a deep breath, then decided to say nothing in case he lost control.

'Yes, my boy,' said Mordecai softly. '*He* saved us then, and *you* will save us now.'

'I c–c–c–can't. I've tried. Fyre and me – we t–tried it at s–school. It opens, but the p–pain's just too much. I don't know how to *keep* it open. How am I supposed to keep it open long enough f–for us to get through?'

'We don't know,' said the Duchess, turning to point at the cat. 'As you can see from poor old Mr Tiddles, we have no idea. Mr Glass opened it for less than a second and *that* happened. We were hoping *you* could tell *us*.'

The wolf pack flew through the streets, their paws barely touching the ground. The white wolf took the lead, loping along almost casually but making her black honour guard struggle to keep up, pink tongues lolling.

The white wolf was both excited and calm. If she had had any human characteristics, she might have likened it to settling down to sit an exam, certain that you knew all the answers. Ever since the boy had reached his Age, and she had sniffed him out of all the possible worlds that the rifts opened into, she had known that this moment would come. It was inevitable. As was the conclusion to their journey – as long as she could keep the boy alive in the carnage that was to come.

And once everyone and everything that the boy held dear had been destroyed, she would use him to open the doors permanently, bringing through both her army and eternal winter.

There was, for sure, no way back without the boy to reopen the doorway. The instant it had snapped shut, leaving one of her most trusted lieutenants half in this world and half in the other, she had known that.

Speed, then, was of the essence. The camouflaging storm which had swept out of the connection wouldn't

273

last for ever, and nor would the sleep it brought with it. And then how long would they last in this world of men and metal and machines?

Yes, they needed the boy, and they needed him soon.

She and her companions bunched their muscles and ran faster and faster.

The prey was almost in their grasp.

Rajesh Patel shifted in his sleep. One part of his brain knew that he was in his cosy little shop with the heater burning brightly on the wall, and yet another part was telling him he was cold, cold, cold. He shook himself and succeeded only in fluffing up his feathers.

Feathers? *Feathers?*

Alarmed, he looked around. He seemed to be standing on an iron girder above a wet, black road. Around him, to his right and left and behind, were similar, familiar bodies, all shivering, all puffing up against the icy air. A host of tiny racing hearts.

He cried out, but the only thing that issued from his throat was a musical chirp.

It was, indeed, a very odd dream – more vivid than any he had had before. And in his dream he dreamed that he'd woken up. Which made things even more confusing. Perhaps the very act of pandiculation would bring him out of it. He tried it: the yawn seemed fine, but where his arms should have been stretching to the ceiling, he saw only two tiny brown wings.

He was a sparrow.

He was dreaming he was a sparrow.

Why not an eagle? A vulture? Some bright and colourful bird of paradise? *In* a colourful paradise?

No, not him; he had to dream he was a sparrow. A boring old sparrow. Sitting in the freezing cold. Under a railway bridge.

This, he dreamed, or dreamed he dreamed, had better get a whole lot better before the day was out.

A sparrow!

What in God's name could he do as a sparrow? he thought. And as if in answer, he squirted a tiny little white worm-like poo onto the girder. A sparrow! Even his poo was pathetic.

John and Fyre were back in the Duchess's flat talking to Kendall Hunter. After the Dobermans had been ushered out of the flat and into the hall, Kendall explained that he was a teenager when they had come through the rift.

'I remember a strange all-over tingling sensation, but that's about it really. Oh, and that it was a lot less cold here. *That* I do remember. It had been pretty much snow, cold, snow, cold, more snow and a little bit more cold. Like it is here now. And lots of running away from wolves. And screaming. There was a lot of that too.'

He was sitting on the coffee table where Mordecai Creed had been perched earlier, his hands cupped around a mug of hot tea. He smiled at the memory. His father stood nearby, on edge, alert. Kendall explained to them that Sarah had set off the previous day to see if Mordecai's suspicions about the wolves were correct. They hadn't heard from her since.

'Can't you phone her?' asked Fyre.

'With what? Didn't they tell you that these flats are a twenty-first-century black hole? A *twentieth*-century black hole, come to that. And even if we had them, they wouldn't work in this,' said Kendall. Only an economical nod of the head indicated that 'this' was the storm. 'We decided early on not to use this world's technology. The thing is, once you start using it, you come to rely on it – and then when it's taken away, you're left with nothing.'

'So how will you know she's OK?' asked Fyre.

'She'll either come back or . . . she won't,' said Fletcher emotionlessly, though the small pause spoke volumes about his true state of mind.

'So wh-wh-what happens now,' interrupted John. 'D-do we just s-sit and wait?'

'More or less.' Kendall obviously found the whole thing slightly absurd. 'Well, we do. You, on the other hand, need to find a way to open those ridiculous mirrors upstairs. Though I'm not looking forward to it if we end up freezing our butts off in yet another god-forsaken hellhole. Can I put in a request for somewhere warm? And clothing optional?'

'The rift is a last resort, we hope,' snapped his father. He was pulling the Duchess's net curtains to one side, peering out across the snowfield where the garden used to be. 'And we don't know that the doors just go from here to there and back again. The only person who might have known was John's fa— Anyway, they could go anywhere. There might be just our two worlds, or there might be three or a dozen or a hundred other worlds out there.'

'So if you – if John manages to open that mirror, you could end up back where you came from,' blurted Fyre.

'Well, yes, or we could go anywhere.' Fletcher turned his gaze away from the window and looked at the young girl coldly.

'*We?* You mean you.'

'If it gets to that point, Fyre, the wolves will quite literally be preparing to huff and puff and blow our house down. You stay, you die. You won't have any choice but to come with us.'

'Oh.' Fyre gulped as if something had gone down the wrong way. She hadn't thought that far ahead, but it was obvious, wasn't it? Goosebumps ran up her arms, and she shivered as a nervous prickle spread from the back of her neck up into her scalp. A new world? It was the scariest thing she had ever faced . . . and the most exciting.

'Knew your mother, you know,' said Fletcher.

'What? Oh, right. You did?'

'Fought against her in the Battle of Carrion Copse, just before the wolves turned against her and she came over to our side.'

'Wow. What was she like?'

'Cold.'

'She could be, yeah, but most of the time she was' – Fyre swallowed down a sob – 'nice, you know? Just . . . *nice*. Sometimes I'd catch her with this faraway look in her eye, staring into space, like she was looking through this world and into another. She always laughed it off. Seems she *was* seeing another world, sort of.'

She looked at John, felt her bottom lip start to tremble, and looked away. He was still angry with her.

'So if the rift is the l-last resort, what's the f-first?' asked John.

'Nothing.' Kendall laughed again. The bravado was now laced with defeat and fear. 'That's the beauty of it. We sit here and do nothing while you tinker around

278

upstairs with your' – he waggled his hands at John like a poor conjuror – 'magic fingers.'

'Kendall!'

'Sorry, Dad.'

'What he's trying to say,' said Fletcher with a harsh look at his son, 'is that we can't rely on you opening a rift; we have to try to hole up here until the wolves run out of puff, as it were.'

'Run out of p-puff?'

'Yes . . . This won't go on for ever – probably only days; hours if we're lucky. There's no way the wolves could have kept the doorway open. Which means that it's closed; what's happening here – this bit of our old world, the magic – will blow itself out sooner or later. When that happens, the storms will stop, the spell will be broken and the country will wake up. Imagine how long a pack of wolves will last then, no matter how many or how big. At least, that's our best guess.'

'We're s-s-sitting in a Norton F-Folgate council flat,' shouted John, whose unease had grown since Kendall's semi-defeated laugh. 'How l-long do you expect us to l-last?'

'Ah, now, I thought you might get around to that,' murmured Fletcher. He crossed to the far side of the window and pressed something on the wall. With a click, a panel at the top of the window dropped down to reveal a metal handle. He pulled it and, with a screeching metallic rattle, a set of steel shutters slid down to cover the whole window.

'We've not been sitting on our hands for twelve years, John,' he said with a grim smile. 'You'll find that Mr Glass's place is the same. Ours too. Yours is about the only place we didn't re-model. And we've added a few other little improvements here and there. Where you're sitting, for instance.'

John and Fyre looked around, seeing nothing but the sofa on which they sat.

'Ejector seats,' said Kendall.

'What?' Fyre started to get up.

'Just kidding!'

'Move the mat,' said Fletcher with an exasperated roll of his eyes, 'and the coffee table, and there's a trap door leading to a cellar packed with food.'

At that point the Duchess shuffled into the room. She was holding a tray piled high with sandwiches. Kendall jumped to his feet to take it from her, leaving John and Fyre staring at the floor in wide-eyed, open-mouthed astonishment.

'Any more tea, dears?' asked the Duchess. 'I've got about ten thousand tea bags under your feet, so don't be shy.'

2
SIEGE

The huge mirror shivered, as if someone on the other side was pushing on it, making it bend to breaking point, only to stop so that it twanged back into place with a dangerous wobble. John ignored it and kept his hand flat on the surface. He closed his eyes, picturing the words and phrases that his grandfather had been teaching him since he was old enough to walk – words that had been passed down from his father.

The mirror was now a huge upright lake; molten metal like the mercury in a thermometer – a silver colour pitted with what looked like crushed diamonds.

'Hruuuuuuarrrgh!'

The pain started as a faint tingling in his fingertips, but then fanned out past his knuckles, past his wrist and up into his forearm, growing in intensity as it went. When it felt like his arm was about to split in two, he pulled away with a jolt. There was a faint *phuuut* and the mirror was just a mirror again.

'Dammit!'

He shook his arm and rubbed his cramping fingers. It felt like the electric shock he'd got when he used a knife to winkle a piece of bread out of the toaster; his hand, wrist and lower arm had ached for hours afterwards. Only now he was being asked to put the knife in the toaster again and again and again.

He looked around at his reflections; at the little red stain that indicated where Mr Tiddles had come to rest after his first attempt to open the rift. He'd managed to replicate what Mr Glass had done – to open the door a sliver – and then it had slammed shut again. He had achieved two things: to make him realize just how far away he was from saving everyone, and to release Mr Tiddles from his predicament. Well, the bits that hadn't fallen through to the other side, at least. As the mirror had changed for that infinitesimal moment, the cat's body had flopped to the floor with a furry thump. He'd learned one other important fact: if a door closes on you when you're halfway across, it slices through your body like a knife through butter. The poor cat's front legs ended in sheared-off stumps of bone, meat and muscle. He avoided looking at the neck completely.

'What the—?'

John whirled round, convinced he had seen something out of the corner of his eye. Nothing. He was alone. The others had left him alone to, as Kendall put it, 'work his magic'. Even Fyre. *Especially* Fyre. He had been horrible to her, he knew. And he also knew she hadn't been spying on him, not really. And yet a small part of him wanted to make her suffer a little longer.

There it was again! Something moving just out of sight. He walked over to one of the mirrors and sat down with his back to it, perfectly still, only his eyes moving, left and then right. What *was* it?

Opposite him, himself, reflected in the other massive mirror. To the sides . . . himself again. Except that when he turned back again, something seemed to change. Was he imagining it, or did the boy sitting there in army surplus fatigues and black boots have a huge wolf's head?

He tried looking round quickly, hoping to catch himself by surprise.

'You idiot,' he whispered when it didn't work.

He got to his feet again, shook the pins and needles out of his hands and placed them back on the mirror's surface. Maybe two hands were better than one? He began repeating the guttural phrases his grandfather had taught him, but there was just more pain – this time a cramp that turned his hand into a claw and forced him to give up.

★ ★ ★

Downstairs, Fyre was getting a crash course in how to shoot a crossbow from Kendall when John walked into the room.

'Fyre? I n–need your help,' he said, then turned and headed off again. Fyre excused herself and went after him. As she entered the mirror room, John was mumbling something to himself, his right hand extended towards the mirror's surface. A million Johns looked up as a million Fyres walked over to him.

'It's useless,' he said, shaking his hand as if trying to loosen it up. His shoulders slumped. 'I can't do it.'

Fyre touched his arm gently. He pulled away, but it was a half-hearted rejection.

'Perhaps you're trying too hard. Where's your grandfather?'

'Next door, b–b–building a machine-gun out of wood and s–sticky tape.'

'What?'

'Kidding! I just don't get it. You're g–g–going to wage a war one day, or withstand a siege, and you arm your-self with b–bows and arrows and a cellar full of t–tea bags? It's s–stupid.'

'I imagine getting hold of guns and stuff might not be such a good idea for people with no ID, no history and no birth certificates.'

'They m–managed to get these flats!'

'Flats you can probably buy with a few forged documents. They're a bit different to guns, John. You know that. They were just being careful.'

'And that's the other thing. Wh–wh–why me? I didn't ask for all this.'

'And I didn't ask for *this*,' said Fyre, pointing at her complexion.

'I know, b–but . . .'

'But there are no "buts", John. You are who you are. People look at me all the time. Never a day goes by when someone doesn't comment. They think they're being clever, or discreet, but I know; I hear them. What am I supposed to do? Complain that I didn't ask for it?'

'I know, I know. You're r–r–right. I'm s–sorry. I'm sorry. It's just f–frustrating, you know? I'm supposed to save everyone – to s–s–save the world from a bloody wolf apocalypse and, well . . . I d–don't think I can.'

'Yes, you can. I believe in you. Your grandfather does. The Duchess is so convinced, she's downstairs making tea as if nothing's happening.'

John laughed at that. He glanced sideways at her. 'Thanks. And, Fyre, I'm s–sorry. About earlier. I was just angry at . . .'

'Everyone?'

'Yes. I'm s–sorry. I shouldn't have said what I s–said. I

d–don't know what I was thinking. I'm so confused. It's like . . . You know, I think that the w–w–wolf *did* poison me. I think Grandpa and the Duchess are right. I think it infected me with s–something without a conscience. I can feel it inside me; it's like a place wh–where nothing matters but *m-m-me*. And it's getting s–stronger all the t–time. But you . . . well, you're the antidote.'

'Thanks,' said Fyre softly. She took John's hand and squeezed it.

He smiled sadly and then a thought occurred to him. 'Oscar,' he said.

'Oh, crap.' Fyre looked disappointed in herself. 'I forgot all about him. Do you think he's alright? I can't believe I forgot about him. The poor thing. I put plenty of food down when I went to school on . . . when was it? Seems like 100 years ago now.'

'Well, he's safer *there* than he'd ever be *here*. And anyway, he's probably fast asleep like . . . like Mr Patel and the rest.'

'I hope so. Can you believe I forgot all about him?'

'Yeah, I can. After all this?' He waved a hand around airily to take in the flats, the mirrors, the wolves . . . the *world* . . . and then pulled it back in to his chest as a spasm of pain shot through it. 'C–come on. I need a b–break; my hand's killing me and I'm g–g–getting nowhere fast.'

Downstairs in the Hunters' flat they found the Duchess making the rounds with a tray laden with mugs of strong tea.

'Tea, dears?'

'No thanks, Duchess,' said John. 'Where's Grandpa?'

'Upstairs in your flat, conspiring with Mr Glass. No luck?'

'No.' John flexed his hand and winced at the residual pain. 'Just taking a break.'

Fletcher and Kendall were on the balcony, peering into the blizzard as if trying to find patterns in the snowflakes. Fletcher nodded at John, took a sip of his tea and turned back to the whiteout.

'S-Sarah?' asked John.

'No sign. Not yet. She'll be fine, though. She's like a ghost, that one. She'll be all right.'

John thought he sounded a little *too* sure of Sarah's safety, but didn't say anything. Fyre just stared out at the snow.

'After all,' continued Kendall, 'she's been keeping an eye on you for years and you never even noticed her, did you?'

'No, never.'

'There you go. She'll be fine. She'll be—'

'Sssh.' It was Fyre: she had thrown back the hood of her anorak and was leaning over the balcony and peering hard into the whiteness. With her savage new haircut, John thought, she looked like some kind of ice warrior princess. 'Can you see that?'

Fletcher, Kendall and John crowded around her.

'What?'

'Over there, right at the end of the street. There's something there. Something big.'

'I can't see a thing,' growled Fletcher. 'Are you sure?'

'I can't s-see anything either,' said John, 'but I c-can hear s-something. An engine? A c-car maybe?'

'Sarah!' Kendall turned to his father. 'Sarah's on a snowmobile; it's got to be her!'

'It hasn't *got* to be anyone,' said Fletcher coolly. 'We wait. Prepare for the worst. Hope for the best.'

'But if it *is* her . . .'

'. . . she'll be here soon. And if it isn't her—'

'It's her! Fyre, can you see anything else?'

'No. Whoever – whatever – it is is just sitting there.'

'I'm going out to get her,' said Kendall abruptly. He turned away, grabbed his crossbow and ran out of the room.

'Kendall! Kendall! Get back here! *Now!*' shouted his father.

There was no reply – just the echo of Kendall's footsteps on the stairs. Fletcher cocked his own weapon and made a decision. 'You two go after him; I'll keep watch from here. Stop the bloody fool going out. If it *is* Sarah, then she's waiting there for a reason. And it won't be good.'

When they got downstairs, they were too late: Kendall was gone.

'What do we do?' asked Fyre.

'We g-g-go after him,' said John, grim-faced. 'Well, I do. You s-stay here.'

'But . . .'

'But n-nothing. I'm going to have to c-close the door behind me, but I n-need you in here, ready, when we get back. OK? Fyre? OK?'

'OK,' she snapped – though as he pulled the door open, he knew she was far from OK.

Beyond the area they kept clear, a towering compacted-ice cliff face had built up. The gardens on either side of the passage were full to the brim with snow that had long ago spilled over the fences. It was both dark and, thanks to the steadily falling snow, light out. The blizzard was like a bunch of white feathers stuck to a jet black canvas.

John's heart was racing as he took a short run-up, and in one smooth, agile bound leaped into the air and landed in a crouch on top of the cliff. He felt giddy and sick at the same time – giddy with adrenalin and sick to his stomach at the thought that perhaps the wolf inside him was winning. Even as he moved off into the blizzard, following Kendall's footprints, he wondered how far it would go. Was he a werewolf? Would he succumb? It felt good, after all – maybe *too* good.

He turned round to check the balcony where Fletcher would be standing guard, but he couldn't see a thing, and trudged on until something large and black appeared ahead. It was indistinct at first, just a small disturbance in the mad snowy swirl.

'Kendall?' yelled John.

Whatever it was sped across his path, then executed a sharp turn and began to head straight for him. Without thinking, his heart almost bursting out of his chest, John dropped into a low crouch. *What are you doing?* he thought. It was as if he – the *real* him, the stuttering, tongue-tied him – had been shoved aside by another John Creed. And that John Creed was powerful, strong . . . *dangerous*. He felt like howling at the moon. The dark shape slowly became more distinct until, just a couple of metres from him, it slewed to a halt. He leaped aside and saw that it was Sarah Hunter on her snowmobile. Sitting behind her, one arm round her waist, the other holding a crossbow, was Kendall.

'Quick! They're right behind me!' she cried.

At that moment, even above the roar of the wind, they heard the high-pitched howl of a wolf.

Owooooooooooooooooooo!

Sarah revved the snowmobile and began to move off towards the flats – then realized that John hadn't moved. She looked back to see him fall to his knees. 'John? John!'

John clutched his head with both hands, grimacing. For a moment he thought he'd been shot in the temple. He shook his head to clear it, but it was too late: he was back in his dream and the white wolf was a lot closer. He could only watch as she bunched up in readiness to spring. The smile was gone, replaced by a triumphant snarl. In that moment he *knew* she was somewhere nearby. He would have waited for her had Kendall and Sarah not leaped off the snowmobile and pulled him to his feet. Together they bundled him onto the back.

'Go go go!' shouted Kendall when he had squeezed on behind John.

Sarah hit the accelerator and they lurched off with a roar that mixed with the wolf howls around them. As they gathered speed, Kendall realized that Sarah wouldn't know about the snow that had built up outside the front door. He tried to shout a warning, but it was too late – the machine plunged over the edge with a plaintive roar.

Kendall threw himself sideways, taking Sarah and John with him, as the vehicle flew into the air, engine whirring uselessly. They landed in a jumble as the snow-mobile crashed into the front door in a screech of glass and metal.

John was the first to come to his senses, despite – or perhaps because of – the pain in his head. He was lying on Sarah and under Kendall, but neither of them were moving. If the wolves didn't know where we were before, he thought, they would now. They might just as well have sent up smoke signals.

He scrambled to his feet, pulling Kendall up, but Sarah lay on her back, dazed.

'We have to get inside,' he shouted in Kendall's ear. 'They're close.'

However, this was easier said than done. The snow-mobile was now a large pile of scrap metal wedged behind the door. Petrol leaked out of the wreckage. The air filled with fumes and, once again, the howl of a wolf.

'Help me!' shouted John, and began tugging at the twisted metal. Kendall squeezed round him and tried to edge it away, while from the inside Fyre was trying to push the door open. Suddenly there was a shout from above.

'Wolf! Wolf!'

Kendall pulled a large machete from his belt and

chopped at the snowmobile until Fyre could poke her head through the gap.

'Kendall!' she hissed. 'Stop, stop! The sparks! There's petrol everywhere!'

He ignored her. John could see his point – get blown sky-high or be eaten by a wolf? It wasn't much of a choice. He slapped Kendall on the back and gave a thumbs up before going across to Sarah, who was starting to stir.

After what seemed like a lifetime, Kendall and Fyre finally forced the door open enough to allow them through one at a time. Kendall went first and reached back to take the half-conscious Sarah from John.

Before John could get through and close the door, a vast black claw snaked in and snared his hood. He fell backwards and felt himself being dragged outside again. This was it, he thought; it was all over before it had begun.

In that instant Fyre stepped forward and grabbed the huge paw that held him. She had no idea what she was going to do; only that she *had* to save John. She sank her fingers into the matted black fur. *I hate you!* she thought. *Hate! Hate! Hate!* To her amazement, the limb turned white as it froze down to the very bone. There was an animal yelp, the razor-sharp claws let go of John's hood, and the paw withdrew. Fyre helped John back inside and pulled the door closed with a thud; the magnetic locks clicked into place.

Their feeling of relief was interrupted by the clatter of boots on the stairs as the others rushed to their aid.

'Well,' said Kendall, pushing his hood back and smiling. 'That went well.'

'What happened?' asked John. 'I thought I was a g-goner, and then it just l-l-let me go.'

'Just be thankful it did. Don't look a gift pig in the mouth – isn't that what you people say?'

'It's a gift horse . . .' John helped Sarah to her feet before turning to Kendall. 'Oh, right, yes, very f-f-funny.'

'It's a natural talent, you know—' Kendall was interrupted by his father's voice bellowing down the stairwell.

'*Kendall! Get. Up. Here.*'

'Sarah?'

'Yeah?' She was still a little dazed and wobbly, but she grinned at her older brother with affection. 'What?'

'Daddy's angry with me. I might need some moral support. Or a gun.'

'Fool,' she said and, with a business-like nod to the others, followed him up the stairs.

John turned to Fyre. 'Are you OK? You saved my life there.'

'I'm fine. I'm . . . fine,' she said. But she wasn't; when John turned to follow the others, she stared at her hand. It looked normal, but she was scared witless. What the hell had just happened?

They had to endure the anger of the Duchess, Mordecai, Fletcher – and Mr Glass, who didn't say much but glared a lot. They were gathered in the Hunters' apartment.

'What were you thinking . . . ?'

'You could have ruined . . .'

'Complete madness . . .'

'What if . . . ?'

While the adults raged, Fyre realized that Sarah was staring at her. She smiled. 'Fyre,' she said, introducing herself.

'Uh-huh, I know,' said the girl.

'Of course. You've been keeping an eye on John.'

'Yeah. Sort of. Interesting hairdo, by the way. Goes well with the, er, well . . .'

'Albino thing?'

'Sorry. Sorry. That was rude of me. Sorry.'

''S OK. I'm used to it. Mostly. You'll get used to it.'

'Oh, but I think you're beautiful,' Sarah insisted. 'I wish I had hair like that.'

At the word 'beautiful', John's ears pricked up. He

looked surreptitiously over at the two girls. Sarah, he realized, was right. Fyre *was* beautiful. Had he never noticed before? He looked back at Fletcher, who was still raging at his decision to go after Kendall. He hoped nobody would notice that he was blushing from head to toe.

'Me?' Fyre was confused.

'Of course you are. Stunning. I can see what John sees in you. I'm surprised to find you here, though.'

'Well, things have changed since you left. Would you believe I'm the Ice Queen's daughter?'

'Huh?'

'And as for you, Sarah Hunter . . .' growled Fletcher with a dark glance in her direction.

'Here we go . . .' Sarah whispered to Fyre. 'Yes, Dad?'

'Come here and give your father a hug,' he said, throwing his arms open wide and cracking an un-characteristic smile. 'We've been worried sick about you. You too, Kendall, you idiot.'

'I g-gotta go,' said John quietly to Fyre. He pointed upwards. 'The m-mirrors need . . . you know.'

'Sure. I'll come with you.'

Sarah caught up with them outside the flat.

'JC?'

'Yeah?'

'Thanks. You saved my life out there.'

'I'll see you upstairs,' said Fyre, and left them alone.

John still found it hard to look Sarah in the eye.

'I suppose you know it all by now,' she said.

'Yeah.'

'I'm sorry.'

'About wh–wh–what?'

'Not telling you. I wanted to, but the others – well, they wanted you to have as normal a life as possible. Funny, eh?'

'It's OK. I understand.'

'I'd be pretty angry myself.'

'Oh, I'm s–s–still angry. B–b–but wh–what would be the point?'

A shrug.

'Are they really here then? It's n–not all in my head?'

'The wolves? Yes, they're here all right. I've seen them. I would have been back earlier, but the snow's changed the landscape completely and my GPS died. They caught up with me at the end of the street. I was wondering whether it would be better to keep going, draw them off maybe, when Kendall appeared out of nowhere.'

'L–lucky for us he did.'

'And for me too. We're going to get through this, JC. You know that, right? One way or another.'

'Yeah, s–sure we are,' said John with all the confidence he could muster. It wasn't much.

'Trust me,' said Sarah, and leaned in to kiss him on the cheek. 'She's gorgeous, by the way.'

'The wolf?'

'No, you dick – Fyre. And she thinks the world of you.'

'She does?'

'Oh dear.' Sarah sighed, shook her head despondently and turned away. '*Men*,' she said, just loud enough for him to hear.

Over the next few hours the flats became a hive of activity. Shutters were drawn down and secured, the carpet in the Duchess's flat was pulled aside to gain access to the cellar, and Fyre and John – when he was taking a break from the mirrors – discovered that Mr Glass's flat was a giant workshop: every room was full of tools and workbenches, welding equipment, lathes and lethal-looking vices. Unfinished or broken frames lay everywhere, and in one corner stood a large generator that throbbed quietly.

John was fascinated. All these years with Mr Glass appearing as just a little round head and a pair of large spectacles through a crack in the door – and now this. The floors were covered in a spongy linoleum, which in turn was covered in wood shavings, small shards of glass, bent nails, blobs of solder and sawdust. On the walls were esoteric diagrams and building plans, most of which might just as well have been Egyptian hieroglyphs or Chinese pictograms.

On one wall hung hooks bearing various tools, in ascending size, small to large. There was a line of spanners, a set of saws, a collection of hammers and, oddly, in a column from top to bottom, again in order of size, five chainsaws. Beyond this were laminating machines, photographs and printers – a forger's paradise.

'What's he b-been building in here?' John wondered as they wandered through the rooms.

'A bomb?' joked Fyre as she studied one blueprint that looked like a nuclear device.

'Don't l-laugh – nothing would surprise me now,' he said quietly. He sounded, thought Fyre, overwhelmed.

She took his hand. 'You were pretty brave out there, you know.'

'You too. And I was b-b-bricking it.'

'We all were.'

'I'm still n-not sure I can do this, Fyre.' With the shutters closed, the storm outside was no more than background noise, and yet still his whisper was almost inaudible. 'What if I can't?'

'Then we're in for a fight and a half, aren't we?'

He shrugged, glad that they were friends again but not sure how to articulate his happiness. Happiness seemed . . . *inappropriate*, somehow.

'I'll go and see if Kendall and Fletcher need any help,' said Fyre, who realized he needed to be alone for a while. And so did she; because he wasn't the only one who didn't know what was happening. The others hadn't seen what had happened to the wolf's paw. But she'd frozen the animal right down to the bone. Any longer and she was sure the leg – arm – whatever you called it, would have snapped off in her hands.

She stopped halfway up the stairs and looked at her hand.

'What the hell have you done to me, Mother?'

Fyre stood on the balcony with the three Hunters, squinting through the snowflakes in an attempt to spot the enemy. The four of them watched silently. Occasionally Kendall or Fletcher would lift his bow and aim into the whiteness, but whatever was out there was keeping its distance. Every few minutes a lonely howl would pierce the noise of the storm. Each one chilled them to the bone.

Below them the metal shutters had been pulled down and the broken window in the front door boarded up. The wreckage of the snowmobile was already partially hidden by snow, like some large dead predator being covered in ash from an exploding volcano, though there was still a faint whiff of petrol.

'I didn't think it was real until now. Not really,' said Fyre, almost to herself.

'Which is why you let John do something as stupid as going out to rescue Sarah,' muttered Fletcher.

'Yeah – sorry about that.'

If Fletcher noticed the sarcasm, he didn't let on. 'Not your fault. Or even John's. But Kendall should have known better.'

'I think he knows that now,' said Fyre, glancing sideways at Kendall, who was miming hanging himself and pulling a face.

'Is he making silly faces behind my back?'

'No.' Fyre tried not to smile but failed.

'Kendall?'

'Sir?'

'Watch the street, please. Snow's so high they might use it to leap up here.'

'They could do that?' Suddenly Fyre didn't feel quite so safe.

'The white one, perhaps.' From behind her in the lounge Mordecai's voice was a deep growl. He was checking a particularly complicated-looking crossbow. 'The rest not so much. Not yet anyway. Keeps snowing like this . . . who knows?'

'You've seen it?' She went back inside and sat down opposite him.

'Her. Yes. Once. Long time ago. Was enough. Is big, like small elephant. Only with claws.'

He pulled back on the crossbow and something locked into place with a click. Satisfied, he put it to one side and picked up another.

'Eyes were worst thing.'

'Eyes?'

'Like honey. Liquid gold. Look right into you. *Through* you.' Mordecai talked as if she had violated him somehow. He looked up from his task and realized that he had alarmed Fyre. He held up a big gnarled hand and slowly made it into a fist.

'But we *will* defeat them. We *will* crush them. One way or another. You have my word, and Mordecai Creed, First Counselman of the Kindred, always keeps his word.'

The rest of the night passed quietly. After shoring up their defences, Fyre and John made their way to the camp beds that had been made up in the Hunters' flat – neither of them wanted to sleep too far from the others – and collapsed into a deep, exhausted sleep.

They awoke seconds later – or so it seemed, though

the light streaming through the curtains told another story – to the sound of running and shouting. John fell out of bed with a thump, and Fyre sat up, bleary-eyed but instantly alert. They pulled on their boots and ran to see what the fuss was about. John snatched up a machete on the way – just in case. He and Fyre were suddenly bright-eyed and bushy-tailed, ready for battle; ready for anything.

Well, almost anything.

They found the Hunters gathered on the balcony with the Duchess and Mordecai. John twisted round to look upwards. Mr Glass was above them, on the top-floor balcony, quietly watching the scene below. He nodded once to John and thrust his chin out towards the scene below.

And what a scene.

'God,' said Fyre.

'God has nothing to do with this,' muttered the Duchess, putting a comforting arm around her shoulders.

The storm had abated during the night; in the pink dawn light the snowflakes fell like thick fluffy feathers. Above, the cloud was still unbroken, but for the first time in weeks it seemed lighter, whiter, as if someone far away had turned on a light.

Below them, spread out along the snowbound street,

were six large black wolves, slinking this way and that, their pink tongues lolling and their breath steaming. They were longer in the body than Fyre had been expecting, like heavily muscled ferrets, and one of them was limping – the perpetrator, and victim, of last night's attack? And bizarre though it was to see them there, Fyre found herself smiling as they curled around the tops of lampposts that stuck incongruously out of the snow. It was as if they'd gone through the wardrobe, only to find the Narnian lamppost almost completely covered. Dig down, she thought, and you'd find the frozen corpse of Mr Tumnus. It was an oddly comfort-ing thought, she realized – all that snow and ice, no doubt courtesy of her mother. Did that explain what she'd done to the wolf's arm?

The wolves, though, weren't the half of it. There were a couple of dozen men, women and children – some in cold-weather gear – just gazing up at the balcony, watching in silence.

'Oh my God,' whispered John, pointing. 'It's Caspar. And there's Cem! And Aziz!'

Fyre looked down. 'And that policeman. Caspar's dad.'

But the surprise they felt at seeing Siimon and Caspar Locke below them was nothing compared to their shock when the white wolf loped into view. She climbed easily up over the ice shelf below, curled like white smoke around Siimon Locke and looked up at the balcony with deep golden eyes.

Whatever their imaginations had conjured up, this was worse. The wolf was gigantic, beautiful, evil; a pure white monster like nothing the world – this world – had ever seen. She smiled – or seemed to – her lips pulled back to reveal pink gums and a row of savage white teeth.

'Gosh,' said Fyre.

Beside her, John was rigid. 'She says she's g-going to huff and p-puff and b-blow our house down. I can hear her in my head. She's *talking* to me. Like in the dream.'

'Like hell she is,' growled Fletcher as he nocked an arrow, pulled back the string and let fly. The white wolf moved with the sort of swift grace that John had shown in avoiding Caspar's iron bar. The black wolves simply retreated, while Caspar, his father and the rest of the crowd remained where they were, oblivious to the danger.

'I'm g-g-going to give the m-m-mirrors another try,' said John.

Fyre watched him go and turned her attention again to the strange immobile figures outside. 'What's wrong with them?' she asked nobody in particular.

'They're the ones who gave themselves over to the wolf,' said Kendall as he picked out an arrow. 'Something in their natures, something inside them, makes them easier to control.'

'Gone over to the Dark Side, eh?'

'What?'

'The Dark Side – you know, Luke Skywalk— Oh, never mind.' What did these people do with their lives that they'd never heard of *Star Wars*? How *far* off the grid do they live? She leaned over the balcony, feeling safer now that the wolves had retreated a little. The white wolf had also wandered off, skipping left or right occasionally to avoid an arrow, and was now sitting in the distance, a great alabaster sphinx. Only those golden orbs seemed to move, flicking here and there as if contemplating her next move.

Below, Caspar and his father were like two statues, one small, one large.

'Caspar?' she muttered under her breath.

At the mention of his name, the boy looked up; his stare was full of such fear and regret that she felt something inside her do a backflip.

He was scared to death.

Next to him, that policeman was grinning like a madman, but Caspar . . . Caspar looked like a boy who had looked into a crystal ball and seen his own death.

DS Siimon Locke had never felt so liberated. His fingers

fiddled absentmindedly with an 'amulet' that hung around his neck on a piece of rough twine. He caressed it, feeling the slight raised nodule where the twine had entered the kitten's decapitated head, and the little misshapen skull, flattened on one side where he had 'tapped' it, and then continued on to where the twine exited the other ear. It was, he thought, a bonzer necklace. And didn't they just love it when you stroked their ears? Hee-hee!

But what was that? Inside his head . . . was that a flash? A sudden image? An image that wasn't his? But who? Ah, yes, yes – he wasn't the only one; there were others – above, below, beside him – and as his tentacles reached out to them, all those other minds bobbed about, touching, exchanging ideas, stories, events, likes, dislikes – dislikes mostly . . . He felt them all bristle with excitement as his images reached them: newborn kittens mewling, the descent of the hammer, the little eggshell skulls all crushed and bloody . . .

Tapper surveyed his new family, his army, his *pack* . . . Christmas had come early: the Colonel was on the parade ground, in a jungle, twin soldiers, a severed head?

No, what's this? Skeletons?

. . . screams in a railway tunnel, a boy's arm bending the wrong way . . .

. . . rock-hard snowballs . . .

. . . the swing of the hammer, a body behind a wall . . .

. . . delicious . . .

And all around, in the sea in which he floated, in the primeval mental soup that seemed to connect them all, there she was. She who whispered of the wonderful things to come, of the Empire of the Wolf and their places in it. *His* place in it.

Locke stood outside the door which kept him from the prize – the scarred boy – and thought so hard that it hurt; it felt as if his brain were floating free and bumping against the inside of his skull.

Think, think, think . . .

He grinned. It hurt the wounds on his face, but he couldn't stop grinning; he didn't know why.

Think.

There's something here we can use.

Ah – there it was: right at the very back of his mind. And then it was nothing but pain, pain, pain, as claws as sharp as scalpels dug away the detritus, dug down into his memories like a dog digging for a bone. God, the pain! It was luscious. It was perfect. It was the mental equivalent of being flayed alive, bits of memory and thoughts sliding down the walls of his mind.

And then she found it. There, sticking out of his self

– whatever it was that made him *him* – the top edge of a box of buried treasure. She dug some more, gripping the edge of it with her teeth.

There! Take it! Take it! I give it to you, whatever it is. Take it.

She pulled and pulled and pulled.

What was it? He watched from afar as she braced herself against his very soul and pulled. Anyone watching closely would have seen a thin line of dark blood drip from Locke's nose and disappear into his moustache. When it dried later it would look like rust.

He finally recognized it: he knew that shape. Knew what she was after.

It was a gun.

He also knew that below that one, if she dug deeper, there were a lot more.

And he knew where to find them.

Tapper Locke turned and began walking away from the flats. As he did so, all the other sleepwalkers followed him, like a flock of birds. Caspar too, and Cem and Aziz.

Up on the balcony, Kendall and Fletcher watched and wondered where they were going.

Locke knew. They were going to the police station, where he would find, in a locked room in the basement, an arsenal of guns.

It wasn't going to be much of a siege.

It was going to be a bloodbath.

Caspar followed his father, but not with any enthusiasm. It wasn't a conscious decision. He could feel the feather-like touch of dozens of minds all working together, thinking together. He didn't like it, not one little bit. After all, his brain was a machine that only had a fast-forward gear, and being stuck with this lot – he knew he had to go along with whatever madness his father was planning or it was curtains for him – was like trudging through treacle. He was the Terminator, after all, and he didn't like anyone messing about with his circuits.

Geography.

What? Where had that come from?

Grimsby is a gap town.

Mr Christmas?

He glanced up to find the enormous proboscis of his Geography teacher wobbling along beside him. The man was dressed in white army survival gear. It could have been anyone but for that nose, especially now that it was the colour of an overripe tomato. God, his nostrils were plugged with what looked like snot ice-cubes.

Like his father, Caspar saw images from all those minds clustered together – but where his father imagined an ocean Caspar saw only a goldfish bowl. His father was swimming in the midst of this ocean of thoughts, but, thanks to his ADHD, Caspar was able to just paddle on the foreshore. For how long, though? After all, it did have its attractions: he felt wanted, embraced, safe in its womblike embrace. And there were all these other minds bumping up against his – all those sleepwalkers, connected, sharing snippets of their deepest thoughts and desires.

Skeletal brothers . . .

Severed heads . . .

Broken arms . . .

The swing of the hammer . . .

The gentle splinter of the kitten's— *Hang on . . .*

That face! That was no kitten!

From the outside he looked like any of the other sleepwalkers – slightly dull-eyed, sly and nasty all at the same time – but inside, Caspar gasped in shock. He rewound the image time and time again: his father raising his faithful kitten tapper, the swish of his arm falling . . . and the look of surprise on his mother's upturned, bloodied face.

His mother hadn't left him!

His father had killed her.

Suddenly the ocean of minds wasn't as benign as it seemed. Suddenly there was a shark in it. Caspar pulled away with a mental shudder and looked around. It was the first time in a while that he had seen clearly, without the wolf's mind dragging him down. His mother was dead, killed in a violent argument with his father. 'Tapped' like some kind of animal. He felt sick.

And then he *was* sick. A mouthful of something acidic and lumpy burst up from his stomach and into his mouth. *Don't spit*, he told himself. *Puke and they'll know. Swallow it. Swallow it now.*

Ahead of him, his father faltered for a moment, looked round, smiled at his son. 'You OK?'

Caspar swallowed, the bile sliding back down his throat, and nodded. He wiped his eyes with the back of his gloves, blinking the tears away.

I will kill you, he thought.

'Yeah, yeah,' he said.

He had to get away.

But even if he did, where would he go?

Rajesh Patel was happy. Happi*e*r. He knew he was dreaming – and dreaming about being a bird wasn't all bad. The weather had cleared up a little, and he and a few of the other sparrows had taken the opportunity to stretch their wings.

He swooped down past the snowdrift that had buried his shop, the cold air thrumming with life. He was asleep down there, in that shop; he knew that. At least, as long as the electricity lasted and the fire kept going. He laughed, and it came out as a trill of musical notes, a full-throated chirrup of joy. Yes, being a bird wasn't so bad.

He landed on the roof parapet. It was lined with a thick layer of snow, like some enormous cream slice. He chirruped again. What would a psychiatrist make of this? he wondered. Standing on the roof of your own shop, over your own sleeping body, quite happy to be a sparrow?

Hang on, what was this . . . ? He hopped daintily along the wall. Below, in the street, a couple of dozen people plodded jerkily along the main road. Who were they? He didn't recognize any of them. No, perhaps the big one in the front – didn't he come into the shop for something? Cigarettes? Newspapers?

And then he saw the wolves, loping along beside them, like ranchers herding cattle – except for the big white one, which had stopped in the street and was looking around, ears twitching, listening.

Patel flinched as a shard of pain pierced his head. It was as if someone had driven a pin into his right eye and was moving it around. He shook his head, ruffled his feathers. It was no good, something was probing his mind, forcing its way in; something bad, something

313

full of evil thoughts, something that was trying to find a foothold.

As he struggled with the 'intruder', a few more sparrows dropped softly out of the sky and huddled next to him. And with that simple act of solidarity he knew what he had to do: he dropped his defences, let the probing mind in. *There! There it is! Open for you! See everything, know everything: see how I failed Ranjeev; see how I will not fail John Creed; see how there is nothing here for you to grab onto, not in this little sparrow brain.*

In the street below, the white wolf snorted, shook her head as if to dislodge some minor irritant and moved on, an almost invisible presence against the snow.

Patel launched himself joyously into the air, pumping his wings as hard as he could, and all around him hundreds and thousands of others did the same.

He finally knew; understood what they had to do. They – he – had to save John Creed.

But how?

3
ATTACK

'Good, good, very good,' roared Mordecai with a huge smile, arms outstretched like a conquering hero. He threw one of those arms around John and hugged him. 'Well done, my boy!'

On the floor in front of them, propped up against a stack of pillows, a small mirror shone silver around the edges, and an incongruous golden glow issued from its centre. John shrugged limply and pointed at the mirror, which he had fetched from their bathroom. To think that only a couple of days before he was using it to check himself for acne.

'It's not m-much help, though, is it? I mean, it's f-f-fantastic if you're ten centimetres tall, but . . . r-really?'

Fyre and Sarah, who had rushed upstairs at the news that John had opened a rift, bent down to peer into it.

Even Mr Glass had come to see. He stood just inside the doorway and smiled, the thick lenses of his glasses shining.

Visible through the frame, looking like a 3D photograph, was a long, curving beach over which a coconut tree bent like a crooked finger. They could hear the faint susurration of waves against sand and a balmy breeze wafted through, bringing with it the faint aroma of tropical flowers and ripe fruit.

'Wow!' said Sarah. 'That's brilliant, JC. This is *huge*. A beach. And it looks deserted. I could get used to *that* quite easily. Does it open to the same place every time?'

'Dunno,' said John listlessly. 'I'm too s-s-scared to close it in case I can't open it up again. I said the r-right words, and then something inside me – inside m-my head . . . sort of, well, f-f-*flexed*. Like a muscle. Hurt like hell. My hand's s-still throbbing.'

'You know that storeroom under the Duchess's flat?' asked Fyre, settling on her haunches and looking mischievously at Sarah.

'Yeah.'

'Did you remember to stock sunscreen?'

'What?'

'Tropical paradise?' Fyre grinned. 'Have you seen my skin?'

John stared at them, dumbfounded.

The Duchess laughed; she was sitting in the corner of the room on a straight-backed chair, nibbling at a tuna sandwich. 'It's good news, John. Allow yourself that. There's still a way to go, but at least now we know that there are other worlds and we don't *have* to go straight back to where we came from. Which is good, because I am far too old to be doing with all this snow and ice.'

John knew she was just trying to make him feel better. It wasn't working.

'Now you bring big guns,' Mordecai whispered. John knew his grandfather was trying to be patient, but there was an urgent note in his voice.

'What happens if you put a finger through it?' asked Sarah.

'I d-don't know; I haven't tried,' admitted John. 'You s-saw what happened to the c-cat.'

'Well, if you don't try . . .' said Sarah, and began to inch her hand through the opening. The room fell deadly silent as her fingers and then her whole hand disappeared through to another world.

'It's really warm,' she exclaimed. 'Here, Fyre, you have a go.'

'Fyre, I don't think—' said John, agitated.

And with that, as Sarah's hand reappeared, the mirror closed up with a noise like the pop of a half-deflated balloon.

'Sorry . . .' said John. 'I think that was me. Lost c-concentration.'

'Try the big one now, JC,' begged Sarah. 'We could go right away.' She put her arm round Fyre. 'All of us.'

John looked at them all in turn: Mordecai, Sarah, Fyre, the Duchess, Mr Glass. The room was silent again, and pregnant with possibility. He shrugged: he'd try his best, but he didn't hold out much hope. He approached the larger mirror, closed his eyes and concentrated. He placed his hands a hair's breadth away from the surface and whispered the words he didn't understand. There was the same flex in his head, the same feeling of tension . . . Yes . . . He opened his eyes. This time?

The mirror became a shimmering lake for a second . . . No, he was losing it . . . Sharp pains stabbed his hands and began to crawl up his arms. It was like a million scalpels carving into his flesh at once. The glass snapped back to reality with a *whoosh*, leaving John standing there, his outstretched hands like claws. He looked at himself in the mirror. He looked like a right tool.

'I can't do it. It sort of gets p-part of the way, b-but . . . it *hurts*. My hands are k-killing me. Look – I can't even open them p-properly. I'm j-just n-not strong enough to f-force it open and k-k-keep it there.'

Mordecai placed his hands on his grandson's shoulders. He looked at him with an easy smile. 'It will come. Don't worry. It will come, my boy. You are Creed, shaman of the Kindred. You will succeed.'

'Don't w-worry? There's a g-g-giant w-wolf outside who wants to kill you and make me its rift-opening slave. How c-can I not w-worry?'

'Perhaps that's the problem,' suggested the Duchess.

'Perhaps,' agreed John with a sinking feeling, 'but if that's the case, then we'll never get out of here.'

Mordecai smiled, and was about to reply when Kendall came skidding into the room.

'John! Duchess! Mr Creed! You'd better come and see this!'

They followed him out, rushing down the stairs to the first floor; they could hear loud bangs outside.

'What's happening?' asked Mordecai as he puffed along behind them.

'It's the wolves,' said Kendall, his eyes big with fear. 'They've got guns!'

They found Fletcher Hunter crouching low on the balcony, forced down below the parapet: the figures below were shooting at anything that moved.

Kendall joined his father, crossbow at the ready. John dropped to his haunches and began to edge out until a sharp rebuke from his grandfather stopped him.

'John, get back! We can't afford to lose you.'

'*I'll* look,' said Fyre, changing places with him. She stood rather than crouched, and poked her head round the doorjamb. What she saw shocked her to the core. The sleepwalkers were now armed with a variety of guns.

'They're not very good shots,' shouted Fletcher above the noise of gunfire, 'but what they're missing in quality they make up for in quantity.'

'John,' said Fyre, 'Caspar's dad is back. He's got a shotgun and he's laughing like a mad person. I can't see Caspar, though.'

John slid up behind Fyre and took a peek. 'Blimey,' he muttered.

For Locke was now a mad parody of himself. His bushy hair and beard were a wild mass of matted tendrils. Frostbite had turned one of his ears into something that resembled a long-dead mollusc, and his nose didn't look much better. It looked like a mushy potato way past its sell-by date.

'Look at his face,' whispered Fyre. Three jagged, bloody scars ran down one cheek. He jerked and giggled and talked to himself as he staggered up and down his line of 'soldiers'. He looked, she thought, like a puppet operated by someone in the throes of a fit.

Under cover of all this, the black wolves began

throwing themselves against the shutters on the ground floor with such muscular ferocity that they made the whole building shake. Somewhere downstairs the Dobermans were all barking and growling.

'You've g-got to start sh-shooting the sleepwalkers,' shouted John over the ruckus.

'Correct,' agreed Fletcher; he was covered in plaster from the walls that were being blasted above him. 'The shutters won't last long at this rate. They'll be inside before we know it if we don't.'

'John?' Fyre was aghast that he would even contemplate the murder of what she thought of as innocent civilians. 'You *can't*! They don't know what they're doing.'

'If we don't, we all dead meat,' said Kendall as he and his father took a quick peek over the wall and were met by a fusillade of bullets.

'But . . .'

Fyre's protest was drowned out by another shotgun blast, followed by an explosion of concrete and a piercing cry from Fletcher. He toppled backwards, clutching his face, blood on his fingers.

'Fletcher!' shouted John.

'Get him inside, get him inside!' With John and Kendall's help, Fyre pulled the injured man into the lounge and laid him on the sofa, where the Duchess tended his wound. Downstairs the great booming thuds continued as, one after another, the wolves threw themselves against the shutters.

'That's it,' said Kendall through gritted teeth as he stared at his father. He snatched up his bow and slotted an arrow into it. 'This is war, Fyre. People are going to get hurt, and it's not going to be us.'

With that he marched out onto the balcony in full view of everyone and took aim. Two or three bullets pocked the walls behind him but he didn't flinch.

John rushed to the balcony door. 'Kendall, what are you doing? Get down!'

In reply, Kendall just smiled his lazy smile and aimed squarely at the head of the shaggy, frostbitten beast that used to be DS Siimon Locke. He increased the tension in the bow, waiting just a fraction too long. Locke, even in his befuddled mental state, knew that the arrow was meant for him. He dropped his shotgun and dived off to his right, immediately rolling away in another direction.

Kendall, though, had other ideas. In one swift movement he stepped right up to the balcony edge, leaned over and released his arrow straight downwards.

The carbon-tipped missile caught the wolf in the nape of the neck and passed right through its flesh like a needle through jelly, severing the spinal cord. The huge black brute collapsed where it stood, blood streaming from the wound. A surprised whimper escaped from its mouth like an unexpected fart. Its eyes glazed over, blood soaked into the snow, and after one more gurgling, bubbling exhalation, it died.

There was a moment of stunned silence.

And then all hell broke loose again.

The white wolf leaped up and snarled in their direction.

John edged back to the balcony and poked his head round the door. He saw Tapper Locke retrieve his shotgun and was still watching – hang on, was that the *Colonel* out there? – when the other sleepwalkers all began firing at Kendall, who was standing admiring his handiwork.

Or at least, he *had been* admiring his handiwork. When the bullets started pinging around the balcony again, he was lying on the floor on top of John Creed.

'John,' he said with a laugh, 'we hardly know each other.'

'That was stupid,' said a voice from inside. They looked up to see Fletcher taking cover against the inside wall. His left eye was closed up, and a trickle of blood dripped down under the bandage on his forehead.

John and Kendall disentangled themselves from each other and crept back into the flat, keeping their heads down as the bullets tore into the wall above them.

Behind them, the wolves and sleepwalkers were moving away, out of reach of the Hunters' bows. Only the occasional bullet thwacked into the walls or broke a window.

'What are they doing now?' asked Fyre. She was sitting looking at John, Kendall and Fletcher as they sorted out bows and arrows. Sarah came to join her, sighing with exhaustion.

'They'll wait for darkness and start again. We've got floodlights, but a few well-aimed shots will put paid to them.'

'And then what?'

'We wait. The plan hasn't changed. We wait and we fight them off as best as we can. And we hope that either the storm lifts or John can open another rift. A *bigger* rift. What did you think of that beach, eh? I could do with some of that, I could. Nothing to do all day but sunbathe and fish.'

'I'm allergic to fish,' said Fyre.

'What? Really?'

'No. Just kidding.'

Kendall, Fletcher and John looked round when they burst out laughing.

'Don't ask,' said Kendall.

'I won't,' agreed John.

'Let's hope we're still laughing this time tomorrow,'

growled Fletcher through his mask of dirt and blood.

John and Fyre went back to their camp beds and tried to sleep. It was still early, but if Fletcher was right, it was going to be a long hard night. And surprisingly, they dropped off almost immediately, exhausted by a combination of fear, information overload, and an excess of adrenaline.

Upstairs, Mordecai Creed and Mr Glass sat on opposite sides of the kitchen table, drinking tea. Glass's mug was decorated with a dodo; Mordecai's boasted that the owner 'hearted' London. In the corner an ancient fridge hummed, stopping with a clatter when it reached its target temperature.

'*Estre penstra el khozu duk?*' asked Glass. He took a sip of hot tea and winced.

Mordecai smiled at him. 'So, we use the Old Language for the last time perhaps? *Dzha*, I think he can do it. Given time.'

'*Jzryuzu timsha?*' – How much time?

'*Chresta? Doyvu?*' – A year? Two?

'*Bashzhru aidritsu, dvroyu.*' – Not very helpful, comrade. Glass smiled.

'*Neh, neh. Jhodritszu neh.*' – No. No. It's not. I know it's not.

They sat in silence, two elderly men who had seen

too much, done too much, known too much. On the wall a plastic clock tick-tocked the future away. After a while Mordecai pushed himself slowly up from the table, his joints creaking in protest.

Glass watched him in amusement. 'When did we get so old, Mordecai?'

'Speak for yourself, old *schtvarich*. Wait here.'

He left the room and could be heard rummaging around somewhere in the depths of the flat. A drawer was opened and closed, and he reappeared clutching an old biscuit tin; the lid showed a soldier in a red tunic and a kilt, for ever frozen in mid-stride. Mordecai placed the tin on the table and sat down.

'Biscuits? How nice. Are we throwing them at the wolves or feeding them?' asked Glass.

'Aaah,' said Mordecai knowingly. He grabbed the tin and pulled off the lid with a clang. Inside, nestled on a bed of straw, were two oddly coloured bright green sausages. Glass whistled appreciatively as Mordecai picked one up and ran it under his nose, inhaling the fragrance.

'Mmmm,' he said. 'Help yourself.'

Glass picked up the other one and did the same.

'Malmar root cigars,' he muttered reverently.

'Exactly.' Mordecai beamed.

'*Zweitszu armishu.*' – Two of a kind. Glass smiled,

sensing Mordecai's thoughts.

'*Finashiza do shemsaul.*' – The last of their kind.

'*Comve doshu?*' – Like us?

The two men rolled the cigars backward and forward on the table with the flat of their hands. Mordecai then produced a cigar cutter and snipped the ends off before pulling a box of matches out of a pocket.

'*Ghanshu?*' – Ready? he asked his companion.

'*Ghanshu,*' echoed Glass, holding the cigar between his teeth. Mordecai did the same, struck a match and held out the flame. When Glass leaned forward and stuck the end of the cigar into the yellow flare, it glowed bright green. As he inhaled, little green sparkles danced around the glowing end.

He sat back in his chair, a beatific smile transforming his normally dour features, then tilted his head back and blew out a thick cloud of luminescent green smoke. Mordecai followed suit, and the two men grinned at each other as the cloud, still glowing faintly, billowed out across the ceiling.

'What in heaven's name are you two doing? I heard you talking in the Old Tongue.' The Duchess appeared so unexpectedly that both men jumped guiltily in their seats.

Mordecai turned a rheumy eye on her. 'You could kill us, creeping up like that,' he said. 'We're not as young as we used to be.'

'Rubbish, you're both as strong as oxes.' She sat down at the table. 'Or you were strong until you started smoking that rubbish.'

Glass settled back down and blew out a smoke ring. The room smelled like someone was burning down a sugar factory in a pine plantation next to a sewage works.

'That stuff stinks,' said the Duchess, waving a hand theatrically in front of her face. 'Are things that bad that you use the Old Tongue *and* get those disgusting things out?'

'Very possibly,' said Mordecai with a smile.

'It'll kill you; you know that, don't you. That stuff is lethal.'

'This, or a wolf . . . well . . .'

'Good point,' agreed the Duchess, holding out her hand. 'I *will* take a puff or two, if you don't mind.'

Mordecai handed over the offending object and grinned like a schoolboy as she stuck it in her mouth and sucked on it. She coughed, blew out yet more bright green smoke and smiled widely.

'So,' she said, 'when shall we three meet again?'

'In thunder, lightning, or in rain?' added Glass.

'Yadda yadda yadda,' said Mordecai.

'You are such a philistine.'

'OK, OK – when the hurly burly's done, when the battle's lost and won. OK now?'

'I take it the malmar root's because we think the battle's lost rather than won?'

'Unless you can think of something else,' murmured Glass.

'And John? Will he still turn, do you think?'

'I think not. But he struggles with it, Duchess. You know this. He struggles all the time.'

'Yes. When he thinks nobody is looking you can see him staring inwards. There is another battle going on there, Mordecai. To be lost or won.'

'He is a strong boy,' stated Glass with confidence. 'A good boy. It's a battle he will win.'

'I hope you're right, Mr Glass, I do so hope you are right.'

'I will keep eye on him,' said Mordecai, taking another huge toke on his cigar.

'So, Plan B?' asked the Duchess.

'Not yet,' growled Mordecai, peering through a miasma of green cigar smoke. 'But I think we are close. Comrade?'

'Agreed,' said Glass quietly.

'And what about the girl?' asked the Duchess. 'Do you trust her now? I do, but . . .' She left the rest of the thought unsaid.

'We have no choice,' muttered Glass around his cigar. 'And John . . . well, John needs her, I think.'

'And what is the alternative, Duchess, my love? Throw her to wolves?'

And then someone began pounding ferociously on the front door.

Fyre and John leaped out of their beds and rushed out to the balcony, where the Hunters were standing guard. The setting sun was a pink salmon sheen, hanging just above the sliver of city skyline they could see through the tower blocks around them. It sent long canyons of sickly light between the buildings, as if the city – such a brilliant white for so many days – had been accidentally washed with something red and it had all leached out.

'What's all the b-banging?' shouted John in a panic as they joined Kendall, Sarah and Fletcher on the balcony.

Fletcher looked puzzled; well, one eye looked puzzled; the other one was closed up, swollen like an overripe peach. 'Couple of kids,' he said. 'Below.'

They peered cautiously over the edge.

'It's Caspar!' gasped Fyre.

'And Davey Leonard!' shouted John. 'Davey!'

At the sound of their names, the two boys ceased their pounding and looked up. John frowned. Where had these two come from? Wasn't Caspar a sleepwalker?

Davey was still wearing his bright red bobble hat. He looked small and vulnerable out there, next to the wrecked snowmobile and the giant wolf that Kendall had killed.

'Fyre!' shouted Caspar.

'John!' shouted Davey.

'We've got more company,' said Kendall. He nodded towards the hooded figure in a grubby yellow snowsuit, which had appeared round the corner of the building, standing just out of range. In one hand it held a long rifle.

'It's Caspar's dad,' said John.

'We've got to let them in,' gasped Fyre.

'No.' Fletcher was unmoved. 'What if it's a trap? Davey's OK, but the other kid . . . ?'

'John? Let us in! John? Pleeease? They'll kill us! I'm sorry, OK? I'm sorry! Please let us in!'

John was shocked. It was Caspar Locke, *pleading* with him, begging to be let in. He looked down on his nemesis, the boy who had made his life a misery. Beside him, Davey Leonard banged and kicked the door.

'John? Mr Creed? Duchess? Open the door! I'm not joking! This is serious! They're gonna kill us when they find out we've gone.'

'We have to let them in,' said Fyre matter-of-factly. She turned to go downstairs, but Fletcher grabbed her roughly by the arm and pulled her back.

'No,' he hissed. 'It's a trap. I'm sure of it.'

'A couple of kids is a trap?'

'Yes.'

'But Davey's one of us,' John pointed out. 'He was g-g-good enough to p-pick pockets with me, but he's not good enough to s-save?'

'Is he? Is he still one of us? And the other one? Jasper?'

'Caspar.'

'Didn't I hear some stories about him and you?'

'Yes, b–but . . .'

'He's got a point, John,' said Kendall gently. For once, his face was serious.

'We've got more company,' said Fletcher, nodding down. The solitary figure had been joined by three other sleepwalkers. All were armed but all just stood there, motionless, watching, gazing at the building as if hypnotized. And wherever the sleepwalkers were, the wolves wouldn't be far behind.

'I'm going to t-t-talk to the Duchess,' said John.

'Do that. She *will* agree with me. Open that door and we all die. Mark my words,' Kendall insisted.

With the pathetic cries of Caspar and Davey ringing in their ears, Fyre and John dashed out to the stairs, where they found Mr Glass, the Duchess and Mordecai.

'Is s-something burning?' John sniffed the air, grimacing.

'Cigars,' said the Duchess.

'Cinnamon p-poo cigars?'

'What's happening?' asked Mordecai.

John told them about Caspar and Davey as they went down. On the ground floor, the dogs were barking at the shouts and pounding coming from outside the door.

'And this is the boy you told me about?' asked the Duchess against the noise.

'Yes.'

'He doesn't sound very nice.'

'He's *not*; I'd leave him out there if it was just him. But he's with D-Davey. Duchess, we c-can't just leave him out there.'

'Fletcher might be right,' said Mordecai firmly. 'He usually is.'

'He's *wrong*,' insisted Fyre. 'Can't you see how scared they are? Still, it's nice to see the windows are boarded up; at least we won't be able to *watch* them being torn apart.'

The Duchess ignored her and disappeared into her flat. She whistled once and the dogs followed her in. Mr Glass slipped away too. Neither, it was obvious, wanted to be involved in whatever happened next. Fyre, John and Mordecai looked at each other.

Then, from upstairs, came the cry they had been dreading:

'*WOLF!*'

Mayhem erupted as the dogs began barking again, the thumping on the door increased, and footsteps clumped down the stairs. Sarah Hunter appeared above them, leaning over the banisters.

'Are we going to open that door or what?'

'Grandpa?'

'Open it, if you must,' snapped Mordecai, clearly against his better judgement. 'But be quick.' He stepped back to let John and Fyre push the button that released the door's magnetic lock. The banging on the other side stopped.

On the balcony above, Fletcher Hunter cursed: a black wolf had appeared alongside the sleepwalkers and was now making its way slowly up the street. Fletcher was puzzled. What was it waiting for?

Downstairs, as the door cracked open and clanged back against the snowmobile, Davey Leonard shot through the narrow gap and collapsed inside. 'Fanks, John . . . Fanks, mate,'

Upstairs, Kendall was, like his father, watching the wolf when something down below caught his eye. A section of the snow in the next garden was moving . . .

John pulled Davey further into the hallway, where

Sarah Hunter reached out and took charge of him. Meanwhile Fyre felt through the gap for Caspar's hand.

Kendall squinted down and off to his right. What was happening down there? Why did the snow seem to be shifting? One of the boys had disappeared through the front door, but the other one seemed to be fighting something.

'I'm stuck!' shouted Caspar. He had grabbed Fyre's hand, but realized that his jacket was caught on the snowmobile. Fyre edged further out through the gap.

John looked up just as she disappeared. '*FYRE!*'

The door clicked shut behind her, but she knew John would open it again. The cold was biting; she realized that she wasn't wearing her boots, and her socks were soon soaked with a mixture of slush and evil-smelling petrol. Caspar was turning round and seemed to be trying to rip his own back off.

At that moment the wolf broke into a run . . .

And the snow that Kendall was looking at exploded upwards as Colonel Christmas, dressed in white camouflage gear, leaped up from where he had been hiding.

'There's someone down there!'

Fyre didn't so much hear as feel the fear and fright in the shout. She reached round behind Caspar, slapped his hands away and pulled. The sharp metal ripped through

335

the back of his Puffa jacket and they both slithered backwards just as John pushed the door open.

'The wolf!' yelled Fletcher Hunter. 'Concentrate on the wolf!'

With that, a dark volley of arrows began winging its way towards the wolf as it raced towards the front door.

Fyre came through safely, but Caspar was suddenly jerked backwards; he let go of Fyre, who fell forward onto her knees.

The wolf had got him! As he was dragged back through the gap, he looked up into the wobbly nose and grinning face of . . . Mr Christmas?

The arrows had managed to slow the wolf down. One had nicked its shoulder and it had veered aside, but it was now only moments away.

'Aim for its—' said Fletcher, but was cut off when the sleepwalkers began shooting again, forcing him to take cover. The wolf picked up speed.

The Colonel was dressed in white, as he had been in the photograph. It *had* been a trap!

'Hello, soldier,' he said to Caspar, who was half in and half out of the door. John and Fyre grabbed him – one leg each – but Mr Christmas had Caspar's chin in some kind of complicated headlock.

'Take your punishment like a man,' he shouted. '*Fee fi fo fum, I smell—*'

'Joringel?' said Fyre out loud, and then whispered to John, 'Have you got him?'

John nodded, grabbing Caspar's other leg and bracing himself against the wall while Fyre shuffled up to the boy's head, which was turning purple.

Upstairs the fusillade continued. The wolf had to be close, thought Kendall. He hoped John and Fyre had the door shut by now.

'Barbary?'

'No! Yes?' The Colonel suddenly looked uncertain, as if he'd woken up from a long dream and wasn't quite sure where or who he was. 'What am I . . . ?'

'Let him go . . .' Fyre gently took the man's forearm, trying to loosen his grip on Caspar's neck. Caspar was gasping now, his tongue protruding, his eyes bulging. Oddly, he was thinking that it was a rotten way to die – like a human Christmas cracker. Christmas cracker! Oh, how he wished he could find the breath to laugh . . .

'Barbary,' breathed Fyre again, her words almost solidifying in the ice-cold air. 'You're better than this. Don't let Joringel win. You were always the best of the two of you, right? Let the boy go.'

The wolf reached the ice-cold body of its companion, hesitated for a second . . . And in that moment the deadened look of the sleepwalkers vanished from the Colonel's eyes.

It was enough.

He let go of Caspar and stepped back, a look of disappointment on his face. He seemed upset with himself. Caspar immediately slammed into the floor, gasping for breath.

The wolf leaped down from the ice cliff with a blood-curdling snarl.

Just as the door slammed shut.

'Barbary!' shouted Fyre. The last thing she saw as the door closed was the teacher turning to face the wolf with a look of extreme peace on his face. She turned, leaped over Caspar, slipped past John, Sarah and Davey and raced upstairs to the Hunters' apartment.

'Don't look,' warned Fletcher, but she did anyway.

The wolf was poised above Barbary/Joringel Christmas, who was sprawled across the broken snowmobile. In the time it had taken her to get up the stairs, the wolf had obviously done its worst. There was a bloody mess in the middle of what used to be his chest, but Barbary/Joringel still seemed to be smiling. The wolf snarled, stretched out its neck and howled.

It was a howl of rage: Mr Christmas didn't have long to live.

'He's a goner,' said Kendall, who had crept up to Fyre's side.

The wolf raised its massive paw – just as the Colonel reached into his pocket and pulled out something small and silver. Even from where she was, Fyre could see the swastika symbol on the side. She looked down at her feet, soaked as they were with water and . . . petrol.

And then she remembered what Barbary/Joringel had said: *Very reliable. Always lights first time.*

'Get down!' she shouted just as Colonel Barbary Christmas flicked the top of his cigarette lighter and the front of the building exploded in a red-and-yellow fireball.

4
TEA AND TREACHERY

Caspar and Davey Leonard were sitting on the sofa. They looked scared, like two old men from a jungle pygmy tribe brought into the limelight of civilisation for the first time.

Mordecai told the story of the wolves, and why they were there, but neither of them seemed to take it in. They just sat there, holding their mugs of tea like shields. It was the only time, John had told Fyre when they popped outside during the telling of the story, that he had seen Caspar lost for words.

Fletcher had come down earlier and given the boys the once-over.

'Don't trust them,' he'd said, and gone back upstairs. Whether he meant *I don't trust them* or *You shouldn't trust them* was open to debate. But, as Mordecai pointed out, Fletcher didn't trust anyone.

The Hunters had stayed in their flat, watching the street for further attacks as the sun finally disappeared, and then turned on the halogen floodlights. Before she went up to join them, Sarah had whispered, 'Well done,' into Fyre's ear.

Thanks to the extra work Mr Glass had done on the front door over the years, it had survived the blast more or less intact – though the windows had to be boarded up again.

'Well, I didn't understand a word of that,' said Davey Leonard when Mordecai and the Duchess finished explaining the situation. Suddenly he was his old positive self again. 'Never mind, though, eh? All's well that ends good, right? Is there any more tea, Duchess?'

John found himself smiling at his friend's . . . what? Audacity? Stubbornness? Stupidity? He didn't care; they had saved little Davey from being torn apart. It had been the right thing to do. On this occasion, at least, his new instincts had come down on the right side.

Meanwhile Caspar sat there and eyed them. The colour gradually came back into his face so that he looked almost normal. He eventually drank the dregs of his tea and put the mug down on the table. 'Thanks,' he said. 'Fyre . . . *John* . . . you saved my life.'

'Did they do wrong?' asked Mordecai, who loomed over the boy like a cat over a mouse.

'Wrong?'

'You were out there with *them* earlier,' he went on accusingly. 'With the wolves and that policeman.'

'That *policeman*,' said Caspar coldly, a shadow passing over his face, 'is – *was* – my father. What else was I supposed to do?'

'And Sarah saw you with the w-wolves, in the cemetery. The rest of us w-w-wanted to leave you out there. Fyre d-d-didn't.'

'I don't blame you; I wouldn't have let me in either.' He smiled his usual charming smile, and aimed it directly at Fyre. 'Thanks, Fyre.'

'So how *did* you g-g-get away?' growled John, fighting the part of him that wanted to tear Caspar apart with his teeth and throw the bits out into the snow. Especially if he kept talking like that to Fyre. God, how that smile *irritated* him.

'I dunno really. I just followed my dad to begin with. He seemed to know what he was doing. But . . . but then we got to that cemetery place and something just seemed to come over me; to take over. You know? It got my dad too, in a *big* way. And while I tried to fight it, he *welcomed* it; invited it *in*. And then . . . then . . .'

'Spit it out,' demanded John. Fyre smacked him on the arm. There was something very wrong with Caspar, she thought. John couldn't see past his hatred, but something really bad had happened to him.

'Go on,' she said gently.

'Let's just say, that's not my dad any more.'

'Yes, we g-g-gathered that.'

Caspar ignored the jibe and kept going, avoiding John's eye and addressing Fyre.

'After that it was, like, I was always trying to outrun it in my head. Then, when they all started getting hold of guns and things, I slipped away. That's when I bumped into Davey. He said he was coming here so I tagged along.'

'These crisps are bare good, Duchess,' said Davey through a mouthful. 'Got any more? I'm starving.'

'Honestly, Davey . . .' The Duchess was grateful for some light relief. 'Look at you. I don't know where you put it.'

'Hollow boots?' he said, spraying the table with wet crumbs. 'Oops.'

John noticed Caspar's lip curl with disdain. He hadn't changed. He might seem grateful to them for saving his life, but John didn't buy it. He would keep a very sharp and wary eye on Caspar Locke.

'So what now?' asked Caspar of nobody in particular.

'Now we prepare for worst,' said Mordecai, moving

towards the door. 'And hope for best. John, you need to keep working on rift. Fyre, see what you can do to help upstairs with weapons. Davey . . . finish your tea, boy. I'm sure Duchess or Fletcher will find you something to do.'

'What about me?' asked Caspar.

'You,' snarled John, 'c-c-come with me. I w-want you where I can s-see you.' Again, he was torn: he wanted to trust Fyre's judgement, but he also imagined himself tearing Caspar's heart out and eating it.

Caspar got up. He wanted to swap insults with this newly-confident Creed but found that his heart wasn't in it.

Upstairs, outside the mirror room, he hesitated. 'What's in here, then?'

'It's the m-mirrors we were telling you about. Weren't you l-listening? Are you s-scared?' John stopped. Something was niggling at the base of his skull, like some little animal burrowing away.

'Scared? Me? Well, I'm not the one who wet his pants when we jumped him in that alleyway.'

'I did not . . .'

Then he remembered. In all the excitement John had forgotten about the reflections. Aziz, Cem, Baz – and Caspar as . . . Caspar as what? Think. Think. Of course, he'd never actually *seen* Caspar's reflection. And now here he was, unwilling to go into a room full of mirrors.

Well, now they would find out. And when Caspar's little wolf head was reflected back at them? Out into the night he would go, and good riddance.

'Inside. Now . . .' John made his voice as menacing as he could, and grabbed Caspar by the shoulder.

'Got a few super powers and now we're pushing people around?' Caspar pulled away with a confident shrug. 'Off the cloth.'

'Get inside.'

'I liked you when you were more of a wimp, you know that?'

It was the final straw. John kicked the door open and pushed Caspar inside. He fell to his hands and knees and skidded across the polished floor. He turned to look at John.

'Was that really necessary?' And then he noticed where he was. He stood up and spun around. 'Insane.'

As he did so, his reflections twirled and mimed 'insane' with him.

'Yeah,' agreed John. For there, in all their glory, were millions of Caspar Lockes with . . . Caspar Locke's face. No dog head, no wolf head. Just that irritatingly handsome face and smug grin.

'What?' said Caspar. 'Were you expecting someone else?'

★ ★ ★

'Here they come!' shouted Fletcher. He nocked an arrow, took aim and let fly. The missile was more or less invisible in the dying light, but its final destination wasn't: a well-padded man holding a handgun went flying backwards as if hit by a truck. He rolled over and lay still.

'The gloves are off then?' said Kendall, also taking aim.

'Sure are,' said his father. 'Either they die or we die. And then this world dies.'

'Fyre won't like it.'

'Fyre can f—'

'Fyre is here, thank you very much,' said Fyre. In her hands she held the crossbow that Kendall had been teaching her to use. 'And she knows when to admit she was wrong. OK?'

'Humph,' said Fletcher. 'There's something of your mother in you after all, eh?' He let fly another arrow. 'Get as many as you can in before they start shooting.'

They took a few more out, but soon enough the gunfire drove them under cover, allowing the wolves to renew their assault on the shuttered windows downstairs.

'Aim for the neck!' ordered Kendall.

But before they could take a shot, the shambling

creature that had been DS Siimon Locke appeared and, with unerring accuracy, began shooting out the floodlights that Mr Glass had fixed up. Soon the area was in darkness again.

'The lights!' shouted Fletcher.

For a moment nobody knew what he meant. They froze.

'Our lights!' he screamed.

And then it dawned on them: with the floodlights out, they were sitting ducks, silhouetted against the lights in the apartment. Fyre, who was nearest, ran inside and hit the light switch, plunging everything into darkness. It was too late: she heard Kendall shriek in agony.

She found Fletcher pressing a cushion against a wound in his son's shoulder. Kendall was dazed but alive.

'Upstairs,' ordered Fletcher. 'Tell Mordecai.'

She ran, not entirely sure what it was she was supposed to tell Mordecai. She found him and Caspar watching John strain to open the mirror. Caspar was open-mouthed in amazement at the transformation of the glass, but also puzzled.

'Why don't you—'

'Why d-d-don't you shut up,' snapped John; and then he noticed Fyre. 'Fyre? What's happened?'

'Kendall's been shot!' she gasped.

Mordecai stepped forward. 'Is he OK?'

'It's his shoulder — it's looking bad down there. They've shot out the lights and . . . What the—?'

A shudder ran through the building and was followed by a shriek of metal.

'The shutters! That's the shutters opening!'

'The Duchess is down there!'

'*Go!*' ordered Mordecai.

John, Fyre and Caspar rushed down the stairs. By the time they reached the first floor they had been joined by Fletcher, an injured Kendall, and Sarah, all armed with fearsome-looking machetes and knives. Sarah, grim-faced, passed Fyre her crossbow.

'That sounded liked the shutters opening,' she said.

'What did you do?' Kendall snarled to Caspar, who put up his hands in mock surrender.

'Me? Nothing. Ask *him*.'

'He was with m-me the whole time,' said John grudgingly, and dashed off down the stairs before anybody else had a chance to move. He rounded the final turn just in time to see Davey Leonard rush out of Mr Glass's flat.

'Davey?' said John, with a horrible sinking feeling in his stomach. In the boy's hands was a large wrench with blood on the end of it. 'What the *hell* are you d-doing?'

'They're gonna win, John! There's nuffin' you can do

to stop 'em,' he whined. 'They said if they let me go and I got in and opened the doors for 'em, they wouldn't do nuffin' to you nor the Duchess.'

'They lied!' shouted John. 'They *lie*! Can't you see that? Oh, Davey, what have you done? You've killed us!'

'No, no, it's not like that . . .' Davey stumbled closer, and John could see there were tears in his eyes. 'Have you seen her, John? She's . . . You can't win, you just can't win. I saved you, Johnny! I saved you!'

John stood there, speechless, as the enormity of his friend's betrayal dawned on him. This was impossible. He would have trusted Davey with his life.

'I'm sorry!' Davey shouted as Fyre, Caspar and the rest appeared. Their presence seemed to jolt him into action. He gave one final, anguished glance at John before dashing into the other flat and slamming the door, locking himself in with the dogs and the Duchess.

'I never liked him,' said Caspar.

'*You* brought him here!' Kendall turned on Caspar, who stood his ground.

'*He* brought *me* here,' barked Caspar. 'Think about it: *he* brought *me* in as a decoy. Bring big bad old Caspar in and you'll never suspect Mr Chirpy Chappy the Chip-Muncher. Right? They used us both!'

'We don't have time for this,' snapped Fyre. 'The

Duchess is alone in there. We have to get in before he opens those shutters too.'

'But if he *came* from over there—' said Caspar just as the door to Mr Glass's flat exploded off its hinges and crashed to the floor, to be replaced by the head and shoulders of a snarling black wolf.

Fyre froze, her mind a blank. She felt her insides turn to water. Sarah fumbled with the knife in her belt and dropped it.

Caspar ran off up the stairs.

John realized he was unarmed. *Idiot.*

Only Kendall had the presence of mind to react. He flipped his machete around, caught it by the blade and, ignoring the pain of his shoulder wound, launched it with all his strength. It caught the beast high up on the shoulder and stuck fast. With a roar, the wolf reached sideways with its massive jaws and tore it loose as if it were a splinter. Ignoring the spouting blood, it turned towards them.

John hadn't yet seen a wolf at close quarters; the sheer size of it was mesmerizing. The head was huge, the jaws looked like they belonged on a crocodile and the shoulders completely filled the doorway. Its breath was rank.

'John . . .' said Fyre. She sounded defeated.

And then a new noise was added to the already

overwhelming cacophony of bangs and shrieks and snarls and gunshots and barking dogs: it was the roar of machinery, like someone starting an outboard motor.

Seconds after *that*, it was joined by the screams of the wolf. Suddenly they were forgotten as the animal began thrashing around in the doorway, trying to turn round but trapped by its own bulk. Eventually, unable to get at whatever was attacking it from behind, it shot forward, the ferocious jaws frozen in a rictus of pain, eyeballs rolling back in their sockets. Fyre, Kendall, John and Sarah tumbled away from it while Caspar watched in silent amazement from the stairs.

'Gross,' he said as it became apparent that the wolf was missing a large part of its back legs. Mr Glass appeared in the doorway. He had a bloody lump on his head and a chainsaw in his hands.

'Help the Duchess!' he shouted before advancing on the writhing animal, whose snarls had turned to whines. 'Now!'

John took a few steps back and threw his shoulder against the Duchess's door; it collapsed, and he went sprawling full length in the hallway. He jumped up and dashed into the lounge. The Duchess was nowhere to be seen, but what confronted him was a living nightmare. Davey Leonard was already dead – a pathetic bundle of blood and rags in a corner of the room. The Duchess's four Dobermans, on the other hand, were alive and well, and hanging onto various bits of yet another wolf. Whatever Davey Leonard had done before he died, he'd been successful. They were *in*.

The dogs looked tiny beside the enormous wolf. One after the other, they were shrugged off and thrown to the floor, only to leap back into the fray, snarling, biting and snapping.

There was no way the Duchess had survived, John thought with a sinking heart.

Despite the onslaught, the wolf wasn't going down. It was covered in bites and scratches, but slowly, inexorably, it advanced towards the doorway. Suddenly it turned and caught one of the dogs as it jumped. The powerful jaws closed around the dog's skull, crushing it like a matchstick, and it fell to the floor like a black rag.

The other dogs hadn't fared much better. One lay on its side, breathing with difficulty, its ribcage flattened; another backed away growling, limping badly. The last one had vanished completely under the wolf's back legs, torn apart from head to tail.

John turned and fled. He reached the main hallway just as Mr Glass finished off the other wolf; the old man was covered in wolf blood and looking a little confused. Perhaps the crack on the head was worse than they had thought. Then John realized: he was wondering whether to help them or go back into his flat to fix the shutters before the other wolves got in – if they weren't in already.

'The shutters!' he yelled.

Mr Glass nodded. 'Tell Mordecai – *Plan B*,' he shouted before disappearing into the flat, chainsaw held high.

Inside, it was dark. The generator was still throbbing away in the corner, though. Which meant that someone had turned out the lights. Someone; not a wolf – that was certain. Mr Glass edged forward, the chainsaw held out in front of him. The shutters had been torn aside, the windows broken. This was not good; he wished he had another malmar root cigar. A noise! Behind him! It was the click of a handgun being cocked.

'Step away from the chainsaw, sir,' said Tapper Locke in his most polite policeman's voice.

In the hall, John turned back to the Duchess's flat to see the other wolf stagger into the hallway. The final Doberman collapsed on the floor and lay still. The wolf, though badly wounded, was still advancing.

John made a decision. 'Run!' he told Fyre, who was just behind him.

But she had other ideas. Annoyed at her earlier indecision, she stood her ground.

'Fyre, we've got to go! . . . Fyre!'

She shrugged John's hands off as he tried to pull her away, raised her crossbow, took aim, pulled the trigger and fired. The wolf, trapped in the narrow hallway and slowed by pain and blood loss, looked up in surprise as the bolt pierced its eye and exploded out through the back of its head. It dropped to the floor like a stone and exhaled one last rancid breath.

'OK,' said John. 'G-good. Yes. Well d-done. Nice shot. Can we g-go now?'

'But the Duchess . . .' Fyre said with a sob.

'Fyre − look at it in there. It's a b-battleground. There's no way she survived that. And the shutters are open. She's g-gone, Fyre. She's g-gone.'

As if to prove his point, the sound of shutters being ripped apart echoed through the flat.

They ran, and were met on the first floor by Fletcher, Kendall and Sarah, all armed to the teeth. Kendall was pale, blood seeping through his clothes.

'Keep going,' said Fletcher. 'We'll be right behind you.'

'I think Mr Glass and the Duchess are—'

'We mourn later,' said Fletcher. 'Go!'

Mordecai met them on the top floor. 'Glass?' he asked. 'The Duchess?'

'Dunno,' said John truthfully. 'But Mr Glass said something about Plan B?'

His grandfather hesitated – just a millisecond, but John knew that a whole history, a whole world, was contained in it; then he was all business again. 'Yes, yes. Come, come.'

He ushered them towards the mirror room, but then veered off into the storeroom that had puzzled Fyre earlier – all those supplies piled up so perfectly . . . But wasn't the storeroom a dead end?

'Where's Caspar?' asked John. He still didn't trust him. If he'd been wrong about Davey, how much more wrong might he be about Caspar? Was it a double bluff?

'In here,' said a voice from the mirror room.

'We don't have time for this,' snapped Mordecai. 'In here, in here. *Now.*'

Sarah turned to look down into the stairwell. She could see jet-black fur as wolves squeezed up the narrow stairs. Cries, shouts, the *pfffut* of arrows drifted up towards them. Fletcher and Kendall, she realized, had had no intention of coming after them. They were sacrificing themselves. She felt a sob well up in her chest.

No. Not now. She was her father's daughter, her brave brother's sister, and she had a job to do. *Take the sadness, take the emptiness, place it in a box, wrap it up, put it away on a shelf. Leave it there, open it later.*

She stayed at her post and waited as the sounds of

battle and the smell of bad wolf breath filled the air.

'We don't have much time,' she shouted, but Mordecai was rattling around in the storeroom, and Fyre, John and Caspar had disappeared into the mirror room . . .

'Has it ever occurred to you, scarface, that you might be biting off more than you can chew?' asked Caspar, indicating the mirrors around them.

'What are you t-t-talking about?'

'All these mirrors. Look at the size of them. You say you can open the little one over there but you can't open these? Well, duh. Why are you surprised? They're enormous. The size – don't you see?' Caspar was insistent. 'It's like asking you to lift a small car when you've only ever lifted a bag of sugar.'

'John, we have to go,' said Fyre. She could see Caspar's point, but now really wasn't the time. Then again, exactly where were they going? They were trapped at the top of a block of flats, with wolves below and nowhere else to hide. 'Look, whatever it is, get on with it. I'm going to see if Sarah's OK . . .'

Sarah wasn't OK.

'You, young Sheila, are under arrest.' A smiling Tapper Locke had appeared at the top of the stairs. 'Come quietly or . . . well, it's going to end in tears.'

Sarah gulped. She had never seen him this close, or

in quite this state. She felt Fyre appear by her side and heard her sharp intake of breath. This wasn't the policeman who had chased her and Davey Leonard through the school. Well . . . it was, but at the same time, it wasn't. For Tapper Locke had become a monster wolf. Or a human with a monster inside trying to get out. Or a monster wearing a human skin two sizes too small.

His yellow ski suit was dirty and torn, the hood ripped away entirely. His hair and beard seemed to join up with the hair on his chest and back: to Fyre he looked like a werewolf from an old black-and-white film. A werewolf in a yellow romper suit? He snarled at them, and his breath smelled foetid, as if he had been eating something dead.

'*Fee fi fo fum*,' he burbled, trying to slip swollen, frost-bitten fingers into the trigger guard of his shotgun. He was unsteady on his feet, his eyes bloodshot, his nose and ears almost unrecognizable blobs of flesh. At the back of her mind Fyre registered the sound of breaking glass coming from the mirror room. It was way, way, way at the back of her mind, though, because, with a garbled cry of triumph, the thing that used to be Tapper Locke forced its digit into the trigger guard and pulled.

Sarah grabbed Fyre's arm and yanked her to one side, dropping into a heap on the floor just as the gun went . . . *click*.

Tapper looked puzzled. He pulled the trigger again and again and again.

Click.

Click.

Click.

He cursed.

John stared at Caspar in astonishment. Caspar was holding the remains of a chair and staring at the mountain of broken glass that now lined one corner of the room.

'I wasn't expecting that,' he admitted with a frown.

'What have you d-d-done?'

'Did that wolf scrape out some of your brain cells when it gave you that scar? What you need is a smaller mirror; something just big enough to squeeze through, right? I thought I might end up with at least one bit that was big enough. And look at this place: it's not like you're short of a bit of glass, is it?'

Caspar paused, saw that John had taken his point, and kicked at the tiny shards that littered the floor.

'John!'

'That's Fyre,' said John, and rushed out to the landing, where he found what was left of Tapper Locke throwing a shotgun to the floor and sliding a large claw-headed hammer out of his sleeve.

'Here, kitty-kitty . . .' He advanced on the two girls, giggling.

John threw himself forward, grabbed one of Locke's arms as leverage and swung himself round behind him so that his knees were in the big man's back. He locked his other arm around his neck.

'Run!' he ordered the girls, and heaved backwards with all his might.

Something cracked in Locke's neck, and he fell backwards, arms flailing. It was a good plan – until they hit the concrete floor with John underneath. Even with his faster reflexes, John couldn't escape in time and hit the ground with a thud. 'Oof!'

He quickly rolled to one side, kicked himself away from Locke and raced after the girls, mostly uninjured and for once, grateful to the wolf for 'infecting' him. 'Fyre? Sarah?'

He found them cowering in the mirror room with Caspar, who was examining the broken glass. He seemed curiously calm and thoughtful.

'We n-need to get out of here,' said John. 'Everyone into the s-s-storeroom. Don't ask me why; we have to t-trust my grandpa. He's g-got a plan.' *Well, I hope he's got a plan: Plan B, whatever that was*, he thought.

It was too late. Tapper Locke staggered into the

doorway and blocked their exit. His neck had an odd bulge on one side and his head sat at an awkward angle, but he was still smiling, and still wielded his cruel-looking hammer.

Caspar reeled backwards at the sight of the shambling, murderous figure his father had become. He was pressed against a mirror, his brain a kaleidoscope of memories and images – his mother foremost among them. He felt nothing but hatred for this man who had lied to him for so long.

And then he had an idea . . .

'Here, kitty-kitty,' croaked Locke. 'Come to the Tapper Man.'

'John?' said Caspar, kicking the broken glass with the toe of his boot.

John was puzzled at first; then he realized what Caspar was getting at. *Of course!* Could he . . . ?

Locke advanced into the room, his wild grin showing blackened gums. In the remaining mirrors, his reflection showed a large grey wolf head atop the yellow ski suit: Locke's true nature.

'Here, kitty-kitty.'

'Do it!' snapped John. He bent down, placed both hands against the broken shards of glass and concentrated. At the same time Caspar grabbed two handfuls of the shattered glass.

'Now,' ordered John, and Caspar tossed the shards as hard as he could at Tapper Locke.

Sarah and Fyre could only watch in awe as the shards began to sparkle and shine in mid-flight.

'He's opened them up,' said Fyre in an awed whisper. 'Every one of them is a door! Oh my God . . .'

John felt a sudden surge of hope. He'd done it!

And where the glass slivers struck, they stuck; leaving tiny bits of Tapper Locke in both universes at once . . .

At least, until John broke the contact.

And then the pieces, like those of Mr Tiddles the cat, were left on the other side.

Locke screamed as little flowers of blood bloomed all over his face and hands. He hesitated but kept coming, the hammer raised.

'Again,' shouted John. His hands were tense, like arthritic claws; he was backed up against one of the remaining mirrors, with the huge man almost upon him.

This time Sarah and Fyre helped Caspar scoop up as much glass as they could, ignoring the sharp cuts, and showered Locke with them. John cried out in pain at the effort, but again, he transformed the shards into a beautiful but deadly shimmering wave that crashed all over their nemesis, covering him from head to toe in a bright silver net.

And again, they stuck.

And again John cut the contact.

This time, though, Tapper Locke dropped his hammer, fell to his knees and put his hands up to cover what was left of his face. Then, with a moan, he pitched forward and lay still, a bright red pool spreading out from underneath his head.

'That's . . . disgusting,' said Fyre, turning away to retch.

Caspar knelt down and threw up. He couldn't look at the mess that had been his father, but he felt nothing but relief.

Sarah, operating on automatic pilot, ran out of the room. There were no sounds of battle from below, so she went to the top of the stairs and peered over. Two huge black wolves, bloody and battle-scarred, were slinking up towards her. She turned and bumped into the others outside the storeroom.

'Inside please, now!' cried Mordecai Creed.

Caspar took one last look at his father and followed the others through the door.

All at once Fyre understood what it was about the room that had been niggling her: the stacks of toilet paper, cornflakes, beans, tuna – they were all false, empty wrappers and boxes stuck together to give the impression of solidity.

'Come through, come through,' urged Mordecai.

'Lock the door!'

They didn't need telling twice; after all, two wolves were advancing down the corridor outside.

Fyre followed the narrow passageway between the false stacks of food. Left, then right; another right. It was like a maze and, she realized when she knocked on one panel of false boxes of oats, not so hollow after all. Round the final corner, they found Mordecai standing at the bottom of a ladder, which disappeared up into a hatch in the roof. There was a way out!

'Quickly, quickly, quickly,' he ordered.

'Grandpa . . . ?' John was confused, but he knew that something was very wrong.

'Plan B,' said Mordecai sadly, looking his grandson in the eye.

'What's behind the stacks?' asked Fyre, though she had her suspicions.

'No matter. All that matters is that you get out of here. As far away as you can. *Now*.'

'I d-d-don't understand,' said John. 'Aren't you c-coming with us? If this is a w-way out, wh-why aren't you c-coming with us?'

'Not this time, my boy. Is something I have to do alone.'

'Oh my God . . .' said Fyre.

'Are you lot coming up?' asked Caspar. He had

already climbed the ladder and was now peering down through the hatch. Behind them, the door splintered a little under the wolves' assault.

'What?' John looked from his grandfather to Fyre, puzzled.

'Remember the plans we looked at in Mr Glass's flat?' she asked him. 'I said it looked like he was building a bomb? Well, this is it. I recognize the layout.'

'A bomb?'

'And you wonder why we didn't buy guns . . .' Mordecai laughed heartily and thumped the false walls. 'TNT!'

'But Grandpa . . .'

'Oh my boy, my boy, my boy – my shining beautiful boy.' The old man, crying now, drew him gently, lovingly, into his arms. 'I have loved you with all my heart, you know that, and I will *always* love you,' he whispered. 'I hoped this day would never come. But now, here we are. Mr Glass is gone. The Duchess is gone. Is time for me to join them.'

John clung to his grandfather, sobbing. 'No! I w-won't let you.' His voice was a muffled moan, and Fyre could see that he was shaking. 'C-come with us. You d-d-don't have to do this.'

The old man held him at arm's length and looked him straight in your eye. John's face was a dirty, tear-

364

streaked mask of anguish. He shook his head from side to side as if just denying everything would make it go away.

'No, no, no, no, no,' he wailed.

'John, I made vow to your father and mother that I would do all in my power to protect you.' He paused, and despite the noise around them his voice fell to a whisper. 'Would you, John, have me *fail* them?'

John wiped his eyes with his sleeve. He could only shake his head. *No*.

'I have to do this and you have to get up ladder. See?' Mordecai indicated a small door low down in the corner of the room, which led to a hidden compartment. 'We have to be sure we get them – no room for error. Now, go.'

'I w-won't. I w-w-won't leave you.' John clung again to his grandfather. 'You're all I've got.'

'Listen to him, John,' shouted Caspar from above.

'Shut up, you!' snapped Fyre.

'Son,' whispered Mordecai, 'and you were my son, John, never forget that . . . but you have Fyre. And Sarah. And – the gods help you – Caspar. *They* are your family now. Go, please, or we *all* die. Remember how much I love you. And I will always be with you. Here . . .' He placed his hand against John's chest, where his heart was. 'Now go.' He looked up. 'Sarah? The factory.'

Sarah, halfway up the ladder, nodded. 'John? We have to go,' she said. 'I'm not losing you now.'

Caspar was long gone. Fyre tugged at John's jacket. 'If you stay, John, I'm staying with you.'

Mordecai, crying openly, took his grandson's head in both hands, kissed him on the forehead, then bent down and crawled through the little false door without looking back. With a click, the wall slotted back into place.

'John, I'm scared,' said Fyre in a tiny voice. 'John? Can we go?'

With a jolt, he pulled himself together and shot up the ladder after Sarah, reaching down to help Fyre up. Below, the door finally surrendered to the wolves, and their howls of triumph filled the room and echoed up through the hatch; John shut it, and turned to find himself in a long empty crawlspace that extended the whole length of the block of flats.

'We need to get as far away as we can,' said Sarah.

'Too right,' agreed Caspar, who was already crab-walking along the roof beams towards the far end of the building. The others followed him.

'Here?' he asked about halfway along. Just above him was an old-fashioned skylight. John forced it open and stood up, poking his head out into the cold night sky.

Here and there a star twinkled. The clouds were dispersing!

He bent back down. 'Nah, the r-r-roof's completely iced over. We'd j-just go straight over the edge. Keep g-going.'

They had gone as far as they could, and had come to the brick wall at the end of the crawlspace. They were wondering where to go next when the head and shoulders of one of the wolves crashed through the hatch. It growled triumphantly and began to pull itself through the hole.

'Now, Granddad . . .' whispered John. 'Now would be g-g-good.'

Down below, out of sight, the hidey-hole door clicked open a little and Mordecai Creed poked his head out. Above him, one wolf was kicking, part way through the hatch, while the other waited patiently below it.

'Pssssssst,' said Mordecai.

The second wolf looked down in surprise . . .

Up in the roof the fugitives dived for cover just as the hatch and the wolf disappeared in the enormous ball of fire that exploded underneath them, hit the roof and then rolled out both ways along the attic.

The noise was deafening, and the heat and smoke and flames flared out like some apocalyptic storm above their heads.

'Stay down!' coughed Sarah.

And then, as quickly as it had come, the fireball was sucked back down into the hole, leaving behind thick, acrid smoke that had everyone coughing and spluttering.

High above them, in the freezing night air, Rajesh Patel the sparrow was soaring wild and free, his little heart pumping in his chest. He watched as the plume of bright yellow flame shot out of the roof's skylight. It lit up the night sky like a flare above an oil rig, making the ochre roof tiles shimmer golden for a moment before disappearing.

John Creed was in there – he knew that.

And it was time to make things right; to slough off a lifetime of guilt.

John Creed needed his help, and he would be there.

And he wasn't alone.

This time he had a few friends with him . . .

Fyre was the first to look up. She was lying awkwardly across two beams, with Sarah sprawled across her. Caspar and John were coughing and rubbing their eyes nearby. Caspar seemed to be bleeding from one ear. Only a thin cloud of smoke still drifted below the eaves – but the hatch was gone; replaced by a huge ragged crater through which they saw the figure of the white wolf.

Mordecai might have finished off the last of the black wolves; but the leader had held back, sensing a trap. Now she climbed up through the hole, gingerly placing her huge paws on the stronger beams, filling the whole of the attic space.

She growled in delight and bared her teeth, hackles raised.

Caspar whimpered a curse.

John stamped his feet.

Fyre looked at him. Was he trying to scare it away? It was a wolf, not a Labrador. He'd be saying 'Shoo!' next.

'Beneath us . . .' he coughed through the smoke. 'Flats.'

They began to stamp on the plasterboard between the beams, but Fyre knew it was too late. They would never break through before the wolf reached them.

Fee fi fo fum . . .

John heard the voice in his head as clear as day. It was the wolf. Triumphant. She began slinking towards them, quiet and confident, stalking prey that had no hope of escape.

Hello, little sparrow, she said to John in the same sing-song voice that had haunted his dreams for so many years. *Long time no—*

Without warning the skylight exploded inwards, and suddenly the crawlspace was alive with a great brown cloud of tiny birds heading straight for the wolf like a swarm of bees.

She staggered backwards in surprise, forced to retreat by the force of the onslaught. She swiped her paws this way and that, but could not beat them all off. In seconds she was engulfed in a swirling, shrieking, stabbing frenzy of beaks and feathers. Round and round the sparrows went, pecking and biting.

In the ensuing tumult, in a moment of clarity that John would remember for the rest of his life, one sparrow appeared out of the madness, landed on his arm, chirruped once, and flew back into the fray.

Finally, inevitably, the wolf backed into the hole created by the explosion and dropped out of sight with an angry howl. With her went the great swarm of birds – so many of them that they looked like smoke being sucked back into a vacuum cleaner.

John, Fyre, Caspar and Sarah broke through the plasterboard ceiling and, one by one, dropped into the bedroom of an elderly couple who, fast asleep, never saw the coughing, bloody, soot-covered figures who fell onto their bed. Quietly, gingerly, the four of them made their way through the flat to the front door, half expecting the wolf to come crashing through the roof behind them. Instead; nothing. They tiptoed down the stairs and, after John had made sure it was safe, they crept hesitantly out into the cold, dark night.

The husband shifted position, turned onto his back, almost surfacing from his dream. He mumbled something, a beatific smile spreading over his jowly old face.

'Chirrup,' he said.

5
THE ICE WOMAN COMETH

'They owned the whole f-f-furniture f-f-factory?' asked John incredulously.

Sarah had led them through a maze of narrow alley-ways to an old building just fifteen minutes away from the flats.

'Sort of. Well, Mr Glass did. He was the boss, but the place ran itself really,' she explained. 'The rest of the Kindred didn't have much to do with the day-to-day running. It was just for emergencies. Times like this. Your grandfather was a great man – he thought of everything.'

The doors and windows were covered in snow, so John had scaled a nearby building and jumped across to the roof, where a skylight had escaped the worst of the snowstorm. He had cleared the snow away, broken the glass and leaped down into a darkened room. He had navigated his way to the front door and opened it, letting them in.

Now Caspar peered at him in the gloom, his face showing disbelief. 'We just got rescued from a giant white wolf by a flock of sparrows and you're spooked by a *factory*?'

'Leave him alone,' snapped Fyre, who was searching around for a light switch. 'Concentrate on now.'

'Yeah, but . . . *sparrows*?' Caspar shook his head.

'There's a generator here somewhere,' said Sarah; she and Caspar moved off into the depths of the factory.

John followed her, still bemused. 'Sarah?'

'Mr Glass started it,' she explained. 'Made furniture and stuff. You didn't think that your pick-pocketing was the only way we made money, did you?'

'Until twenty-four hours ago I d–d–didn't know there was a "we", let alone that there was any m–money. Grandpa didn't—' He choked up and couldn't go on.

Sarah stopped in the darkness and laid a comforting hand on his arm. She had forgotten, she realized, that John was just thirteen years old, a boy.

'Oh, John,' she whispered, just as the generator coughed and put-putted and roared into life.

'Found it,' shouted Caspar.

The lights stuttered, blink–blink–blinking before finally giving out a blindingly bright light. John shielded his eyes from the sudden glare, and saw Fyre slip her sunglasses over her eyes. They were in a cavernous building dotted with shrouded furniture. Sarah strolled over to one of the shapes and dragged back the heavy tarpaulin to reveal two gleaming red snowmobiles.

'Tra-laaa! Our ride out of here.'

'Where will we go?' asked Fyre. She sidled up to John and hugged his arm.

'Anywhere b-b-but here. And we won't have to w-wait long; I saw stars through the storm clouds. I think it's ending. If we g-get away, we can just wait it out.'

'First things first,' said Sarah, jumping aboard one of the machines and looking at the door, which was still half covered with snow. 'How do we get these things out of here?'

'Well—' said John.

But he never got to finish his sentence. Suddenly a window erupted in a shower of glass as the white wolf burst through and landed, catlike, in the middle of the room. With one swipe of her paw she swept Sarah and the snowmobile to one side. The machine tumbled over and over, throwing its rider across the room; she slammed against a wall and lay still.

The wolf, covered in blood and now missing an eye, snarled and looked around. She took one step sideways

374

and swiped again; this time her paw caught Fyre as she ran towards John, sending her pin-wheeling across the floor.

John faced the wolf – the animal that had killed or maimed everyone he had known and loved; that had murdered his parents and scarred him for life. He felt his scars throb in white-hot anger.

'R-right. You and m-m-me then,' he said and, crouching like a wolf himself, launched himself at her. Taken by surprise – no human had ever attacked her first – she slithered backwards and bumped into something that stood at the back of the factory, dislodging the dustcover.

John flew through the air and punched the wolf on the nose as he went past. He landed on all fours, rolled agilely, and jumped upright. *That was it?* he thought. *A punch? I'm dead.*

As the wolf slunk round the room to face him, he looked about for something to use as a weapon. Nothing. He backed up, bumped into someone. It was Caspar, who thrust Sarah's machete into his hand.

'Behind you. Mirror,' he hissed, and disappeared into the shadows again.

John kept one eye on the wolf as she stepped sideways, looking for the best angle of attack, muscles tensed. The majestic animal now looked like a large white dog that had been caught in an avalanche, he thought. Her missing eye flopped about just below the socket like a blob of jelly on a rubber band. John tried to stay on her blind side.

Slowly they circled each other, the wolf occasionally feinting forward, only to be forced back by the machete. As they changed position, John saw what Caspar had been talking about. On the other side of the factory there was a mirror – a version of the one that Caspar had smashed back at the flats; obviously a prototype made by Mr Glass but left at the factory.

If he could open it . . . Yeah, *then* what?

And there, next to it, he saw Fyre. She was struggling to her feet, only half conscious, using the frame to haul herself upright. If the wolf saw her . . .

John attacked again, at the very same instant as the wolf. This time, though, he rolled under her at the last moment, and slashed out with the machete as they passed each other.

It didn't work. The wolf had anticipated his move, and the machete was torn from his grasp. One of the wolf's back legs raked the air and caught John's left hand, throwing him off balance.

He crashed into the base of the mirror, which tottered alarmingly. Fyre reached out and righted it, pulling John to his feet at the same time. Blood dripped from his hand, and the wolf smiled the smile that John had been dreaming about for so many years. She was confident now. The human was unarmed, injured, *powerless*. She howled her delight to the heavens.

John put one hand behind him, searching for Fyre. Instead he found smooth, cold glass under his palms. He thought of his grandfather, of the Kindred language, and felt the glass shiver. It was no good – his hand hurt too much. The effort was always painful, but with his hand injured like this . . .

And then there was another feeling – or a non-feeling: of a pain-numbing cold.

He glanced down to find Fyre clinging to his arm, an intense cold radiating from her hand. The mirror rippled, the usual shimmer taking on a frozen look. Whatever Fyre was doing was numbing his hand, keeping the pain at bay. He felt a surge of power rush through him, and he spoke the Old Tongue again, this time with more confidence.

'*Pahtech dreyschi chaoimh!*'

Of course! What had his grandfather said? That it was shortly after Fyre's mother turned up in the Kindred stronghold that his father had managed to solve the problem of the rift.

It had been Fyre's mother and his father who had

opened the doorway. Together! The cold! It was the only way to deal with the pain!

And here they were – doing exactly the same thing.

This was *destiny*. This was *fate*. He and Fyre, *together*, opening doors to other worlds.

He grinned stupidly at her, but she only had eyes for the wolf. With a vicious snarl the creature went back on her haunches, an enormous bundle of muscle and anger, and sprang across the room.

John felt another massive surge of power flowing through him. He felt elated, almost joyous. His hands – now far too cold to feel any pain – tingled with excitement and fear. And as they did so, a rift popped open, and stayed open. John waited a second longer, and then leaped to one side, taking Fyre with him as the wolf descended. With a surprised yelp, she whistled past him and plunged through the opening.

But not before twisting round, catching John's hood with a claw and pulling him through as well.

John shot out a hand and caught hold of the ornate frame of the mirror. Whatever was on the other side, it was night-time, and gravity was not in their favour. The wolf disappeared with a yelp and a faint thud somewhere below.

John struggled to haul himself back through, but he was exhausted and his grip began to slip. He felt a sharp pain as claws raked his leg from below. The wolf! If she got a better hold of him, he was dead!

And with that he felt his control of the rift waver. If he lost it now, there'd just be a set of severed fingers left on one side and the rest of him at the wolf's mercy on the other. He tried to hook an elbow over the frame. It was no good – he didn't have the strength. His hands were killing him. He was going to fall . . .

And then Fyre and Caspar appeared in the frame. They grabbed John's arms and began pulling him back into the factory.

'Up you come, scarface,' said Caspar. 'If you disappear, nobody's going to believe *any* of this.'

EPILOGUE
HAPPILY EVER AFTER . . .

'And that, children, was The End. And they all lived happily ever after.'

The speaker was a white-haired old lady wearing a long black woollen dress and a baggy black cardigan. She was sitting in a comfortable but threadbare armchair which looked, to her audience, almost as old as the occupant herself.

In front of her, sitting cross-legged on the carpet, were a dozen or so fresh-faced children. They all gaped, wide-eyed, in utter silence, as the story came to an abrupt end.

They were in a room with high vaulted ceilings and stripped-back industrial brickwork. Desks and easels were scattered here and there, piled high with books and paper and pencils and all the other bits and bobs of a normal classroom. Jars of muddy water crammed with paintbrushes lined a shelf, and colourful pictures of happy-looking stick people under bright yellow suns adorned the walls. On the wall a sign declared: KINDRED FAMILY SCHOOL.

For an old factory it looked very cosy.

Next to the old lady, fixed to the wall, was a large mirror with an ornate carved frame.

'John Creed,' she whispered into the awed silence, 'grew up to be a fine young man and a great warrior, and he and the Lady Fyre have been hunting the white wolf ever since.'

'Miss?' A hand went up; a tiny slip of a girl with grey eyes and blonde hair.

'Yes?'

'Miss, what happened to Kendall and all them others?'

'Ah, yes, well, that was all very sad. Mr Glass perished after the Tapper Man got into his flat. Fletcher and Kendall Hunter fought valiantly but were eventually overcome by the remaining wolves when they found their way in through Mr Glass's flat. But of course, once that happened . . . what came next?'

'Plan B!' shouted a high-pitched voice from the back.

'Yes, indeed, Marie. Plan B. But, please, put your hand up when you answer a question; it's not ladylike to shout.'

'Sorry, miss.'

'So, knowing what Plan B meant, the badly injured Kendall helped his dying father down the stairs and they hid . . . Can anybody guess?'

Silence. But she could hear the ticking of young minds.

'No? Well, they hid in the cellar. With the Duchess!'

'Oooh.'

'Yes, you thought she had perished too, right? Well, when the Duchess saw what the traitor Davey Leonard had done, she knew she couldn't fight the wolves off by herself, so she hid in the cellar and locked it tight behind her, only letting Kendall and Fletcher in when they gave the secret knock. And that, sadly, is where the brave Fletcher Hunter passed away, in the arms of his loving son.'

'But it's all rubbish, that is.'

'Is it, Aaron?'

'Yeah, you just made it all up,' said a boy of about eleven who had got to his knees and now crossed his arms cockily across his chest.

'Did I?' The old lady smiled.

'Yeah. Course. And there's no such thing as the Tapper Man. Grown-ups made him up just so as we'd be good.'

'We did? Well. You might be right. But everyone's heard of the Great Freeze, right?'

The children nodded their heads sagely. Nobody listened to Aaron anyway; he was always moaning and questioning things. They had all heard about the Great Freeze – when the country had stopped and lots and lots of people had died. It was the stuff of legend. And it was true.

'Well, there you go, then.'

But Aaron wasn't so easily placated. 'What about the sparrow man?'

'Mr Patel?'

'Yeah, him.'

'Well, the lovely Mr Patel fell asleep during the freeze and never woke up again. It was very sad. But I like to think he's with us in spirit. In fact, I have something to show you.'

And with that, she reached into one of the pockets of her voluminous cardigan and, very carefully, pulled out what looked like a dirty ball of fluff. She beckoned the children forward and held out two hands, cradling whatever was in them as if it were the most precious thing in the world.

The children crowded forward and gasped.

In her gnarled old hands she held a salt-and-pepper coloured sparrow. They could see its tiny chest beating fit to burst.

'Now, now, children, don't frighten him.'

The bird was old – impossibly so – but its eyes were bright with excitement. It fluffed its feathers up, flapped its wings and opened its beak in a funny approximation of a yawn.

Pandiculation.

The old lady stood and reached up to allow the bird to perch on top of the mirror.

'That could be any old sparrow,' argued Aaron. 'And anyway, it's just a fairy tale. I'm too old for fairy tales.'

'Ah, we're never too old for fairy tales, Aaron. Though you might be right: some of that story might have been made up – but not *all* of it. There's always a nugget of truth in fairy tales. Remember that. Anyway, that's it for today, children. I see some of your parents are waiting outside already.'

'Walk! Walk! *Walk!*' said the old lady as the children rushed for the door and freedom. It didn't make any difference. Within minutes the room was empty, and the old lady eased herself out of her chair and made her way to a door at the rear of the classroom. On the other side was a large warehouse-sized room dominated by a huge mirror. As she closed the door behind her, the mirror began to shine with an eerie light, first diamond hard, then liquid silver and then nothing, a doorway only.

And through it stepped a young woman with bright orange hair, dressed in army fatigues and carrying a complicated-looking bow. Following her was a handsome man with jet-black hair. As they came through, they nodded respectfully to the old lady.

There was a short pause, and then came a muscular woman, also in camouflage greens. Her savagely chopped hair was as white as unsullied snow, her skin deathly pale. She wore matt-black snow goggles and carried a small crossbow. When she was through, she snapped the goggles up onto her forehead to reveal white eyelashes and pale, pink-rimmed eyes.

'Good news, Duchess,' said Fyre.

'Really?'

Fyre moved to one side, and through the glistening mirror stepped a tall, mousy-haired man who moved with a sinewy grace. He was wearing black boots, black cargo trousers and a dirty black T-shirt.

Across one side of his face were three ragged scars.

And in his hand he held the severed head of a giant white wolf with one half-closed golden eye.

'G-g-got her,' said John Creed.

THE END

GRYMM

KEITH AUSTIN

*Jacob and Mina have moved to the creepy town of
Grymm where:*

THE BUTCHER IS BLOOD THIRSTY
THE BAKER IS HUNGRY,
THE MILKSHAKE HAS MAGGOTS IN IT.

*Then, overnight, their baby brother disappears and no
one, not even their parents, seems to notice.*

What is the terrible secret of Grymm?

TURN THE PAGE FOR A SNEAK PEEK...

1

Jacob Daniels is twelve years old and none too impressed with his sister. Make that *step*sister. Right from the start let's get that clear – as clear as the clearest and most expensive, most flawless crystal. Jacob is adamant about that. Just because his mother and *her* father have shacked up, it doesn't mean she's family.

Not by a long shot.

No, sir.

No way. Not in a million years.

That's not why he thinks she's an idiot, though.

It's because she thinks she's a witch.

Yeah, sure. And Jacob's Harry bloody Potter.

Wilhelmina Lipton is fourteen and a Goth, a teenage Morticia Addams. Her mousy hair is dyed cat-black and backcombed until she looks like the Bride of Frankenstein (according to Jacob, that is). She wears shocking white make-up, black clothes and a silver ring in her nose (that caused a few family arguments, it must be said). On a chain around her neck hangs a small, five-pointed star, a pentacle.

Jacob doesn't understand why she can't just have her name there, or a heart, or some sort of locket. Honestly! What *does* she think she looks like? She's obviously watched too much *Twilight*. Jacob calls her a witch because he knows how much it irritates her. He calls her *Wilhelmina* for the same reason.

She's not, though, OK? She's 'Mina' to her father and to all her friends. Always has been, always will be. And if her new *stepbrother* 'Jakie' doesn't shut his face, she's going to turn him into a big, ugly frog. Well, a frog anyway; he's already ugly. And what's with the hair? There must be half a tonne of gel on it – he could take someone's eye out.

Yeah, well, *she* can talk. And why doesn't she stop calling him Jakie? She only does it because she knows he hates it . . . And another thing—

'Will you two pack it in?' Mary, Jacob's mother, has turned in her seat to glare at them. Mina's father is trying to steer their well-worn four-wheel-drive and map-read at the same time. 'You're upsetting the baby. George, will you tell them? They're upsetting the baby. Again.'

Ah, now here's something – the *only* thing – that these two sworn enemies can agree on. Everything else pales into insignificance. Their newborn half-brother, Bryan, perched in his bright new blue booster seat between them, might look like any other baby – a pudgy white dough-boy with big eyes the colour and shape of those scented blocks they put in toilets – but he's really the devil's spawn, sent to Earth to make their lives even more miserable. During the nine-hour drive from the city, the little monster has already somehow broken Mina's mobile phone and vomited over Jacob's T-shirt and shorts.

Then there's the stink. How can something so *small* smell so *bad*? That's what Jacob wants to know. Maybe he'll take him in and ask the chemistry teacher when school starts again after the summer holidays.

Mina, on the other hand, has had a year of biology at secondary school and is fascinated by what happens between Bryan's mouth and Bryan's bum. Maybe that's next term's project: Bryan and his fatal effect on biodegradable matter. Perhaps they could dissect him.

And then there's the crying. Morning, noon and night; the thing never stops caterwauling. It was like listening to a vet de-sex a cat, without anaesthetic. They went to bed at night with his sobbing in their ears, and woke up the next morning to a dawn chorus of yowling that frightened birds out of trees and attracted wildlife from miles around.

'He's just a bit colicky,' their parents had explained, gazing at their little bundle of misery with tolerant smiles. It was sickening to watch.

Bryan, according to his loving half-brother and half-sister, never seemed to stop grizzling unless he was eating something he could turn into radioactive waste. Even Mina's father, a geologist with kind eyes, a bushy grey beard and even bushier ginger eyebrows, made jokes about taking samples of his son's poo to his new job at the mine. 'I could get them to run a Geiger counter over it; tell them it's a new strain.'

And what a strain it was. Every so often Bryan would turn purple, and veins would stand out on his head with the exertion of pushing another toxic bundle into his nappy. It was a performance that never failed to make Mina's top lip curl in disgust. She would bet anything that her father hadn't been this *goo-goo*, *ga-ga* when *she* was a baby.

So they bicker on through the sun-blasted desert, throwing up a long billowing plume of red dust behind them that makes their 4X4 look like it's ablaze and they're trying to outrun the flames.

But the Liptons and the Danielses aren't fleeing from a fire.